The Birdcage Quilts

a novel by

Jan Cerney

American Quilter's Society
www.AmericanQuilter.com

Located in Paducah, Kentucky, the American Quilter's Society (AQS) is dedicated to promoting the accomplishments of today's quilters. Through its publications and events, AQS strives to honor today's quiltmakers and their work and to inspire future creativity and innovation in quiltmaking.

EXECUTIVE BOOK EDITOR: ELAINE H. BRELSFORD
EDITOR: NATE M. BRELSFORD
COPY EDITOR: ADRIANA FITCH
GRAPHIC DESIGN: SARAH BOZONE
COVER DESIGN: MICHAEL BUCKINGHAM
PHOTOGRAPHY: CHARLES R. LYNCH

Cover photo credit: Catalog # H-572
Mission School, Ft. Totten Indian Agency (Devils Lake Indian Agency) 1881

Photograph by F. Jay Haynes

American Quilter's Society
www.AmericanQuilter.com

Additional copies of this book may be ordered from the American Quilter's Society, PO Box 3290, Paducah, KY 42002-3290, or online at www.AmericanQuilter.com.

Text © 2015, by Author, Jan Cerney
Artwork © 2015 American Quilter's Society

Library of Congress Cataloging-in-Publication Data

Cerney, Janice Brozik.
  The birdcage quilts / by Jan Cerney.
    pages ; cm
  ISBN 978-1-60460-178-7 (softcover : acid-free paper)
  1. Quilting--Fiction. 2. Women missionaries--Fiction. I. Title.
  PS3603.E74B57 2015
  813'.6--dc23
                    2015002642

CHAPTER 1

Deadwood, South Dakota, 1899

Deadwood bustled with activity as a new day unfolded in the gulch. Once known as a rip-roaring mining camp, Deadwood was doing its best to downplay a dusky past. Prospectors had once swarmed its creek banks searching for gold. Whiskey had flowed from the saloons like water through sluice boxes, and questionable characters had inundated its streets. But the times were changing.

Kat unlocked the doors to the Birdcage Saloon. Marley and Scrooge, Kat's parrots, chatted a good morning from their separate cages.

"Hello, guys," Kat greeted. "Ready to entertain the customers?" She reached for the birdseed under the counter and sprinkled some into the cages. She watched as her feathered friends pecked at their breakfast and scattered fragments onto the wood floor. She frowned at the mess they were making.

When Kat was sure the birds were as happy as possible

in their limited space, she kindled a blaze in the stove and made a pot of coffee. She inhaled its enticing aroma while she pushed in the chairs around the tables and swept the scattered birdseed from the floor. After the coffeepot boiled awhile, she filled her stained cup and sat down at the table in a pensive mood.

A half hour later, Jennie, the barmaid, pushed through the saloon doors. "There's coffee left in the pot if you want some," Kat said, barely glancing up from the cards she had begun to deal herself.

Jennie filled a cup and joined Kat at the table. "You look deep in thought this morning. What's the matter?"

"I couldn't sleep again last night. Since Jet's been in prison, I have been thinking of him—so alone, probably cold and miserable in his cell."

Jennie sipped her coffee. "Yeah, that would be tough."

"I have an idea for you."

"What do you have in mind?"

"Remember when I told you about learning to sew while I was at the mission?"

"I remember."

"Well, I've been thinking of a quilt for Jet, but I just can't get much done after I finish here at the saloon, and he needs it before winter. He'll appreciate something to wrap himself in to ease his nights."

"Surely he has some kind of blanket in his cell."

"I suppose, but it's not something made especially for him. Besides, I would make it extra warm." Kat wrapped her arms around herself.

"Not a bad idea."

"When can you help me?"

"Help you! Me? I can barely thread a needle."

"It will take forever by myself, Jennie, and I have to get it to him soon."

"Kat, I'm really sorry, but I'm too tired after I get done

with work here."

"I was thinking we'd make it right here in the saloon."

"The saloon?" Jennie nearly choked on her coffee and coughed. "How?"

"We have days that aren't too busy, mornings especially. I'd have to find a sewing machine to bring in here and—"

"Oh, Kat. I don't know about this. What do you want me to do? Remember, I can't sew."

Kat tapped her red fingernails on the table. "You can cut, can't you?"

"Well, yes."

"Perfect. I will have lots of pieces for you to cut."

Jennie rolled her eyes. "And how do I do that?"

"I'll give you patterns—templates. You trace around the templates with a pencil and then cut on the markings. I sew the pieces together into a quilt block, and eventually sew the quilt blocks into a quilt top."

Jennie shook her head. "That sounds like a lot of work. You must really like this guy to go through all this."

Kat's face grew solemn. "Jet's alone with no one to care for him. He's an alright sort of guy, better than I've met for a long time."

Jennie heaved a sigh of resignation. "If it's that important to you, I'll help you out. Besides, you're paying me for my time."

"Great. Now all I have to do is come up with a pattern." Kat drummed her temples with her fingertips. "Wish Cassandra and Minnie were here. They would give me some ideas." Kat suddenly swept her cards into a stack. "Could you watch the place while I go out?"

"Where are you going?"

"To find a sewing machine." Kat grabbed her shawl and thudded down the boardwalk. She shivered, but not because of the cold. She couldn't forget that look on Jet's face when the jury read the verdict. Jet looked like he was going to collapse. She knew what it felt like to be so alone. Kat barged into the general store, saying, "I need a sewing machine, Mel."

"You need a what?"

"A sewing machine."

"I have one over here. It's a great model. Quite, uh, ornate—"

"Does it sew?"

"Why, of course."

"Then I'll take it. Could you have someone deliver it as soon as possible?"

"Well, sure, if that's want you want."

"Would today be too soon?"

"No, no. I can do that for you. To your house?"

"To the Birdcage."

"Oh, to the saloon?"

"Yes, the saloon. Do you have any quilt patterns here?"

Mel pointed to a box on the counter. "Over here."

Kat rummaged through the box looking for the easiest pattern to assemble. She decided they were too difficult for a novice like her, so she stuffed the patterns back into the box.

"Are you having any luck?" Mel asked from behind the counter.

"No. They're too complicated. I'd like something a little simpler."

"My wife is in the back room unpacking some new dishes; let me ask her to come out. Corella!" he yelled. No answer. "She can help you, I'm sure. Corella!"

"No, that's okay—" But before she could get the words out, Mel had left. *Oh, great,* she thought to herself. *Here comes the snub I always get from these uppity ladies who think they're better than a saloon girl.*

Corella seemed to emerge from nowhere. Kat wondered if the shopkeeper's wife had simply slipped into the store from the street behind her, or if she had been eavesdropping from the top shelf next to the bundles of twine all along.

After all, Deadwood folk tended to hide in plain sight.

"May I help you?" Corella asked. A look of annoyance appeared on her face as though she had been terribly inconvenienced.

"Well, maybe. I was looking for an easier quilting pattern than what you have here. Oh, and Mel went back to fetch you."

"I see." Corella tilted her nose a tad higher. "You are going to make a quilt?"

"Yes." Kat straightened her shoulders. "I know how to sew. I have quilted before," Kat replied, blushing faintly at her fib.

"I know of a few simple patterns. I could draw them out for you, if you wish."

Not wanting to accept her help, Kat swallowed the knot of pride. "Thank you. Let's see what you can do."

Corella led her to the counter near the cash register where she took a piece of paper and drew out a Log Cabin pattern. "This pattern is very old. What do you think?"

"It's just straight strips. I see no problem with it."

"The length and arrangement of the colored strips determine the whole appearance of the quilt." Corella shaded in the strips to demonstrate some variations. "Placing darks on one side and light colors on the other will make a pleasing arrangement."

"I'll keep that in mind. How about material?"

"Choose the colors you like, and I will calculate what you might need."

Kat took all of an hour to select what she wanted and the amount she needed. After Corella wrapped her purchases in brown paper, tied the package with string, and sent her on her way, Kat briskly strode back to her place of business. She entered the saloon and waved her bundle of quilting supplies.

"You're really going to go through with this quilting notion of yours, aren't you?" Jennie asked while drying a glass.

"There's no reason I can't do this. Let me show you the pattern. It's called the Log Cabin, Corella told me—"

"Corella? You had to get help from Corella?" Jennie slapped the bar with her hand. "Oh, this is funny."

"Stop it." Kat's face became as red as her hair. "I had no other choice."

Jennie rested her hands on her hips. "Frankly, I'm worried about you."

"Why?"

"You're becoming too domestic. A man usually has something to do with that."

Kat lifted her chin. "I admit I'm interested. I'm not getting any younger these days. Anyway, as I was about to say, we'll have this pattern put together in no time."

"We?"

"Like I said before, you can do the cutting. All you have to do is measure the strip length to make templates from cardboard, lay them on the material, and cut them out. I'll do the rest."

"Oh, Kat. It sounds like a lot of work," Jennie whined.

"I'm paying you for your time, aren't I?"

"Yes, but it takes both of us just to keep this business going."

"We'll work on the quilt only when we aren't so busy, and we might as well begin before tonight's rush. You're right, though. Customers come first."

Jennie rolled her eyes and sighed in disgust as she listened disinterestedly to Kat's instructions.

"Now cut as accurately as possible," Kat said, shaking her finger at her.

"When will you get the sewing machine?" Jennie asked with scissors in hand.

"Today, I hope. We'll be ready for it if we already have some pieces cut by the time it gets here."

———

After about two hours, Jennie had cut a stack of strips as the card players began to shuffle in the saloon. One man pushed open the swinging door, stopped short, and bellowed, "What's going on? Ain't this the Birdcage?"

"Come on in, Rio," Jake the bartender said. We've been waiting for you."

"Looks like the Ladies Aid. Don't know if we should stay." Rio halted in his tracks with no apparent intent to approach the card tables.

Kat piped up. "We won't hurt you. Nothing's changed."

"Promise me you won't start marching and telling us we shouldn't drink."

"And ruin my business?" Kat laughed.

Rio delivered one more sideways glance before he and a few men who had entered the Birdcage Saloon behind him swaggered to the farthest card table. "Hey!" Rio shouted. "We need a dealer over here."

"Would that be me or you?" Jennie whispered to Kat.

"I'll take it," Kat told her. "You can deal the next table." Kat left Jennie, who continued to cut strips, and headed for the card table.

Just then, Mel and a boy stepped into the saloon carrying the sewing machine. "Where do you want this?" Mel asked.

"Over there by Jennie." Kat pointed. "Are you sure it works?"

"Corella threaded the needle and tested it before I brought it over."

"Then I'll try it out tomorrow. Thanks, Mel." Kat continued toward the table where Rio and the other men were waiting. She could feel their eyes on her as she approached.

"What are you up to?" Rio asked. "I never knew you were the sewing kind. Are you making bandages?" He laughed. He was rather good-looking and lean, which reminded Kat of

Jet, but his hair was sandy brown and his complexion lighter.

"It's just a project I'm working on." Kat didn't know Rio all that well. It wasn't very long ago that Rio had begun to frequent the Birdcage. She knew he had an interest in her, which she tried to squelch. "Don't worry, it won't interfere with your card playing," she said, cracking open a new deck of cards.

"Now don't get sore at me." Rio winked.

"It's not your business anyway." She peered out of the corner of her eye to see how he took her remark and happened to meet his hard glare.

"Is this a nice way to treat your customers?"

"I thought you were here to play cards." She kept her tone firm.

"Yeah, I guess so. Deal me some good ones."

Kat dealt cards for several hours. Rio didn't win many games, but he didn't seem to mind. Before he left, he tipped his hat to Kat. She didn't like the way he said, "I'll be seeing you," and she made a mental note to stay clear of him.

———

Before Kat and Jennie returned to their homes after closing, Kat said, "We need more help with the quilt. Most days we'll only have about an hour to work on it."

"And where do you suppose we'll get any help? No respectable lady who sews is going to come in here with her needle, thread, and thimble."

Kat chuckled. "I suppose you're right, but I wasn't thinking of respectable ladies. Anyway, all the interruptions are setting me back."

"All your business is setting you back, you mean."

"You have a point. What am I complaining about? Business is good."

"I've been thinking. If you do get this quilt made, how are

you going to get it to Jet? They probably have standard items, so I doubt the prison officials will let him have it. They might think you've hidden knives in it! Hey, now that's an idea..." Jennie's eyes twinkled as she laughed.

"Oh, quit now. I've thought about that, too—I don't mean the knives. But I may have some connections to get the quilt through to Jet."

"Who would that be?"

"Ed, Jet's attorney. I suppose I should write him and ask for his advice."

———

At midmorning the next day, Jennie brought two acquaintances to the Birdcage and introduced them to Kat.

"I've seen you around," Kat said to Cilla, the young woman whose brown eyes were too large for her thin face.

"I work part-time at the Prospector Saloon."

"You can sew?"

"I know how to thread a needle."

"That's a start."

Cilla nodded to her companion. "Aggie knows the most about sewing."

Kat studied Aggie for a moment. "I've seen you at the Miner's Restaurant."

"I work there once in a while. I clean at the Prospector most days," Aggie said. Her gray hair was pulled back in a bun, and she clenched a stogie between her teeth. "We didn't bring our sewing boxes. It'd ruin our reputation," she said with a straight face.

Kat smiled. "I can't pay you gals."

"We know. Let's say we owe Jennie a favor," Cilla said.

"Must be a big one," Kat said.

"I understand this quilt's for a man?" Cilla teased. "Is he good-looking?"

Kat nodded. "As long as you like the tall, dark, and handsome type."

Cilla laughed. "That'll make the task easier. Where is he, anyway?"

"In prison," Kat said.

"Prison? What did he do—or would you rather not say?"

"He used to rustle cattle."

"Ah, I knew a few of them in my day." Aggie rolled her cigar to the other side of her mouth. "Most of them weren't such a bad sort."

"His name's Jet. He fell in with a bad crowd and tried to quit, but the ringleader wouldn't let him." Kat took a deep breath. "He kidnapped Jet and forced him to do another job. The leader was killed when they got caught at it, which gave Jet the chance to surrender himself. He was taken in, tried, and sentenced to a year."

Aggie wore a puzzled expression, and Cilla stared at Kat intently. "Wow. Interesting story, but a little short. How did you meet up with him in the first place?"

"We shared a stagecoach on my way back from Cleveland, but he was pretending to be a tailor at the time. Are you sure you want to know all of this?"

"I adore love stories," Cilla prompted.

"This isn't exactly a love story. We didn't get to that part before he was hauled off to prison."

Cilla held her hands to her heart. "Unrequited love, even better."

Kat wasn't sure she should be telling these strangers her personal story, but she was in too deep now to quit. "We were on our way from Pierre to the Black Hills. It's funny now that I think of it, but all of us in that stagecoach reconnected later." Her voice trailed off for a while.

"How do you mean?" Cilla asked, unwilling to give up on the tale.

"Like I said, it's a long story. Let me start with Jet. He was dressed in this awful suit and told everyone he was a tailor on his way to Deadwood. I played a game of cards with him and won. We didn't say much more to each other, and when we got to Deadwood, we went our separate ways. Then I got curious about his tailor story and went to the Deadwood tailor shops to look for him. I couldn't find him, and no one had ever heard of him. One day, I saw him riding down the street dressed in a cowhand's outfit, so I called out to him. He just kept riding. I didn't see him again until the mission."

"Mission?" Aggie said.

"You see, two other passengers on the stage were newlyweds from the Cheyenne River Reservation. They were honeymooning in Denver. They run the Cheyenne River Mission. I happened to leave my special compact on the stage, and the driver found it and gave it to the lady, Evangeline, since I had already left for Deadwood on another stage. Evangeline and her husband, Elijah, found the picture of my sister, me, and my niece hidden inside the compact. When they showed it to the other ladies at the mission—lo and behold—Minnie recognized me from the Fort Pierre Deadwood Trail, from when I was just a teenager! When they mailed the compact back to me, Minnie enclosed a letter and invited me for a visit." Kat stopped to gather her thoughts.

"So you visited?" Cilla asked.

"I did. My sister was involved in an accident in Cleveland, where she lives, and she asked me to take care of her daughter. I didn't think a Deadwood saloon was a good place for a little girl, so I took Minnie up on her offer and met Miranda—my niece—in Pierre, and then traveled upriver to the mission. It was there that I saw Jet for the second time."

"Destiny. It was destiny," Cilla said, her brown eyes growing even larger.

"Maybe it was. I hadn't really thought of it that way. He was working for the Bar Double B Cattle Company and his boss, Ed, insisted that his hired hands attend church every

Sunday. That's when I saw Jet for the second time. Now, how likely is that? After the service, I went up to him and asked him what was going on, and we saw each other every Sunday after that until he disappeared."

Cilla slowly sat at the table beside Kat. "Disappeared?"

"I didn't know he was gone until Ed came to church one Sunday without him. He told me Jet had just vanished, yet with all his belongings still at the ranch. We found out later from Tex, a man I met on that same stage with the others, that he and a stock investigator rode up on Jet and a gang rustling cattle. Ed was really concerned about Jet and offered to be his defense attorney."

"But he didn't get him off?" Aggie asked.

"No, but at least he got a reduced sentence. He's in Yankton prison, and I want him to have a warm quilt." After a moment, Kat added, "I learned to sew and make quilts while I was at the mission."

"I come from a big family and learned to sew to keep from wearing tattered clothing all the time," Aggie told them. "I could be of some help to you."

Kat was hoping Aggie would provide more information, but decided to press on. "Do you ladies want to begin today?"

"I'll have a go at it for a while," Aggie volunteered. "Looks like a new sewing machine you have here." Aggie ran her hand over its smooth, varnished surface.

"It is. Come on over here, and I'll show you what I'm doing. This is the Log Cabin pattern," Kat said, holding up a completed block.

"Are the stripes supposed to be the logs?" Cilla asked.

"I assume so," Kat said. "Let's follow the arrangement I started in the first block." Aggie sat at the sewing machine, her stogie smoldering. Kat's gaze glued to the cigar stub wedged between Aggie's lips. *Strange woman. I hope she doesn't burn up the quilt before we're done.*

CHAPTER 2

The sewing group gathered at the Birdcage Saloon for their second week of sewing. The Log Cabin quilt was already taking shape. Aggie was sewing on the last row of blocks when a small, white face peeked through the swinging doors.

"Who's that?" Kat asked the group, gesturing toward the partial doors.

"Oh, I think it's Ling Li," Jennie answered, getting up to visit with the young girl. She pushed the swinging door aside and greeted Ling Li, who was distinguished by her porcelain face and almond eyes. Jennie exchanged a few words with the young woman and returned to the sewing table alone.

Kat stopped cutting the bias strips to bind the quilt and looked up at Jennie. "Who was that?"

"I've taken her under my wing recently," Jennie explained. "Ling Li was born in Deadwood to a family with a laundry business. I met her there."

"Can she speak English?" Kat asked.

"She can. Her family returned to China several years ago. Her mother remained there with several of Ling Li's brothers and sisters. Ling Li came back to Deadwood with her father. Her mother has wanted to return for a long time, but can't because of that Chinese Exclusion Act."

"Poor girl. She must be frantic," Kat said.

"She's a timid little thing. Her father takes good care of her, but she's lonely," Jennie explained.

"I suppose she is. There are not very many Chinese women left in Deadwood anymore. Most have gone back to China," Kat added.

"She needs someone to talk to. Whenever she has a problem, she usually comes to me. She doesn't want her father to know I am her friend." Jennie rolled her eyes. "He probably wouldn't approve, thinking I'm a bad influence."

Kat frowned. "You're one of the nicest people I know. Anything we can do to help her out?"

"She could use more friends, but like I said, we're really not at the top of the social ladder." Everyone laughed. "She met a man," Jennie said. "He's Chinese, too, but she's afraid to tell her father. I don't know what to advise her."

"I wouldn't know what to say, either," Cilla said.

Aggie stretched the completed quilt across the table. "Looks mighty good, I'd say."

"It does," Kat said. "Now, we need to decide if we are going to quilt or tie it. Tying is easier and faster, but quilting is so much prettier. What do the rest of you think?"

The women shrugged.

"You're the ones who will be doing the work," Kat reminded them.

Aggie rolled her cigar to the other side of her mouth. "I say let's do it right. Let's quilt it."

"We'll need a quilting frame." Kat sighed. "I suppose I'm going to have to visit Corella and ask her about one."

"Let me ask around. Someone at the Miner's Restaurant

surely has one or knows about one," Aggie offered.

"Until then, let's pin the top, the batting, and the underside together. If Aggie finds a frame, we'll be ready," Kat said.

"Who knows how to quilt?"

The ladies shook their heads.

"Not to worry." Secretly, Kat was anxious. Making the small, even stitches would be tedious and time-consuming, not to mention the wear it put on the fingers. She would just have to accept whatever result they could manage. Besides, Jet wouldn't know if the stitches were perfect or not.

The women spent the next several hours pinning the quilt layers together while customers began to fill the saloon. They lit cigars and rolled cigarettes in preparation for an afternoon of card playing. Smoke curls began to fill the air when Clem came over to where the women were working. He shuffled his feet several times before speaking. "I have a suggestion for you ladies. You can take it or leave it."

"What is it?" Kat asked. Clem hardly ever interfered, so she knew it had to be important.

"I think you should put up some kind of partition between you and the main part of the saloon. That way the customers don't know what's going on. They really don't like to come in here when you're sewing. They think there's some kind of ladies' meeting going on."

"I suppose they don't. Maybe we remind them that they're still under their wife's thumb." Kat laughed. "You have a good idea. Could you and Jake put up something?"

"Sure. All we need is some support points and building paper. It wouldn't be anything permanent. You intend to stop sewing after this quilt's done, don't you?"

"We do. I have a business to run. Can't spend all my time quilting. You tackle that project whenever you wish," Kat told Clem as he walked back to the bar.

"I like the idea of a partition, too." Jennie said. "Sometimes I feel like I'm out of place. And you know, I think I might have an idea about who can help us with the quilting now that she wouldn't be seen."

"Who's that?" Aggie asked.

"Ling Li. Do you know the Chinese make quilts, too?"

"I had no idea," Kat admitted. Kat put in her last pin for the day. "Looks like we'd better get back to work, Jennie. The card tables are beginning to fill."

"Do you want me to take Rio's table?" Jennie whispered.

"No, he'll still holler for me to come over and deal."

"It's too bad he doesn't do something so Jake can kick him out...for good."

"He's too smart for that. I can't understand why he just doesn't give up," Kat said. "I've made it clear that I'm just not interested. There are plenty of other saloons in town."

"You know what would help your situation?"

"What?"

"Well, we deal as a courtesy. The days of legal gambling are gone, so let the card players deal for themselves. That's probably why Rio hangs around. He's too lazy to deal his own cards."

"I suppose you're right. Old habits die hard for me, but what would I do with my time?"

Jennie laughed. "Sew."

———

Jennie had talked Ling Li into helping with the quilt as soon as Clem and Jake constructed the partition. "I hope we aren't going to get you in trouble," Jennie said.

"Don't worry. If my father does find out, he'll just be mad for a little while. He always forgives me. I did tell him I was helping a friend with her quilting, but I didn't tell him where." She covered her giggle with her petite hand.

By the time Ling Li joined the effort, the quilt layers had been pinned together. Aggie had a crude quilting frame delivered to the saloon. Working together, the ladies secured the quilt onto the frame and pulled it tight.

Kat demonstrated how to take small stitches and where to place them. "Use your thimbles," she said, "or you will stick your fingers. I guarantee it."

The women soon became frustrated with the tedious chore—except for Ling Li, who proved to be adept at the craft. She made small, even stitches and never complained about how slowly the task advanced.

"You've quilted a lot, haven't you?" Kat observed.

"I have done many. I learned at a very young age," Ling Li said. "I'm also very good at embroidery."

"We're glad you joined us. I think in maybe one more week, we should be done with this quilt. Ling Li, you could embroider our names on it if you want."

"I don't want our little sewing meetings to end," Cilla said. "I have enjoyed our time together and actually learned to do something useful."

"We don't have to quit, do we?" Aggie said. "I know of some down-and-out people in Deadwood who could use a quilt. But, of course, this is your saloon and your decision," she said, glancing at Kat.

"I've cherished our time together, too," Kat agreed. "I suppose we could make another quilt or two. Maybe we should tie them this time, rather than quilt them. Who do you have in mind for the first one?"

Aggie threaded her needle. "There's this lady who takes care of neglected kids. She doesn't have much to go on, and I think she could use a quilt."

"Aggie takes food to her from the restaurant," Cilla told them.

"Hush! You weren't supposed to say anything." Aggie shrugged. "It's food that would be wasted, anyway."

"You have a good heart. You just don't want anyone to know," Cilla added.

JAN CERNEY

Aggie chomped firmly on her cigar and scowled.

"Perhaps it's time for all of us to help someone out," Kat said. "I certainly could do more."

"There's the people in Chinatown. I know of several families who could use a quilt," Ling Li said.

"Ling Li, I heard you have a fellow!" Cilla sang the last word.

Ling Li hung her head.

"You've embarrassed her," Jennie scolded.

"It's all right. I'm just not used to talking about myself to...strangers." Ling Li lifted her head to peek at them.

"Don't think of us as strangers. We're your friends," Cilla said, trying to smooth her abruptness.

"I met Cheng at the laundry," Ling Li explained. "Father doesn't even know I am interested in him. He's been coming in every day. We try to meet when my father is in the back room."

"Would your father approve of him?" Kat asked.

"I don't know. I actually don't know much about him or his family. Father would be the one to find that out."

"Has your father already chosen someone for you?" Jennie said as she peered up from her sewing.

"He has. It's the son of one of his friends." Ling Li hung her head. "He's in China."

"So that means he's coming here someday?"

"No. I think we'll be returning to China soon."

"Oh, I didn't know you would be leaving, too," Jennie said. "So many of your people have left already."

"Since the gold rush is over, my people have gone back to China or to the big cities where there are other Chinese. We will have to move someday, too. My father says times are changing."

"It's a bad time to become interested in someone," Cilla commented.

Jennie tapped her chin with her finger in thought. "Well,

18

if Ling Li married him, she wouldn't have to leave. Right, Ling Li?"

"Father would insist we leave, too. I have to obey my father," Ling Li confessed.

"If you don't know Cheng very well, I think we are all getting ahead of ourselves talking marriage," Kat advised. "Maybe he's not even the right man for you."

Jennie adjusted her thimble. "When are you supposed to see him again?"

"In about an hour. He'll be stopping by the laundry to pick up some of his clothes."

"I suggest we all go over to the laundry and meet him, too," Jennie said, her eyes lighting up.

"Are you all mad?" Aggie interjected. "None of you are her mother. You shouldn't be sticking your noses into her business."

"Well, as her friend, I feel responsible," Jennie said.

Ling Li lowered her head. "I didn't mean to cause trouble. If you want, you can come over to the laundry and see Cheng."

Jennie didn't need another invitation. "Let's go. We need a break anyway." With that, Kat, Jennie, and Cilla left their quilting and followed Ling Li out of the saloon. Aggie stayed behind, grumbling.

The women entered a very simple building constructed near the creek. A few of the patrons were arguing with an employee who was collecting for the laundry service. After the disgruntled customers left, Jennie asked Ling Li why they were so angry.

Ling Li shrugged. "They think our prices are too high." Ling Li took over the ironing while they all waited for Cheng to make his appearance.

Eventually, a young man with a queue entered the laundry. Ling Li made an unobtrusive gesture that this was Cheng. Kat listened and watched as the couple spoke in

Chinese and shared a few laughing moments before Ling Li retrieved his bundle of laundry from a shelf. She presented him with the bill, to which he did not take offense.

When Cheng left, Jennie quickly approached Ling Li. "He's good-looking and very mild-mannered. Where does he work?"

"In a mine."

"Why might your father not approve?" Jennie asked. "He has a respectable job."

"You don't understand. Marriages are based on family connections, and Father has his heart set on someone I have never met in China," Ling Li objected.

"That's too bad," Jennie commented. "I believe love is the reason for marriage."

Ling Li nodded. "I'm not being a good daughter. I need to do as my father says." Her face saddened.

Kat searched for words that would comfort Ling Li, but she couldn't find any. Instead, she and the other women waved a farewell to Ling Li and left the laundry.

"What a sad situation," Jennie confided to Kat.

"Yes, but it's their way of life. We shouldn't interfere."

"I suppose you're right, but I still think we could do something to help her out. If she and Cheng are in love, they should be together."

Kat frowned. "Jennie, leave well enough alone."

———

The Birdcage customers had finally become used to the fact that Kat and her help were not going to be dealing cards anymore. During the slow days, Kat found herself returning to sewing projects as soon as she ran out of things to do. The sewing group had finished the border and sewed it to the Log Cabin quilt. After Ling Li embroidered their names on the quilt, Kat wrapped it up in sturdy, brown paper and sent it by stagecoach to Ed, Jet's former boss. He had promised that he would deliver the quilt in person to Jet on his next visit to the prison, just ahead of the worst of the winter weather.

The sewing group had been collecting money for material to make the next quilt for the neglected children. They decided to make one small crazy quilt from the scraps left over from the Log Cabin quilt. Still, they needed material for the back. Kat left the saloon for Mel's general store the next morning. She hoped Corella wouldn't be there.

"Oh, good morning, Kat," Mel said when she walked through the door. "What can I help you with today?"

"I need material," Kat said. She inspected the shop, paying particular attention to the dark corners to make sure Corella wasn't nearby.

"Hmmm. You haven't finished your quilt yet?"

"We have, and we're making another." She could tell that Mel wanted to know who it was for, but she wasn't going to tell him. Kat quickly chose two bolts of fabric—one blue and one pink—and took them to Mel for measuring.

"Ah, is someone expecting a baby?" Mel asked.

"Not that I know of."

Mel, slightly bewildered, dutifully cut the fabric she wanted, wrapped it in paper, and handed her the bundle. "Well, good day, then."

"Thanks, Mel," she said after paying the bill. She walked directly back to the Birdcage with her bundle and disappeared behind the partition. It would be some time before the ladies joined her. That gave her time to play around with a crazy quilt design. This quilt would not require such a rigid pattern, but rather imperfect shapes sewed around a centerpiece. This time, they would have to sew the scraps onto a square block of fabric. Kat had found an old bed sheet they could use for the square blocks.

While Kat was sewing a crazy quilt block, she thought

about her slowing business. Dealing cards was one of the more enjoyable tasks of her workday, but she had known for years that the authorities would eventually crack down on gambling. Since she had taken over the saloon, she had seen the negative effects of gambling and drinking on individuals and families. But what else could she do? This was all she had known. Unless...

"Clem, are you busy? Could you come in here a minute?" she asked, as though her thoughts might instantly evaporate.

"Just a minute."

Kat heard him clomping toward the partition.

"What can I do for you?"

"Have a seat. I have an idea."

"I'm ready," he said, placing his hands on his knees.

"Business has been declining lately."

Clem nodded.

"I can't give up the business just now, but I am wondering if we could increase our profits by selling food."

"Food? Who's going to do the cooking, and where? I don't see a kitchen."

"I know there are a lot of details to work out, but if we serve one meal a day, we could perhaps keep the customers here a little longer. Perhaps someone could use my house to prepare the meals and bring them over. If it catches on, then I'll have to do something else. You don't cook, do you?"

Clem laughed. "I'm a confirmed bachelor. I had to learn to do some cooking, but I can't promise anyone would enjoy it, let alone pay for it."

"So what do you think?"

"I'll go along with it if that's what you want, but you need to find a cook."

"Thanks, Clem. I'll start looking." She smiled. "I knew I could count on you." After Clem returned to the bar, Kat continued sewing the quilt block until the women arrived.

She showed them the completed block and explained her process. "We need to cut out twelve-inch blocks from this old sheet. I cut out one for this block." Kat placed the sheet between Cilla and Jennie.

Ling Li took the completed block in her hand. "I could add embroidery to each of these. It would make the quilt especially pretty."

Kat handed Ling Li the embroidery floss left over from the Log Cabin. "See what you can do while Aggie and I sew more blocks."

"Why don't you make another one, so I can watch," Aggie suggested.

Kat sat up to the sewing machine, sewed on a centerpiece and began to sew the scraps around it. "Would you happen to know of someone who is looking for a cooking job?"

"Maybe," Aggie said. "Where do you need a cook?"

"I'm thinking about serving one meal a day here at the Birdcage."

"What for? There are plenty of restaurants in town."

"I thought it might help my business."

"Well, I can cook," Aggie admitted.

"Would you consider working for me? Do you have time, say, for the evening meal?"

"I'd have to quit at the Prospector, which isn't a bad thing. Cleaning is hard on me at my age. But you don't have a kitchen here," Aggie pointed out.

"No, but I do at my house. I thought the meal could be cooked there and brought here to the Birdcage. Want to give it a try?"

"Sure. Just tell me when to start," Aggie agreed. "I don't cook fancy—just plain, rib-sticking food."

"That's all I'm interested in. Just let me know when you're free to begin cooking, Aggie."

The ladies continued to talk, and Ling Li had finished

applying embroidery to the block using oriental designs. Kat praised her. "It's simply beautiful, but I suppose we should wait until all the blocks are sewn together before the embroidery is added. We are so lucky to have found you."

Ling Li bowed her head with gratitude. "I must be going now, or Father will miss me."

"Customers are beginning to arrive, so I suppose we'll also quit for the day. Thanks again, everyone, for coming by," Kat said as she straightened up the space.

Kat crossed the partition and walked out to the tables, which were filling rapidly. She noticed Rio with a man she had never seen before. She maintained her distance and slipped behind the bar. In spite of Kat's unfriendliness, Rio pushed back his chair, approached her, and leaned his elbows on the counter. "Kat, how about a round of drinks at our table. We're all mighty thirsty."

"I'll send Jennie over," she said. She was careful not to look up from her ledger.

"No, we'd rather have you come over. This here's our favorite place, you know."

"I know, Rio. Why is that so?" Now Kat looked straight into his eyes.

"Because it has the prettiest redhead in all of Deadwood."

"I'm not your type, Rio. I don't want to be rude, but I'm not interested."

Rio's face stiffened. "You are an unfriendly one. We might have to find another saloon if that's how you're going to be." He leered. "I hear your boyfriend's in prison."

Kat's heart began to pound. "What did you say?" *Who could have told him? Hardly anyone knew,* she thought. "What of it?" she managed to say.

"Good news has a way of traveling fast. You're all alone, little lady."

"Are you threatening me?"

"Take it any way you'd like." He laughed. "Never mind the

drinks. I'll find a saloon that wants my business." Rio swaggered out of the saloon. The stranger followed, but not before he glanced back with chilling, steel-gray eyes.

Kat shuddered as Jennie stopped at the bar for a tray of drinks. They shared a look of disgust. "Remind me to buy a gun tomorrow," Kat said with determination in her voice.

CHAPTER 3

A week later, Kat and Aggie met to discuss the Birdcage Saloon's first dinner. They both stood in the doorway of Kat's tiny kitchen. One look at the walls confirmed the meticulousness that had afforded Kat so much success in her business. A multitude of clean utensils hung from pegs. The oven contained a stack of assorted pots and pans. There was no food to be seen; it was stashed in cupboards and boxes and tins, except for the few dried onions and herbs that hung from nails on the back porch. Aggie ascertained that Kat made the best use of her limited space and already felt a bit sorry for the mess she was about to make.

"Do you think you can cook in this small kitchen?" Kat asked. As she watched the unkempt woman stride into the kitchen, a dab of white ash tumbled from the end of that perpetual cigar and silently splashed onto the otherwise flawless floor.

"Why, sure. The Miner's actually isn't much bigger. Now, what shall I cook for tonight?"

"We'll try to keep it simple. Roast beef sandwiches might work for starters. I don't know how many of the customers will eat on this first try, so just cook up what I have in the icebox. When it's gone, it's gone. The bread's in that box on the table. I bought it from the bakery this morning. I'll send someone over later to help you deliver." Kat began her short walk to the saloon, but not without a twinge of apprehension.

Residences could only get so large in Deadwood, a town built between the slopes of a gulch among the Black Hills. Kat's small house was wedged into a string of homes lining a terraced hillside. Wooden stairs clung to the dirt banks for those wishing to reach Main Street on foot. Kat had used these stairs without fear for her safety even in the wild early years of the town's short history, but now Rio's threats echoed in her ears.

Did he just want to scare me simply because I rejected him? she wondered. *That had to be the reason, but what about the stranger with him? I've never done anything to him.*

The stranger's evil eyes frightened her the most. She didn't tarry on the stairs and was relieved when she reached Main Street and, finally, the Birdcage. Jake was preparing for a big night at the bar. Clem had not yet arrived. Jennie, Cilla, and Ling Li were busily sewing.

"About time, Kat," Jennie teased. "Is Aggie ready for the big night?"

"I believe so. I'll send Jake or Clem to help bring over the food closer to dinnertime."

Jennie pulled Kat aside and whispered, "Are you still going to get that gun you were talking about?"

"I have to, but don't tell anyone else about this, especially the ladies." Kat placed her hand on Jennie's shoulder and Jennie nodded. "Thank you. I don't want to frighten them." She watched Jennie take Aggie's place at the sewing machine and crossed the partition to find Jake washing bar glasses.

"Jake, I have something to ask of you."

"Anything, Boss."

"I need a gun," she whispered.

"A gun? What kind of gun?"

"Quiet!" she hissed. "I don't want anyone to hear. I need to defend myself."

Jake stopped wiping, set the glass down on the counter, and looked at her quizzically. "I don't understand. What's going on?"

"It might be nothing, but Rio threatened me about a week ago."

"He did? You should have told me then," Jake said, rolling up his sleeves.

"I didn't want to cause trouble. Anyway, he left with another fellow who gave me the creeps."

"How did he threaten you?"

"Rio somehow knew that Jet is in prison and that I live alone. It was just the way he said it. Maybe I'm exaggerating what I heard."

"Probably not. I never cared for Rio, the way he treats you. I was always hoping he'd start a brawl so I could sic the sheriff on him."

"Well, anyway, I'd feel better if I could carry a gun. I was hoping you would buy one for me."

"Do you know how to use one?"

"Somewhat."

"Oh, that makes me feel better. When do you want it?"

"As soon as possible."

"I'm going to show you how to use it. The last thing anyone wants is an accidental discharge—or a misfire."

"Okay, that's probably a good idea. Would today be too soon?'

"If you let me off work for a few minutes, I'll go buy you something. Are you thinking about a pistol?"

"I want something for my purse."

"A derringer, maybe. I'll see what I can find."

"Take whatever money you need from the till, Jake. You can go now." It wasn't until after Jake disappeared through the saloon door, leaving Kat alone at the bar, that she realized she was shaking. She wasn't in the mood to work on quilts, but she rejoined the ladies on the other side of the partition. She forced herself to cut a few more white squares from the old sheet and trim the blocks Jennie had completed. Yet, for the first time, quilting with her friends could not preoccupy her troubled mind.

———

Jake returned to the saloon later that morning. Kat left the ladies to speak with him. "You have it?" she asked softly.

"I do, but I'm not giving it to you until I show you how to use it."

"Let's slip out now. It's about time for lunch anyway." Kat gathered her purse as Jake hurried out from behind the bar to prepare his buggy. He was reaching toward the door when Kat shouted, "Oh! Jake! I need you to help Aggie bring the food from my house later on."

———

Kat and Jake rode through the dusty streets of town until they were surrounded by vast wilderness. Jake stopped near what appeared to be a deserted log cabin. They both knew it was most likely built by one of the early miners, and there was a good chance that the miner was now either dead or far from Deadwood.

Jake helped Kat out of the buggy and told her to stay put while he looked for something to use for target practice. Soon he returned with an armload of rusty tin cans, which he lined up on a fallen tree. He opened a case, revealing two weapons. "Are you ready for this?" he asked Kat.

"I don't think I have a choice."

"Remember, these are short-range weapons. You have to fire when you are close to your target. Even though they're small, they can be deadly if used properly. There are two of them in this set because this particular model fires only two shots. If you miss, or if the gun misfires, the other gun is your backup." Jake paused to ensure that Kat was listening.

She nodded.

"This derringer has two barrels. See?" Taking the gun in his hand, Jake explained how to load the ammunition. "There, now you have two shots."

"Let me load it."

Jake unloaded the small-caliber rimfire rounds and let Kat load the gun. "I advise that you fire this gun every once in a while to get used to it. Are you ready to shoot?"

"I am."

"Let's get close to our targets. Remember, this gun is not for long distances." They approached the cans perched on the fallen tree trunk. "You don't actually aim with this weapon; just point and shoot."

Kat tried to take his advice, but naturally felt compelled to aim instead. She learned what Jake meant when she jerked the trigger. The loud report rang in her ears and caused her heart to flutter.

"Try again, Kat."

She nodded. *What am I doing with a gun in my hand?* She squeezed the trigger once more. This time she came closer to knocking the can off the log.

"Reload. Do it again," Jake said.

Kat managed to hit three of the cans with eight shots. "This is harder than I thought," she admitted.

"I know. That's why I think it's foolish to have a gun. More than likely, you would be killed before getting a shot off."

"Thanks a lot for the confidence," Kat retorted.

"I don't mean anything by it, but I hope you never have to use the derringer."

"I see what you're getting at. Suppose we'd better get back to town."

Jake left the cans where they were. "Maybe we'll come back sometime for more practice."

———

As the crowd began to assemble that same evening, Kat was tidying up the workspace at the quilting table. She rose and pushed in her chair. The other women had packed up their things and left, except for Jennie, who was wiping tables. Kat felt the knot in her stomach clinch when she crossed the partition. A quick glance around the room assured her that neither Rio nor his eerie friend was there. She sighed as she approached the bar.

"He's not here tonight. At least not yet, anyway," Clem said.

"No, not yet," Kat echoed. She wondered if she would be able to use the derringer in an emergency. The gun at least gave her the sense that she was in control of the situation. That would have to do for now.

———

Night after night, Aggie's hot meals produced feeding frenzies. Kat acquired a sense of urgency to transform her saloon into an eatery, and the ambition replaced her anxiety over Rio, who hadn't shown his face in weeks. She hired workers to add a lean-to kitchen off the rear of the saloon. Aggie continued to cook, and the customers devoured whatever she made. Although Aggie wasn't able to help with the quilting much anymore, Kat now had more time to sew than ever. The quilt was nearly complete and business was good, in spite of the unfinished kitchen, impending winter weather, and fierce competition from the numerous restaurants in Deadwood.

During one of the rare quilting sessions in which Aggie was present, she confessed, "I'm glad you decided to add a kitchen. I can cook full meals now without having to worry about delivery. The kitchen's right here and handy, and maybe that will leave me more time to quilt."

"We have just about finished this crazy quilt," Kat said.

"That quilt is sure to be appreciated. Want to come with me to present it?"

"I'd love to see the children."

"What's left to do on the quilt?" Aggie asked.

"The binding has to be sewn on. Ling Li might have a little more embroidery to finish. I'll ask her when the ladies arrive."

Aggie glanced at the regulator clock on the wall. "Suppose I should get back to your house and check on the stew. I'll be back at about noon." As Aggie left the saloon, she waved at Cilla and Ling Li, who were on their way in.

"Sure wish Aggie could help us more," Cilla said.

"Once we get the kitchen done, she might be able to. Projects like these can be a strain on anybody. We could just give up our sessions after we finish this quilt," Kat proposed. "I never even intended to make this an ongoing project back when we started."

"No, I don't think we should," Ling Li said softly. "I like a change from the drudgery of the laundry. It's hard work, the washing and the ironing."

"What do the rest of you think?"

"I think Ling Li is right. It's fun," Jennie agreed. "I'm learning to sew."

Cilla nodded.

"Well then, let's finish this quilt, and then we can move on to another if you would like," Kat suggested.

"Do you have any ideas for the next one?" Jennie asked.

"I believe Ling Li suggested we make a quilt for a needy Chinese family."

"I did suggest that," Ling Li said.

"Do you know of any Chinese quilt patterns we could use?" Jennie asked.

"I do. The Chinese Lantern is very pretty and simple."

"Chinese lanterns sure are pretty. They make a place seem so festive," Jennie said. "Could you draw the pattern for us?"

Ling Li took a piece of paper and pencil and drew a pattern that clearly resembled actual Chinese lanterns. "What do you think?"

"I think it's beautiful," Jennie said. "Would we need oriental print fabrics?"

"Yes, it would be best. There is a Chinese mercantile here in Deadwood that sells such fabric."

"Would you have time, Ling Li, to stop by the mercantile with us and pick out some cloth when we deliver the quilt?" Kat said.

"I could meet you after I get some ironing done," Ling Li said as she put away her embroidery thread and needle. "Father is displeased when I take too much time from my work."

———

With the crazy quilt finally finished, bundled, and in hand, Aggie and Kat set out along the streets of Deadwood. They waved at Ling Li through the window of her father's shop. Ling Li joined them for the short walk to the Chinese mercantile.

Neither Aggie nor Kat had shopped in this mercantile until now. The shop's sandalwood incense perfumed the air with a spicy fragrance. Once inside the shop, both Kat and Aggie perused the imported merchandise while wind chimes tinkled soft melodies. Kat scanned the shelves with gaily packed novelties and discovered colorful, hand-painted ceramic tableware and paper decorations. She lingered, and Ling Li quietly identified the rice and soup bowls, teapot, saucepot, tea cups, soup spoons, and even a wine warmer, all decorated with various patterns and tranquil scenes. Less decorative earthenware and stoneware were arranged beside the porcelain pieces. Kat moved on to the personal items: medicine bottles marked with Chinese characters, tooth-brushes, combs, hairpins, earrings, clothes, hats, shoes, and more. Kat stopped to admire the ivory toothbrush handles.

Vibrant ceremonial items caught Kat's attention in an-other part of the store. She had seen the colorful Chinese fu-neral processions led by bands from Chinatown to the cem-etery at Mount Moriah. She was often mesmerized by the brass band's cacophony mingled with the mourners' weep-ing, accentuated by firecrackers intended to ward off evil spirits. And who in Deadwood was not aware of the Chinese New Year festivities? These ceremonies attracted many non-Chinese spectators from the surrounding area. Even Kat had once gone to the Chinese section of Deadwood during the Chinese New Year to take part in the celebration. Kat recog-nized the items used for such festivities on the store shelves and fondly stroked the banners, fans, and candles. She gri-maced at the noisy firecrackers that would keep the town awake all night. Finally, Kat was drawn to what seemed to be the brightest arrangement on the shelves—the Chinese lanterns.

Ling Li led them past what seemed like miles of silks to the cloth prints they would need for the quilt. Ling Li explained that the pretty fabric designs were influenced by the majesty of her homeland. Kat was impressed. The three women agreed upon the most pleasing color scheme and then purchased the necessary amount of cloth.

Afterward, Ling Li returned to the laundry, and Kat and

Aggie went on with the widow's quilt.

"I found that very interesting," Kat remarked to Aggie.

"I guess so. I see it every day."

Kat hesitated to ask Aggie what she meant because she suddenly realized she had no idea where Aggie lived, or anything else about her. She had found it best to generally avoid such questions in Deadwood.

"Here we are." Aggie stopped abruptly in front of a ramshackle building that leaned toward the east. Aggie knocked on the door and greeted the woman who introduced to herself as Cora. Kat noticed that the woman seemed aged beyond her years and suspected she hadn't worn a new dress in decades.

Cora invited them into her sparsely furnished dwelling. Five young children expectantly gathered around them for a handout.

"I have no food for you today, but perhaps tomorrow," Aggie said. The children frowned but remained in the room.

"My neighbor brought me a rabbit. It's in the stewpot. It will do for us today," Cora explained.

Aggie handed the quilt to Cora. "Here's a quilt for you. Five of us women made it."

Cora took the quilt and tested its heaviness. "The children can use it. They all sleep in one bed," she said with her unchanging, dour expression. "Want some coffee?"

"I need to be going," Kat blurted out. Cora didn't impress Kat in the least. *Why was she caring for these children? She obviously didn't have the means*, she thought.

Aggie stared at Kat. "I suppose I should be about my business, too. I'll bring you all something to eat tomorrow. I work at the Birdcage tomorrow. I should be able to scare up something for you." She looked sideways at Kat. Cora nodded, and the two women left.

"She didn't even thank us," Kat pointed out indignantly. "You would think she'd be more grateful."

"We don't help others for the thanks."

"Well, maybe not, but it's nice to know that someone is appreciative."

Aggie shrugged as she parted company with Kat, walking along Main Street toward Chinatown.

But Kat, still miffed with Cora's attitude, plodded toward the saloon. Eventually, out of curiosity, she turned around to see where Aggie was going, but the woman had vanished.

Two curious ladies, Kat thought. She pondered their strange behaviors all the way back to her saloon. Once inside, she pulled Ling Li aside. "Have you ever seen Aggie in Chinatown?"

"I see all sorts of people in Chinatown, not just the Chinese."

"Yes, but I'm wondering if Aggie lives there."

"Why do you ask? Is she in trouble?"

"Not that I know of. I guess I just need to know more about Aggie. In fact, I hardly know anything about her."

"I don't wonder about such things."

"So you're saying you have never seen Aggie in Chinatown?"

"I...have seen her."

"What does she do there?"

"That is her concern, not ours."

"So, I gather you don't want to tell me anything?"

Ling Li nodded.

"All right, then I'll quit asking." But Ling Li's answer had piqued Kat's interest. Kat didn't consider herself a meddler or a conniver, but she decided she wasn't going to leave this matter alone.

CHAPTER 4

Several days later, when Aggie finished preparing the meal, Kat asked what she was going to do for the rest of the day. Aggie shrugged and replied that she didn't have any plans. Kat wished her well, and Aggie left the saloon and strode down the street. Kat watched through the window, and when she thought Aggie was far enough ahead of her, she quietly followed. Aggie turned around once, and Kat ducked into the nearest store until Aggie continued walking toward Chinatown. Kat's heart thumped wildly as she neared the lower end of Main Street, where she very seldom visited. Careful to remain out of sight, she watched Aggie enter a building Kat did not recognize. Kat was torn. She didn't want to search the building in case Aggie were to come out and find her snooping.

After debating her plan of action for some time, she chose to instead enter one of the Chinese restaurants in view of the building into which Aggie had disappeared. Kat wasn't hungry, even though the restaurant tempted her with the aroma of oriental spices and fried food. Instead, she ordered a cup of tea and a pastry and watched the door from her window table for two hours. She had decided to give up her stakeout when Ling Li entered the restaurant.

"What are you doing here?" Ling Li asked in astonishment.

Kat was taken by surprise and found herself completely at a loss for words. "Oh, I'm...I'm having a cup of tea."

"I see that. But what are you really doing here?" Ling Li said as she sat at the table. "You're spying on Aggie, aren't you?"

"Yes, I guess I am. And you know where she is, don't you?"

Ling Li nodded.

"Are you going to tell me what she's doing? I know which building she went into, although I don't know what it is. Please tell me, Ling Li."

Ling Li fidgeted with her hands. After a slight hesitation, she said, "It's a Chinese gambling establishment."

"What's Aggie doing in there?"

"She's a dealer."

"How do you know?"

"My uncle owns that building."

"Isn't gambling only for men?"

"It is, but they let her in for some reason."

"The law isn't concerned?"

"No, I guess not," she said as the waitress came and poured Ling Li a small cup of tea.

Kat leaned in closer to Ling Li. "I'd like to see inside a Chinese gambling hall. I've been told they play different games than we do."

"The Chinese have been gambling since ancient times. It's just a part of who we are," Ling Li explained after taking a sip of tea.

"What's their popular game here in Deadwood?"

"Fan-tan, I am told."

"Do you know how they play it?"

"No."

"What would happen if I walked into their gaming establishment?"

"They'd walk you right back out."

Kat frowned.

"You sure are determined, aren't you?" Ling Li said.

"I guess so. I hate unanswered questions, although I'd say you are pretty determined yourself."

Ling Li tilted her head. "How so?"

"You come and go as you please. You're not afraid of your father."

"I was raised here and went to the Deadwood schools. I learned not to be so submissive."

"Do you really want to return to China?"

"My family is there, and so is my mother. I hope Cheng will return, too."

Kat glanced through the window toward the gaming hall. "No one is going in or coming out."

Ling Li heaved a sigh. "I shouldn't do this, but I may be able to sneak you in through the back way. We couldn't actually enter the gaming, but you can see what they're doing."

"You would do that for me?"

"On one condition. You can't tell anyone, or I will be in such trouble."

"I promise. What do we do?"

"There's a rear entrance to a kitchen. Since I'm family, we won't seem suspicious, but we'll still have to be silent. If we're discovered, we'll need an excuse."

Kat nodded. "But I don't understand how that will do me any good."

"You'll see when we get there." Ling Li gulped the last of her tea. "Just follow me."

The women paid their bill, left the restaurant, and backtracked on Main Street until they had circled around to the rear door of the gaming hall. Ling Li carefully pushed the door open into the makeshift kitchen. A stale odor penetrated the air. Unwashed dishes filled a dish pan. Ling Li held her finger to her lips while she led Kat to a pantry. Ling Li silently removed a large pot from a shelf to reveal a hole large enough to peer through. As the ladies stood quietly, they could hear the voices in the gaming hall. Ling Li motioned for Kat to look through the peephole.

Kat sidled up to the pantry shelves and peered through the hole. She saw a multitude of tables, each with a dealer and a number of players placing bets in the center of the table. She watched as the dealer dipped into a container and placed a handful of glass counters under a metal bowl. When the bets were placed, the dealer removed the bowl-shaped cover and, taking a bamboo stick curved at the end, raked counters into groups of four. It took a while for Kat to determine how the game worked. She eventually determined that whatever number of counters remained was the winning bet.

Before she stepped back from her view, she surveyed the players. She spotted Aggie with ease. The end of that characteristic cigar bobbed with every move she made. Kat's gaze floated along with the cloud of smoke hovering over the table, and then a sight so startled her that she jumped back from the peephole and bumped into the wall behind her. Covering her mouth in fear that they would be detected, she stood silently while Ling Li looked through the peephole.

"I don't think anyone heard you."

Kat sighed with relief.

"What did you see?"

"Let me look again." And again, her body trembled, though she was able to muster more control this time. Rio and the stranger were sitting at Aggie's table! They were playing fan-tan right along with the Chinese. She watched

Rio push back his chair and saunter over to Aggie. He said a few words to her and left. The stranger followed.

Kat silently mouthed, "Let's go," to Ling Li, who put the pot in its original place in the pantry. Once outside, Kat explained what she had seen.

"Rio? You saw Rio?"

"Yes. Let's try to follow him."

"You're crazy—"

Kat jerked her to the front of the building. Luckily, the two men were in no hurry. As Kat peeked around the corner of the building, she drew back quickly and bumped up against Ling Li. Kat grimaced. "They're right outside the building." Both women shrank back against the structure.

"What do we do now?" Ling Li whispered.

"You got me on this one. I don't know." They soon heard the men's spurs jingle down the boardwalk. Kat peered around the corner and then shrank back.

"This is a crazy idea," Ling Li said. "Go back to the Birdcage and let me follow them. I live here; it wouldn't look so suspicious if they were to turn around and see me."

"Maybe you're right. I don't want an incident with Rio. Do be careful, Ling Li. If you learn anything, come back and tell me at the Birdcage."

"I'll return to the Birdcage either way."

Kat and Ling Li separated. Kat turned around one more time to see Rio and the stranger heading deeper into Chinatown. Ling Li followed closely before she strode toward her place of business.

Once back at the saloon, Kat busied herself while she awaited Ling Li's return. She took over Clem's job of washing glasses and sent him to sweep the floor. "What's the matter, Kat? You sure are jumpy," Clem said.

Kat wondered if she should say anything and remembered her promise to Ling Li. "I'll tell you when I get some more information."

"It's about Rio, isn't it?"

Kat nodded. "He's still in Deadwood, but I can't say any more than that for now."

"So we need to remain alert?"

"Yes, we do."

"Should I talk to the sheriff?" Clem offered.

"He really hasn't done anything other than make a threat. I say we just wait around a little longer until Rio shows his hand. I have a feeling there's more to this than a passing interest in me."

In the time it took Clem to sweep the saloon floor, Kat had finished washing the glassware and wiping the tables. They were ready for the night crowd, although the establishment was so quiet, Kat was almost at peace. Just when she had placed her elbows on the bar and leaned forward to take the stress from her sore feet, Ling Li emerged through the swinging doors of the saloon and motioned for Kat to join her in the sewing area. Kat approached and whispered, "What did you find out?"

"I had to wait while Rio and his pal stopped at a saloon to have a drink or two. I just about to give up when they finally came out and continued their walk down the street. Both men entered a shack on the edge of Chinatown."

"That's all they did?"

"Yes. But guess who else lives in that shack?"

Kat's eyes widened. "I have no idea."

"Aggie."

———

The following morning, Kat lingered over her coffee and reread the letter she received from Jet the day before. She was pleased to read of his surprise when Ed delivered the quilt and loved hearing that he had been enjoying it very much. The nights, he wrote, were cold, and the quilt warmed him. Other than that, Jet did not have much to say. But what was there to say about prison life that would be fit for her eyes to read?

Kat wanted so much to write Jet about Rio's threat, but of course, there was no use. Jet was locked up, and there was nothing he could do about her predicament. She placed the letter back in the envelope and left it on the table. She departed from her little house on the terraced hillside, holding the purse that hid the derringer.

The frigid morning fog reminded her that the harsh winter weather wouldn't hold off forever. She pulled her cape closely around her. The familiar stairs were damp, and as she glanced down to carefully place her steps, she saw a stiff piece of paper on one of the ledges. She hadn't noticed it before, so she stooped down to pick it up. Her heart jumped into her throat as she read, "Hi, little lady. I plan to visit you soon. Hope you're friendly this time."

The note wasn't signed and wasn't addressed to anyone in particular, but she knew who it was from. She reached for the derringer in her purse and decided it would be safer to continue on to the Birdcage than to return to her house.

Clem was sitting at the table drinking a cup of coffee when Kat opened the swinging doors to her saloon. "Good morning, Kat. What happened to you? Looks like you've seen a ghost."

Kat shakily handed him the note she had found on the path. "What should I think of this?"

Clem scanned the note and wrinkled his brow. "Of course it's easier for me to say, but I think Rio is playing games. For some reason, he's trying to rattle you."

"But why? I've done nothing except to turn him down."

"Some guys just can't stand that. He's one of those ornery characters. Maybe you should talk to the sheriff. He might know something about him and that friend of his."

"Perhaps you're right. Mind the store while I'm at the

sheriff's office." In those few short minutes, the wind had picked up and the temperature seemed to be dropping. Then again, maybe she was just chilled at the thought of Rio and the stranger with the steel gray eyes. She pushed open the door of the office to find Sheriff Briggs in quiet slumber, seated with his feet propped up on his desk.

"Busy night, Sheriff?" Kat shouted to wake him.

"What—oh, hi there, Kat. Yeah, it was. Ruckus down the street." Sheriff Briggs removed his feet from the desk, rubbed his eyes, and adjusted his large form in the chair. "Trouble at the saloon?"

"No, not really. I'd like to talk to you for a minute."

"Okay," he said, removing his feet from the desk. "Need some coffee?"

"No, thanks."

"Mind if I have some while we talk?"

"Go right ahead."

Sheriff Briggs poured himself a cup of steaming, black brew while Kat sat across from his desk. "Okay, I'm ready," the sheriff said when he returned, stifling a yawn.

"Do you know a guy by the name of Rio? Strongly built, sandy hair, walks with a swagger. He has a friend with dark hair and steel gray eyes. Doesn't say much."

"Yeah, I've seen them around town. They manage to stay out of trouble."

"Do you know anything about them?"

"No, I haven't had the occasion to really get to know them. Why do you ask?"

"This fellow, Rio, used to come into the Birdcage on a regular basis, usually alone." Kat caressed her purse. "He always wanted me to do the dealing at his table. I tried to avoid him, but finally I had to tell him I wasn't interested. He threatened me and said he knew my friend Jet was in prison, and that I was all alone."

"And who is Jet?"

"A man I met. He was arrested for cattle rustling and is in the Yankton prison."

"For how long?"

"A year."

"Let me get this straight. You're interested in Jet, not Rio?"

Kat shifted in her chair, feeling uncomfortable talking about matters of the heart with a stranger. "Yes, well, anyway, this morning I found this note along the stairs where I walk down the hill from my house. I don't know what to think about it," she said, handing the note to the sheriff.

Sheriff Briggs scanned the brief note. "It's not signed."

"I know, but it's from Rio," Kat insisted.

"Does Rio come into your saloon anymore?"

Kat shook her head.

Sheriff Briggs thumped the note with his thick hand. "I can't arrest him on this little bit of information, but I see he has put a fright into you. I'll scout around and see if I can find him and his friend, keep an eye on them, maybe ask a few questions. Until then, keep me informed if anything else happens."

"Thanks. I will." Kat rose from the chair and clutched her purse. She knew the sheriff would frown on her for concealing a firearm, but she felt a little better after talking to him. At least he was aware of her situation, and if anything happened, he would know the story. She just hoped the sheriff wouldn't blab her predicament all over town. The less people knew about her, the better.

———

The women had gathered for their quilting session by the time Kat returned. Cilla and Jennie were cutting pieces out of bright fabric for the Chinese Lantern quilt. "Where's Ling Li?" Kat asked.

"Don't know," Cilla said. "She's usually here by now."

"This quilt is turning out to be a beauty," Kat commented. "I'm thinking we should give this one to Ling Li for her hope chest."

Jennie sat at the sewing machine to begin another block. "I agree. She's going to marry sooner or later."

Not long after that, Ling Li rushed into the saloon in tears. "Cheng is in jail!"

"In jail? I was—" Kat caught herself. She didn't want them to know she had visited with the sheriff. *Was that the ruckus the sheriff was referring to?* she wondered.

Jennie stopped sewing. "What for?"

"The sheriff and his deputy raided an opium den and took him to jail last night. If Cheng had just paid the fine, he could have walked away. But instead, he decided to protest by spending time in jail," Ling Li explained. Tears streamed down her cheek.

"Did you know he smoked opium?" Jennie asked.

"No. But it's typical. It helps the men relax."

"I don't like that opium," Kat said.

"But it's part of Chinese culture," Jennie said, "like alcohol and tobacco are part of ours."

"I just don't want him to be in jail like a shameful criminal." Ling Li hesitated and put her hand to her mouth. "I'm sorry, Kat. I didn't mean to say that."

"Don't worry about it," Kat said. "Jet did rustle cattle at one time, but I don't think of him as a lowly criminal."

"My father wouldn't like me being interested in someone who's serving jail time," Ling Li said.

"But didn't you just say that using opium is a common thing to do?" Cilla asked.

"Not to my father. Spending time in jail is worse."

Kat nodded. "I see your dilemma."

"I'd like to go visit him in jail, but I know father wouldn't like that, either. I worry that they aren't taking care of him."

"Sheriff Briggs is a decent man," Kat said. "I'm sure he'll treat Cheng fairly."

"I hope so. Some men are prejudiced. One time, some white men attempted to cut off his queue."

"You do have cause to worry, but I'll bet the sheriff will let you see Cheng if you really want to," Jennie said.

"I'll have to talk to my father first. I can't go behind his back anymore. I need to be honest with him."

"They say honesty is the best policy, but sometimes I don't think it works that way," Jennie said. "What did you say that Cheng does for a living?"

"He's a miner."

"What if we found him a job that would elevate his social standing? Perhaps he would appeal to your father then?"

"How would we find him a job?" Cilla spat.

"I'm not sure, but I do know a few wealthy Deadwood citizens hire house servants."

"From miner to house servant...I'm not sure I see much improvement," Kat said.

"Well, let's see. I guess Cheng would rub elbows, so to speak, with Deadwood's elite, even if he is their servant."

"I don't know how Cheng would feel about our plan. I'll have to ask him," Ling Li said.

"Good idea. Then get back to me," Jennie said. "We'll get to work finding him another job."

CHAPTER 5

Kat was examining the inventory of liquor bottles under the counter when she heard the jingle of spurs approach the long, mahogany bar. Clem was busy on the other side of the saloon, so she stood up with pad and pencil in hand to help the customer.

"What could I get you—?" She stopped short.

"Hello, Kat," said the tall, dark, and slightly thinner Jet.

She stood speechless for a moment and the color drained from her face. "I didn't expect you to turn up like this. You never wrote you were coming."

"Sorry for the shock." His eyes lingered on her a moment. "Let's...sit down," he urged. Her wobbly legs carried her around the counter to his outstretched hand. She took it, and her eyes remained locked with his as she followed him to the table.

"I didn't expect them to let me out early on good behavior, like they promised, until a few days before I left. There wasn't enough time to get a letter to you."

Her eyes still held to his face, searching every nuance. "It's hard to believe you're out of that place. How are you?"

"I'm okay, although it will take a long time to forget. Your letters and the quilt kept me going. Ed wrote me a few times, too. This is the second place I came after getting my walking papers."

Color began to return to her face. "And where was the first place?"

Jet laughed. "I see you haven't lost your spunk." He chucked her under the chin. "I stopped at the ranch and talked to Ed. I had to find out if I still had a job."

"Do you?" was all she could manage to say. She couldn't believe Jet was sitting beside her.

"I do if I want it, but I'd like to stay around here and get to know you better until I have to leave."

The thought of him staying sent shivers up her spine. "Stay in Deadwood?"

"Yeah, if that's okay with you."

"I guess I never thought about you staying here. I mean, I'd like you to."

"There for a minute, I thought you didn't want me around."

"No, it's not that. You just took me by surprise."

"I'd have to find work, and I suppose no one is going to hire me for just a short time."

"I know a lot of people who could use temporary help if you're not fussy about what you do."

"No. I'll take whatever I can find."

"How about working in a tailor shop?" she said expressionlessly. Then she smiled, and he laughed again at her teasing. "I'm so glad you're free. I was worried about you." She stroked his pale, drawn face.

"It was no picnic, that's for sure. But I survived, and I'll be darned if I'll go back there again."

"Where are you staying?" she asked with concern.

"Nowhere, yet."

"We have several vacant rooms above the saloon. Let's go up, and you can choose which room you want."

"I can't pay much."

"The room's free as long as you take me to supper once in a while. I'd invite you over to my house, but I'm not much of a cook."

"You have to be better than what I ate in prison. In fact, I'm yearning for a nice, juicy steak covered with onions." He grasped her hand before they climbed the stairs to the four rooms at the top.

Just the feel of his hand let her know he cared. A tingling surged through her body. Finally, he was here beside her—but she wasn't sure what to do. She inhaled deeply to steady herself. "Clem and Jake each have a room up here. But the two on this end are empty." She opened the door to each one. "Go on in and have a look." She waved him to the small rooms, each neatly furnished with a bed, chair, and wash-stand. She watched him as he entered the room nearest the stairs to give it a cursory glance.

"I can't tell you how good this looks to me after spending almost a year in a prison cell. I felt like I was going to suffocate. A terrible feeling it was...one I'd like to forget."

She couldn't imagine what such confinement would be like. "You'll be comfortable here." She glanced down at the small satchel and the quilt he was carrying. "Now, how about I buy you supper?"

"I should be the one buying, but I need a job first."

"We'll take care of that tomorrow. But for now, let's go eat. I know a restaurant that can fry you up the best steak in town."

Jet nodded. "With onions?"

"You bet." Kat couldn't resist slipping her arm through his, but he appeared tense and unyielding during the remainder of their stroll to her favorite restaurant. They chose a table in a dimly lit corner. A waitress brought them the house special, steak and fried potatoes.

Jet ate with relish, savoring each mouthful. Kat pushed her food around her plate, and she didn't disturb him with conversation. It wasn't until he finished his meal and was halfway through his apple pie that he spoke.

"So where is it you think I could find work?"

Kat slid her plate to the side, wiped her mouth with a napkin, and waved away the slice of pie the waitress offered her. "Jobs are plentiful in the mines and sawmills. Jake or Clem could tell you where to inquire."

"I told Ed I'd be back to help with the fall roundup. He'll need me then."

She nodded. "The mines and sawmills are extra busy in the summer. You surely can find work for as long as you want." Kat paid the bill and they walked around the town in the pleasant glow of the moon.

"What a beautiful evening," she murmured.

Jet deeply inhaled the pine-scented air. "It's funny how a person takes an ordinary day for granted. You never know what a gift a day is until it's taken away from you. I have my life back. I don't want to mess it up again."

"You won't. Just stay away from bad company." She wanted to link her arm in his, but this time she didn't. He obviously needed to be left alone for now. "This is where I live," she told him as they climbed the last few steps before her little house. Her cat watched them from the railing of the porch. "Want to come in for a while?"

"No, I'm going to head back to the saloon, get a good night's rest, and begin job hunting in the morning."

"Good luck," she said, disappointment edging her voice. "I always have a pot of coffee on. If you don't leave too early, stop and have some."

He turned and walked away. She watched his form, slightly bent with weariness, and picked up her purring calico cat off the railing, snuggling him against her face.

Odd behavior, she thought, *for a man who wants to get to know me better.*

———

Discussing the day's events over supper had become a routine for Jet and Kat. They took turns buying supper, usually frequenting three of their favorite places. Once in a while, they ate at the Birdcage. When the weather permitted, they walked after their meal or hired a buggy and took a ride outside town. A month of companionship had deepened feelings between them. She had grown accustomed to his presence, even though he didn't have much to say about his past or his prison experiences. They mostly discussed Jet's new job in the mine. Kat secretly hoped Jet wouldn't remember his promise to return to the Bar Double B Ranch. She liked having him around.

One evening after a scrumptious supper of fried chicken, biscuits, and gravy, the couple lingered over coffee.

"I hired a rig tonight. Thought you might enjoy a drive this fine evening."

Kat ground her teeth at this slight annoyance. Jet always assumed. Why didn't he ask her before making plans? "Any place in particular?"

"There's this trail near the mine I thought you might enjoy. Very scenic."

"Okay, as long as we're back by ten. I have to take over for Clem at the Birdcage."

Jet paid the bill and escorted her out of the restaurant to the awaiting buggy. The night air cooled as it often did in the hills. The pines released their special scent. She drew her shawl over her shoulders as soon as she settled into the buggy seat. Jet snapped the reins and the horses clomped down the street. A few of the town residents waved to them as they drove out of town and onto the rough trail.

"You've been very quiet tonight," Kat remarked.

"Guess I have something on my mind."

He's thinking of leaving, she thought. Her heart raced as she searched for something to say to hold him.

After they had driven a great distance from the town, Jet stopped the buggy on a hill so they could watch the sky's hazy pinks and blues slip behind the western edge of the earth. "Simply beautiful, isn't it?" she murmured.

"Yeah ... Kat, I've been thinking about us all week."

"You have?" She diverted her eyes from the sunset to him. His face blended into the shadows in the background.

"We seem to get along together, don't we?"

She nodded. "We do."

"Have you ever considered leaving Deadwood for good?"

"Why would I do that? I have a business here."

"I know you do. That's the problem."

"The problem?"

"I'd like to return to the ranch, but I want you to be with me."

She glanced at him, surprised that he was talking this way.

He took her hand, then blushed. "Would you consider marrying me?"

"And live at the ranch?"

"Well, not at first. I thought maybe you could stay at the mission, and I would come to be with you whenever I can get away from the ranch. It would be closer than Deadwood."

She moved away from him, her heart hammering. "I don't want to sell my business or my house. It's made me a good living. We'd...we would have no home."

"You could lease the business and close up the house for a few months."

"Yes, I suppose I could. But I've worked too hard to just leave everything. Besides, I don't think we could live on your wages." She jingled the bracelets on her wrists. "I'm used to living better than an ordinary ranch wife."

Jet frowned. "So you're turning me down?"

"No, I didn't say that. But I'm not ready to give up everything I've worked for. I'd like to be with you, but let's talk this through."

"I can't go back on my promise to Ed. I'll have to leave soon."

"In other words, you're leaving with or without me?"

"I'll have to."

"How long will you be gone? Would you come back?"

"I...don't know. Deadwood's okay for a while, but I prefer the open country. Is that going to come between us?"

"I'm not sure, but I know Deadwood will never be the same if you leave."

"Would you be willing to go with me?"

"I have to give it some serious thought. I'm sure Clem and Jake would lease the saloon."

"If you absolutely hate it, we could come back. You'd still have your business."

"But you said you prefer the wide open spaces."

"I do. We'll just have to compromise somehow."

"If I decide to go with you, we would be married?"

"I was thinking that's what you'd want."

"Like I said, I'm going to have to do some thinking."

"I understand. How much time do you need?"

"To think?"

"No, for a wedding! All women want one, don't they?"

"Most, but not me. I'll just dress up in something nice, we'll get our picture taken, and then visit the justice of the peace. Wait a minute! I didn't say I was ready for marriage."

Jet ignored her. "That's all you would want for a wedding?"

"That's it," she reassured him.

Jet let out a long sigh of relief.

Kat became irritated. "You're relieved, aren't you?"

"Yeah, I thought you'd make me dress up in a fancy get-up."

She clipped her words. "You're not off the hook that fast."

"What do you mean?"

"You have to wear something decent. Hmm. You still have that suit you wore when I first met you?"

"I thought you hated that suit. Oh...I get it." The corners of his mouth formed a smile. They both started laughing.

CHAPTER 6

The following morning, Kat arrived at the Birdcage late. She hadn't slept much for thinking over Jet's proposal. It was toward dawn that she had fallen asleep, but only after she had decided to accept. *What would it hurt to try the ranch?* she had thought. She wasn't getting any younger, and she had to admit she did love the man. She knew Deadwood was her home, but there was still a chance she could change Jet's mind about the ranch.

Kat received a particularly friendly greeting from Aggie upon entering the Birdcage. Now that the new kitchen had been added, Aggie could cook up a full meal with all the trimmings. And best of all, she no longer cooked with the cigar in her mouth. Kat guessed the Miner's restaurant broke her of that. Aggie could make a tasty meal out of next to nothing. Savory aromas had replaced the dank odor of alcohol and tobacco smoke in the Birdcage. Kat's mouth began to water as the smells emanated from the kitchen.

"Can't wait to eat," Kat told her.

"Sit down, and I'll bring you coffee and a piece of cake I just frosted."

Kat had no objection to resting a minute longer. She let Aggie wait on her. The coffee tasted fresh, and the cake was light and airy. The frosting was the creamiest concoction Kat had eaten in years. Kat smiled at her help as she forked the last crumb into her mouth. She was indeed fortunate, she thought. However, suddenly, she sensed impending loss. She began to realize how much she would miss her employees and the Birdcage if she were to leave with Jet.

Kat watched Jennie and Cilla take care of the customers. They certainly didn't need her help. She accepted a second cup of coffee from Aggie and began to rethink her decision. She mused about her business and life in Deadwood. She hated to leave her life and friends in the bustling town. But, on the other hand, she would probably lose Jet. She doubted she could come between Jet and his commitment to Ed, and she was frenetically weighing her options.

Ling Li glided through the swinging doors of the saloon. Her eyes shone brightly. "I'm here to work on the Chinese Lantern—or is everyone too busy?"

"I can help." Kat left the table and sat down beside the sewing machine to cut the templates. Kat liked the feel of the slippery material under her fingers but found it more difficult to cut and sew. "I like this material, Ling Li. But I don't know about sewing it."

Ling Li smiled. "Here, let me do the sewing, and you can do the cutting."

Kat gladly let her take over, but the cutting didn't go much better. She couldn't seem to function well with the lack of sleep. In about an hour, they had completed several blocks. "They are beautiful," Kat said. "So expensive looking."

"I'm pleased, too," Ling Li said, smoothing the last block.

After Aggie put the food away and cleaned the kitchen, she came and sat beside Kat at the table. "Ladies, I've decided to move on and find another town."

"What are you talking about?" Kat sat dumbfounded.

"I'm afraid I won't be cooking here anymore."

"Haven't I paid you enough?"

"Oh, it's not that. I don't like to stay in a place too long."

"You can't just leave me high and dry," Kat insisted. "Who's going to cook tomorrow?"

"I'll see if I can round up somebody to help you out. Are you and your fellow going to be here this evening?"

"We're going out to supper and coming back here afterward. Why do you ask?"

"Just in case my replacement wants to come by and talk to you."

"Well, I hope you find one. I don't know what I'll say to my customers," Kat said. "You're putting me in a bad way." She had a notion to withhold some of Aggie's wages for the inconvenience, but she had a feeling Aggie needed that money. After all, she had been a valuable asset to the Birdcage. She pushed her chair away from the table, went to the till, calculated Aggie's pay, and shoved it into her hand. Aggie shrugged, gathered up her things, and left with a haphazard wave. Kat fumed under her breath about misjudging people when Jennie came over with a quizzical look on her face.

"You look mad, Kat."

"I am. Aggie just up and quit with hardly an explanation. I can't believe some people. I knew she was a little different, but I didn't expect this."

"So are you doing the cooking tomorrow?"

"Me? I should say not."

Jennie stifled a laugh.

Kat frowned. "Aggie said she'd find someone, but I can't trust her with that. I suppose I should plan something."

"She sure could sew, too. Her absence will set us back."

Kat sighed. "We'll just have to do the best we can."

Kat's mood improved when Jet came back from work,

cleaned up, and took her out for supper. She couldn't wait to tell him about Aggie.

"You shouldn't be surprised," Jet said after he heard her story. "You didn't know much about her anyway. People hide all sorts of things about themselves."

"You're right. I'm foolish to become so upset. But there's one thing bothering me."

"What's that?"

"What could Aggie have been up to in Chinatown?"

"Chinatown?"

"Well, I wanted to find out more about her, so I followed her." Kat hurriedly explained the incident with Ling Li at her uncle's gaming house. "Then Ling Li followed Rio and the stranger."

"Where did they end up?"

"They went to Aggie's shack in Chinatown. Ling Li knew where Aggie lived, but she wouldn't tell me before. I guess she thought it was none of my business."

"So there's some connection between this Rio fellow and Aggie?"

Kat nodded.

"Didn't that make you feel a little nervous, having her sewing and cooking for you?"

"Well, I didn't know any of that at the time. Besides, everyone in Deadwood has some kind of hazy past. I was never afraid of her."

Jet fumbled with his fork. "Have you given any more thought about us?"

"Yes. All night."

"Couldn't sleep?"

"No. Could you?"

"I did. Had to, or I wouldn't have been able to do my job."

"Funny how men can push emotion to the back of the mind," she said under her breath.

"What did you say?"

"Oh, nothing."

"Well, what did you decide?" His voice cracked with anticipation.

"I'm still not clear on what I should do."

"You love me, don't you?"

"I do, but you're asking me to give up everything I know to live in some desolate place."

"Minnie and your other mission friends do it."

"That's different. They're missionaries. They don't own a business like I do."

Jet shook his head. "How about going back to the Birdcage?"

Kat nodded and threaded her arm through his as they left the Miner's Restaurant. Once back at the Birdcage, Jake brought two mugs of foaming beer to them at the table. The couple was sitting in silence, sipping the beer when Rio and the stranger burst through the door.

"That's the man I was telling you about," she whispered.

Kat gasped. Her heart thudded against her chest when the stranger purposely strode over to their table. His face was set in a firm, cruel line. Rio kept his distance, his legs spread in a defiant stance. The color drained from Jet's face as he stood up to meet them. Jet cleared his throat and instinctively reached for guns that were not at his side. The two men stared at one another before anyone spoke.

"Jed," Jet said.

"I've been waiting for you for a long time," Jed said in a low tone.

"I suppose you blame me for your father's death."

Jed nodded.

"I wasn't the one who fired the shot. You know very well it was the range detective."

"If you were truly with us, you'd have fought harder and protected our father."

"You have no way of knowing that it would have done any

good or not."

"You can't deny you betrayed us."

"I told Tom I didn't want to go. He just wouldn't leave me alone."

Some of the customers edged toward the door. "Stay put," Jed shouted. The patrons slowly backed up to where they were before. Jed pulled out a gun that was concealed under his vest and waved it toward them. "Jet and I have a score to settle, and my brother Rio will make sure no one interferes."

Kat gasped, realizing what those two reprobates had been up to all that time. Fighting to keep herself from freezing on the spot, she reached for her handbag. The derringer was still inside. She knew it hadn't been fired for some time. *Would it still work? Is my hand steady enough? Is my will steady enough? Does Jet have a gun on him, too?* Her mind whirled, knowing if she didn't do something soon, Jet might be killed. She quickly surveyed the positions of Rio, Jed, Jet, and herself. Rio stood sentinel at the front door. She was within a few inches of Jet. Jed was in front of her at close range.

"I spent a year in prison for something I was forced into," Jet said. "I already paid my dues."

"Not for our father's death." Jed leveled the gun at Jet. "But you will now."

Kat whipped the derringer out of her purse and fired. She saw the instant blaze of gunfire, heard two sharp reports, and blacked out.

———

Kat awoke to a maze of darkness, sudden flashes, confusion, and hollow din. "I think she's waking up. Kat, stay with us," someone pleaded. Kat could barely hear the faraway yet familiar voice. She battled against the haze that was pulling her back to the depths. It took all her strength and determination to open her eyes and focus on the person beside her on the floor. She was beginning to remember. *It's...Jet!* He was stroking her arm. "What happened?" she said weakly.

"She might be confused," someone said.

Jet nodded. "Do you remember Jed and Rio coming into the saloon?"

Kat sorted through her thoughts, trying to remember. "The derringer. I had the derringer. I wanted to protect you."

"You did your best. You put your life on the line."

Kat's mind began to clear enough to see blood oozing from Jet's leg. "Your leg. It's bleeding."

"Jed shot me."

"And Jed?"

"You pulled you gun, fired, and grazed his shoulder. But he escaped with Rio."

"So they're still out there?"

"They are."

She clutched his arm. "You're still not safe?"

"Sheriff Briggs is looking for them."

A doctor rushed into the saloon and knelt near Kat. He examined her and placed his hand on Jet's shoulder. "She'll be all right. Now let me bandage your leg."

"What happened to me?"

Jet stroked her hair back from her forehead. "You fainted."

"I fainted? When you needed me the most, I fainted?"

"It's all right, Kat. You saved me, that's all that matters."

"Someone help these two to my office," the doctor ordered. "I want to keep you under my watch, at least for the night."

Kat felt weakness and nausea wash over her, and she offered no resistance to the doctor. She was thankful that no one was killed this time, but she couldn't forget that Rio and Jed were still out there.

———

A week later, Kat faced her first day back at work with some trepidation. She still couldn't believe that someone had actually entered her saloon with the intent to kill. The saloon seemed like a different place to her since the shooting. She didn't enter the Birdcage with the confidence she once had. Her old friends Clem, Jake, and Jennie greeted her as always, but sympathy was in their eyes.

"I don't know if I'm ready for this," Kat blurted out.

"At least no one was killed that night," Jennie consoled. "You have to remember that."

"The worst part is that Rio and Jed are still loose and might come after Jet again. This time, they might actually kill him. How can I get married with that on my mind?"

"The sheriff put out a warrant for their arrest," Jennie said. "Maybe they will be brought in soon, and then you won't have to worry about it."

"Come, sit down. I'll bring you a cup of coffee," Clem told her. "We're so glad you're back."

While Clem poured the coffee, Jet descended the stairs from his room. Kat looked up and caught his reassuring smile. "I thought you'd be at work by now," she said.

"I asked the boss if I could come in a little late. I knew you might need me here."

Kat shook her head. "I didn't think I would be so rattled to come back. I'm not as strong as I thought I was."

Jet sat beside her and stroked her arm. "You don't have to be strong all the time."

"And how is your leg?"

"It's healing," he said rather flippantly.

Kat grasped his hand. "Tell me more about that night."

"Are you sure you want to stir it up again?"

She nodded.

"Everything...happened...so fast," Jet explained. "When you pulled out the derringer and fired, I think I froze. I had no idea you had a gun on you. Jed didn't either. I think that was why he ran off. We were both distracted because it was so unexpected."

"So I did some good after all?"

"Yes, you did, but you could have been killed." Jet's face grew pale. "I didn't know you cared for me that much," he teased.

"Of course I do."

"Now, tell me about the derringer."

Kat hesitated. Jet wouldn't like this story. "When Rio started his threats, I had Clem buy me a gun. He wasn't keen on the idea, but he said he would on the condition that he could teach me how to shoot it. One day, he took me out to the country for target practice. I've carried it in my purse ever since."

"What threats?"

"Rio knew about you being in prison. He insinuated that he and I should get together, and then he left that note that scared me to death."

"Yeah, Clem told me about it. I guess I have a confession to make."

"A confession?"

"Now, don't get mad, but Clem told me on the sly what was happening around here with Rio."

"He did?"

Jet nodded. "I believe I had a right to know. Besides, he was worried for your safety. He didn't tell me about your gun, though."

"I see."

"Are you mad?"

"No, I guess not. You were just interested in my safety."

"You're one gutsy lady. Wish you would've told me."

"And let you worry? You couldn't have done anything about it when you were in prison."

"I know, but I still would have liked to have known."

"So that's why you had your gun on you?"

"Well, yeah." Jet hung his head.

Kat's expression became serious. "I'd die if anything happened to you."

Jet reached for her hand. "I feel the same."

Kat wiped away a tear, embarrassed at her moment of weakness. "What happened after I fainted?"

"I heard someone shout that the sheriff was on his way. Then Rio and Jed headed for the door."

Kat tugged at her earring. "I'm unclear on one point. You know Jed, but not Rio?"

"That's right. Jed was with us on many of our forays. He's a mean cuss, just like his father. I didn't even know Tom had another son."

"Wish we didn't have to worry about another run-in with them."

"I know, but I'll bet they cleared out of Deadwood. Let's put this behind us," Jet pleaded. "Do you feel up to talking about our wedding day?"

"I will after I get over the shock of all this. One thing I do know is that I definitely want to marry you. I almost lost you forever."

Jet took her in his arms. "It's okay. We're in no big rush."

———

After Jet left for work, Kat forced herself to focus on business. "It's good to be back," she told Jake, plopping herself on a bar stool. "But I don't know if I can put in a full day yet."

"You don't have to," Jake said. "We have it covered."

"Who did you get to cook? Or did you give up that notion of mine?"

"Ling Li took over," Jake informed her. "She's even cooked a few Chinese dishes, not that the customers especially appreciated them."

"What about the quilters, Jennie? Have you been working on anything?"

"We have. We didn't know if we should start anything without you, but we finished up the lantern quilt. I know we talked about surprising Ling Li with it, so I put it away and said we wouldn't give it to anyone until you came back."

"How's it going with her feller?"

"She finally broke the news to her father. He's concerned about Cheng's background. Whether there will be a wedding or not remains to be seen."

"Do you gals have any other quilt projects in mind?"

"Ling Li suggested the Chinese Coin quilt. Since we enjoyed making the Lantern Quilt so much, she thought we might like the Chinese Coin quilt. It's a strip method that turns out beautifully. Or so she says."

"That sounds interesting."

"I don't imagine you feel like quilting?"

Kat heaved a deep sigh. "I can't say I feel like doing much of anything right now."

"You just sit there and watch us work," Clem joked.

Kat smiled. "I can manage that." It felt good to be back in her old, familiar routine. She had been in limbo too long. She didn't realize how much she relied on her business and her friends to make her life meaningful.

As soon as Clem and Jake left and returned to their tasks, Jennie sat down beside Kat. "Now, what about this wedding?"

"The wedding? Oh, it's not going to be anything fancy. We will probably be married by the justice of the peace. That should do nicely."

"Is that all? No party or reception? You must have a wedding cake," Jennie insisted.

"And who's going to come?"

"You have enough friends to celebrate."

"Oh, I don't know. I'll have to talk to Jet. We haven't really had time to make plans, with the shooting and all. One thing is certain; I have to start feeling better than I do now."

"I understand. Is there anything I can do for you in the meantime?"

"You're doing it now. I want you to be my bridesmaid. Go ahead and order yourself a dress and hat. I'll pay for it."

"Do you mean it?"

"Of course I do," Kat insisted.

"What color?"

"Anything your heart desires. And in the meantime, you can keep an eye out for something I can wear, something in ivory."

"I'd be happy to. Oh, what fun!" Jennie said as she returned to work.

Just then, Ling Li came into the saloon carrying a bag of groceries. "Hi, Kat. It's so good to see you up and around. We were worried about you."

"Thanks. I appreciate you doing the cooking and such."

"You're welcome. I drew out the pattern for the Chinese Coin quilt," Ling Li added, handing Kat the sketch. "If you feel like it sometime, you could dabble with it."

"Perhaps within a day or two. I suppose I should muster enough energy to go over the books. What's for dinner?"

"I tried a few Chinese dishes. They don't go over very well, but my wonton soup is usually a hit. I thought about making a big pot of wonton soup and sandwiches for tonight."

"Soup sounds good to me."

A short time later, Kat noticed Cheng enter the saloon and walk to the kitchen. Jennie stopped to talk to him, and Cheng left soon after. Kat said to Jennie, "I see Cheng is no longer in jail."

"No," Jennie laughed. "The Chinese can hold out longer than anyone I know. Cheng wouldn't pay the fine, and the sheriff figured it was costing more than it was worth to keep Cheng in jail, so he released him," she explained.

"How long did Cheng hold out?"

"About two weeks. Seems like that impressed Ling Li's

father, too. Maybe things are going better between her father and Cheng."

"Perhaps. I'd like to ask more questions, but I think I'll wait for Ling Li to be here. I finished the books this morning, and I think I'm ready for a nap. Jet won't mind if I use his room upstairs. He doesn't lock it, does he?"

"I don't think so. You do look a little pale," Jennie said. "I might slip out and borrow some fashion books for the afternoon. Maybe when you wake up, we can go through it together."

"That would be fun. See in you a little while," Kat said as she climbed the stairs to Jet's room. She didn't realize she was so weary until she laid down on his bed and covered up with the Log Cabin quilt she and the other ladies had made for him while he was in prison. She snuggled under the quilt, which blanketed her with warmth and security that quieted her restless mind.

———

Kat awakened to the thud of Jet's boots on the stairs. "What a pleasant surprise," he said when he opened the door to his room.

Kat rubbed her eyes and pushed herself into a seated position. "I didn't think you'd mind. I suddenly felt so tired."

"Not at all."

She yawned. "How was work?"

Jet sat on the edge of the bed. "I'm happy to have a legitimate job. Mining is hard, and I don't intend to do it for the rest of my life. Actually, this mine is looking like it might play out soon, and I'll be searching for another job."

"You intend to return to the ranch this fall anyway."

"I do, but I want us to go back together as husband and wife."

"Jennie's bringing fashion books to the saloon so we can

order dresses. I asked Jennie to be my bridesmaid. Who will stand up for you?"

"I don't know. I haven't given it any thought. The only guys I know are Clem and Jake. How can I choose one over the other?"

Kat frowned. "That's a tough question, unless I choose another bridesmaid."

"And who might that be?"

"There's Cilla and Ling Li. Oh, gosh—that's two. At least I don't have to consider Aggie. She was a funny one. I've been thinking about how strange it was that Aggie left town around the same time Rio and Jed came gunning for you."

"Yes, that is strange. Didn't you say both men were seen at her house?"

Kat nodded. "You don't suppose they're..."

"Could be. Tom never mentioned Rio or Aggie—only Jed. So how might they be connected?"

"We may never find out."

"No, I suppose not. Anyway, what are we to do about your bridesmaids?"

"I should decide before we look for dresses. I think I'll just stick with one."

"But what do I do?"

"Choose Clem. Jake won't mind."

"Okay with me."

"Did you happen to see Jennie downstairs?"

"Yeah, I think she was looking at those books you were talking about."

"I better go down and talk to her. Want to go out for supper?"

"Sure. How long will it take you?"

"I'll just take a quick glance and then look more tomorrow," Kat promised as she left him to clean up for supper, but not before she kissed him on the cheek.

"Jennie, have you found anything for us?" she asked when

she reached the bottom of the stairs.

"I have. Come and look at these two." Jennie opened to the pages she had marked. "I was thinking of this pale lavender for myself, and maybe this ivory gown with the high neckline and tapered sleeves will work for you," Jennie suggested.

Kat thumbed through a few more pages of ivory dresses. "I must say, Jennie, you made the right choice. What about hats?"

Jennie turned to another book and flipped to several marked pages. "I know how much you like hats. Here's one with an attached veil."

"Perfect. Now, what about you?"

"I like this lavender one with the white feathers."

"We have a lot to work with here. I will look over them again tomorrow. Jet and I are going out to supper at the Miner's Restaurant." She smiled at Jet when he strode toward the women.

"I'm ready when you are," he said.

"Let's go. I actually have an appetite tonight," she said, hooking her hand in his arm.

The night was pleasantly warm as they arrived at the Miner's Restaurant. The scent of pines drifted past them to the gulch below. Deadwood had just installed new streetlamps, which illuminated the town in a soft glow. The couple chose a table next to the window.

"What do you recommend tonight?" Kat asked the waitress.

"Fresh trout is our special."

"What do you think, Jet?" Kat asked.

"Fry them up crisp," he said.

"I see that the owner is here tonight," Kat said. "I wonder if he knows anything about Aggie?"

"Do you suppose he'd tell you anything if he knew?"

"I'm going to give it a try," Kat said. "Let's see if he will come over and talk to us."

Kat soon returned to the table with the owner. "Jet, this is Mr. Lockert."

"Pleased to meet you, Jet," Mr. Lockert said as they clasped hands. "Call me Aaron."

Jet nodded.

"How are you two doing?" Mr. Lockert asked. "Of course, I heard about the shooting in your establishment. I was sorry to hear it."

"We're both recovering, but the shooting has left us with unanswered questions."

"I understand you would like to know more about my former employee, Aggie Brown."

"We would," Kat said. "Do you think that was her real last name?"

"Probably not. I get a lot of workers with common last names. Many are trying to escape their pasts. As you know, Deadwood has always been notorious for characters on the run."

"Aggie was cooking for me at the Birdcage and then quit suddenly. She said she would find a replacement, but she never did. Oddly enough, the shooting occurred the same day Aggie had decided to leave," Kat explained.

"I'm sure you know Aggie wasn't one to talk about herself. She simply did her work. I had no complaints," Aaron said. "She did pilfer leftover food. I found out she took it to those less fortunate, so I never said anything."

"When did she come to work for you?"

Aaron wrinkled his brow as he tried to remember. "Over a year ago."

"Did she talk about a family?"

"It seems to me she did mention a husband, but I think he was killed somewhere."

"Can you remember his name?"

"Let me think. What did she call him?" Aaron closed his

eyes and pressed his fingers against his temples. "Tom. Yes, it was Tom."

Jet started at the revelation, and Kat merely nodded. "Did Aggie speak of any sons?"

"There were two men in here from time to time. She always insisted upon waiting on them. I can't tell you their names. They seemed to know each other."

"Was one blond, kind of a smart aleck; the other had dark hair and steel gray eyes."

"Yeah, that's them."

"Could they have been her sons?" Jet asked.

Aaron shrugged. "They could have been. I just don't know."

"You don't know where they came from?"

"Let me see. What did she say? She did say something about the Black Hills reminding her of the hill country where she used to live."

Kat sighed. "That could have been anywhere."

"I'm sorry I don't know more. You could probably inquire about her from her former neighbors. You know where she lived?"

"I do. Thanks for your time," Kat said as he left their table.

The waitress brought the trout, which was fried exactly to Jet's liking.

"We didn't find out much more than we already knew," Kat said while buttering her bread.

"We do know that Aggie was Tom's wife. She probably cooked for you just to keep an eye on us."

Kat shivered. "I suppose she did. That gives me the creeps."

"I wonder if Rio and Jed still rustle cattle..."

CHAPTER 7

After leaving the Birdcage Saloon, Aggie skedaddled back to the shack she was renting, gathered up the few things she owned, filled a couple of satchels, and loaded her buggy. She had become used to packing up and leaving at a moment's notice when she was married to Tom. No matter where they were living, Tom had always been on the wrong side of the law. At first, she pleaded with him to turn straight so she could settle in one place with their two boys, but he couldn't live like regular folks. Aggie thought about settling down after Tom was killed, but her two sons had taken up where her husband left off. She couldn't desert them, so she continued to cook and care for her sons, even though it meant continuing to live as an outlaw herself.

Aggie climbed aboard her buggy and settled in for the eastward ride out of the Black Hills. She hadn't asked Rio or Jed why they wanted her out of town. She just did as they told her. She spat the cigar stub out of her mouth and fumbled around in her bag for a fresh smoke. She lit it and inhaled with gusto, reflecting on her short stay in Deadwood. She had begun to appreciate the Black Hills and felt that she could have spent more time there. She suspected that her boys felt that they needed to even the score with Jet. She didn't even believe Jet was responsible for Tom's death.

She had kept to the trail all day. Her sons had promised to catch up with her sometime after dark. Now it was after midnight, and Aggie thought she could hear riders following fiercely in the distance. She placed a rifle beside her and settled back against the seat while her horses plodded along the moonlit trail. As the sounds neared her buggy, she picked up the rifle and held it in her lap. The riders slowed when they reached the buggy. They were so close behind her, she could smell the horses in the breeze, and their cloud of dust tickled her nose. The riders flanked the buggy in wide arcs, when she could finally see the features of her sons, Rio and Jed.

"What's that gun for? You didn't recognize us?" Jed asked.

"Well, I wasn't sure. A lady can't be too careful these days. Jed, are you sporting a bad shoulder?" Aggie asked when she saw the bloodstained bandage.

"Yeah, you're gonna have to look at it, Ma. Maybe even dig the bullet out."

"What are you up to? Are we being followed?" She quickly turned to look behind them.

"I suspect so. We didn't kill anybody, but we might've wounded a man and a woman." Rio said.

Aggie's face reddened. "A woman?"

Rio cowered with her retort. "I don't think so, but I had to do something. She aimed for Jed."

"What woman?" Aggie demanded.

"Kat," Rio answered.

Aggie clenched her teeth. "She's a good woman. You were after Jet, her fellow?"

"Yes," Jed said.

Aggie was quietly relieved that no one was killed. She

didn't want her sons to be murderers. Besides, she was beginning to like the women at the Birdcage—Jet, too.

"I never counted on them having guns," Jed confessed.

Aggie frowned. "Rustling cattle is one thing, but murder is something else entirely. I'm disappointed in you two." She clamped down on her cigar.

"But Ma, we're sure no one died."

"Yeah, but you're wanted. Let's take care of that shoulder soon."

Jed was slumped over in the saddle. "I can go a little further."

She shook her head. "We need to settle somewhere out of sight so I can take care of you."

"There's nothing out here for miles," Rio said.

"Let's head toward the river breaks," Aggie motioned. "Find a spot to hide for a while. The law is surely after you."

Aggie and her sons diverted from the trail and descended to the breaks below. *I'm too old to be running from the law,* she told herself as her buggy bounced over the hilly terrain. *These sons of mine will never learn. How can they? They don't have brains in their heads,* she thought angrily.

"Make sure to cover the buggy tracks," she yelled to her boys. They quickly complied and used brush to sweep away the tracks for at least a mile back.

Soon, traveling over ridges and between trees became too difficult in the buggy. Their only alternative was to abandon it temporarily and proceed on horseback. Rio arranged the branches he hacked off the bushes to cover the buggy. "That's the best I can do, Ma."

"Alright. It might buy us some time if they ride this way," she said. Aggie gingerly mounted a horse she had unhitched from the buggy and rode with Rio and Jed to the river. Eventually, they came to a heavily-wooded area of pungent scrub cedar where they could remain concealed.

"I hope this is far enough." Aggie sneezed at the cedars

as they made camp for the night. Rio built a small fire to boil water for sterilizing the knife Aggie would use to cut out the bullet.

"I hope it isn't too deep," Aggie said as she scrutinized the hole in Jed's shoulder. She approached the task without any trepidation. Digging out a bullet didn't intimidate Aggie in the least. She had done it many times to her husband and his outlaw friends. Out of habit, she carried her medical implements with her wherever she went.

While she was laying out the medical supplies, Rio brought the bottle of whiskey to help deaden his brother's pain. Fortunately for Jed, the bullet was near the surface of his skin. Aggie had little trouble lifting out the slug. She bandaged it and covered him with one of her crazy quilts, thinking of the days when she had cared for him as a small boy. *Where had the time gone?*

"We'd better let him rest here tonight and continue on in a few days," Aggie suggested.

Rio unrolled his bedding beside the dying fire. "The law might forget about us by then."

"I hope so. You know how I feel about killing," Aggie reminded them. "Rustling isn't so bad, but keep in mind that if you're caught, you will serve jail time. No way around that, and I imagine it won't be a picnic. Just because your father was on the wrong side of the law doesn't mean you have to follow his lead."

Jed grunted in response and then fell asleep in a whiskey-induced stupor. Rio reached for a stick and drew in the dirt, deep in thought. Aggie, sensing he wanted to talk, waited in silence.

"I liked that redheaded saloon gal," Rio said. "She wasn't interested in me, just in that Jet fellow. I could picture her and me, married, out on a spread somewhere with a nice herd of cattle. Guess it was foolish to think that way. You, me, and Jed will never be able to settle anywhere now, unless we leave the state. Maybe Texas. Jed has different ideas."

"What ideas?" Aggie asked cautiously.

"He heard from a friend of his that it's easy rustling cattle southwest of Pierre. Wide open spaces. Cattle roam free for easy pickings. We are supposed to hook up with this friend of Jed's."

Aggie shook her head. "You're playing with fire. One of these days, you're going to end up like your father. Then what am I going to do?"

"Maybe I'll do this one more rustling job for a little money and leave for Texas," Rio said, tossing the stick away and wrapping himself in his bedroll.

Aggie carefully spread the dwindling embers apart, not wanting to draw attention to their camp. Then she curled up in her pallet of blankets on the ground. Sleep was slow to overtake her. Her thoughts of what lay ahead kept her awake.

———

In the morning, Aggie assessed that Jed would not be able to ride for at least another day. She sent Rio to keep watch on the trail from a high point. While Aggie tended to Jed, she occasionally scanned the heights in hopes of spotting Rio. It was late afternoon when he returned.

"Well, what did you see?" she asked him.

"A posse."

Aggie's heart skipped a beat in fear. "They're gone?"

"We lucked out. Sweeping the tracks confused them. They backtracked, but I'm not saying they won't come near here again."

Toward evening, Jed said he was ready to travel. Aggie agreed. Traveling at night would render them less conspicuous. Aggie and her sons packed up their camp, backtracked to the buggy, and uncovered it. Jed rode with Aggie and tied his horse to the back of the buggy. They kept to the trail all night, and by daybreak they searched for another place to hide out.

"How much farther is it to the rustlers' camp?" Rio asked his brother.

"I don't know for sure. They're somewhere along the White River. Murdock said he would be watching for us during the night."

"There's surely somewhere to camp in those river breaks." Rio pointed to a river south of the trail.

"Let's head that way and hope no one notices," Aggie said as they turned to the south. Soon they reached the river bottom. The site provided their two foremost needs, drinking water and concealment. After caring for the horses, they spent the daylight hours sleeping under the cottonwood trees in preparation for another night's journey.

The next evening, Aggie clenched the cigar between her teeth, her body aching from days on the trail. She so desired to leave the jolting wagon and settle into camp for a few days. She wished she were back at the Birdcage, cooking up a fine meal for the customers. Even that old shack in Chinatown appealed to her now.

––––––

Murdock located the runaway family on the trail later that evening. He led them to the hideout on the river. He signaled their arrival to a sentinel on a high butte. The waning moon shed enough light to see the well-established hideout tucked between the clay buttes and the wooded bottom land. Murdock assured the newcomers they would talk after a night of rest. He jerked his hand and nodded to indicate where they were to set up for the night. He then retreated to his tent. Neither Jet nor Rio were tired enough to sleep, but they bedded down anyway under the rustling cottonwoods to await dawn.

The next morning, Aggie awoke to the smell of wood smoke and frying bacon. She counted six men and two women in the camp, aside from herself and her sons. One of the women, Vernie, seemed to hang onto Murdock's every word and movement. Clearly, Vernie had joined the rustlers a short time ago. Aggie mused that Vernie was probably running from a life of drudgery and overwork, or maybe even from a mean father. She had no doubt that the excitement of a rustler's life and the haphazard attention of a man old enough to be her father suited Vernie's needs for the season. *Such a young and pretty thing,* Aggie thought, *to be with such a grizzly, old coot.*

Aggie pinned some loose strands of her hair and caressed her wrinkled face, remembering her soft skin all those years ago. Now it seemed to her that it didn't take long for the elements to age her. Perhaps she had been attracted to Tom the same way that Vernie was to Murdock. Aggie's youth had been far from perfect. That life with Tom was far from easy, but she knew she would be clothed, fed, and led on a life of adventure.

The other woman was much older, near Aggie's age, and possessed the look of resignation. She wound her unwashed hair into a tight knot and wore a soiled skirt with a belt tied around her thick waist. She sported a lackluster expression while frying flapjacks for the camp's breakfast.

After breakfasting on pancakes, bacon, and hot coffee, Murdock brought the camp together and introduced Rio and Jed as the trustworthy sons of his friend Tom. He assured the group that there was no need to worry about the loyalty of these two. Murdock then explained his plans for a rustling job. Aggie listened while he described the unsettled area targeted for their next caper. Aggie thought he made it sound too easy, and she noticed her sons smiling at the prospects.

When the men gathered around for more definite in-structions, Aggie gathered the tin plates and brought them to the dishpan and introduced herself. "I'm Aggie. My sons are Rio and Jed."

"I'm Leona. So you were Tom's wife."

"I was, but he was killed. Did you ever meet him?"

"Yeah, once. Ornery cuss."

"He was. Not so much when he was young. Rustling hardened him," Aggie said.

"Are you married?"

"No, not anymore."

Aggie waited for a longer explanation but Leona didn't offer more. "How long have you been in this camp?"

"About a couple of months. After another rustling job, we'll move south for the winter."

"My sons and I would like to go south, too." Aggie didn't offer any more explanation, either.

Leona glanced at her with a puzzled look. "You traveled during the night?"

"We did. Like you, we aren't exactly friends of the law."

The corner of Leona's mouth twitched to a small grin.

"Here, let me help with the dishes," Aggie offered, shift-ing her cigar to the other corner of her mouth. "I've cooked for restaurants before."

"With that cigar in your mouth?"

Aggie laughed. "Yeah, until a customer found cigar ashes in his mashed potatoes. Then I had to give up the cigar until after work."

"Funny story. I usually cook all the meals. Vernie...well, Vernie doesn't do much of anything other than fix her hair and sashay around the men."

Aggie picked up a soiled dish towel, turned it over in her hands, and began to dry the dishes. "Seems to me she has eyes for Murdock."

"Murdock is an old fool. He still thinks he's young and

flatters himself having a young filly hanging all over him."

Aggie sighed. "Guess we don't have that power over men anymore."

"No, and I wouldn't want to. Too complicated. Where did you cook?"

"I cooked in a few Deadwood restaurants. Ever been there?"

"Once, but not for long. It's too dangerous to stay anywhere very long," Leona explained.

"I know what you mean. I would have hung around Deadwood, but we had to leave. It was a good job at a decent place. Sometimes I wonder what it must be like to live somewhere for a long time."

"Ah, we're not the settling kind." Leona finished the last dish, threw out the dishwater, and turned the pan upside down on a weathered bench. "Come into the cabin; I'll show you something."

Aggie followed her into a cottonwood log cabin expecting to find it matching the exterior. Instead, she stopped short with her mouth gaping.

"What's this? Why, it looks like you've lived here forever." The place had been swept and scrubbed, and the walls were lined with colorful quilts of varying patterns. On one wall she identified the Log Cabin. She saw the Churn Dash pattern hanging on another wall. More quilts had been folded and placed around the room. "You live here alone?"

Leona nodded. "I used to live here with Murdock until he thought I was too old. I kicked him out when he started making eyes at other women. The cabin is all mine. I earned it for all the years of faithful service to this gang of rustlers."

"You haven't been in this country for all those years?"

"No. We operated in Utah and Idaho in the early days. They used to call me the Queen of the Rustlers. I was young and pretty then, and I could ride like the wind and was good with a gun. Murdock loved me then, too, but something happened as time wore on. I used to even plan our rustling jobs." Leona shook her head. "Now I cook and live alone, although Murdock lets me tag along. I suppose I should be grateful. How about you?"

"About me?"

"What kind of life have you had? I'll bet we have a lot in common," Leona said.

"I've never been called the Queen of the Rustlers. I may have been young once, but never pretty. How did you get that name?"

"I was one of the few women who actually rustled cattle." Leona stroked one of her quilts. "You see, in winter, we'd hide in a big valley called a 'hole.' If lawmen came by, they would be seen and taken care of. Many were too scared to venture our way. We were isolated from the rest of the world." Leona sighed. "It was so peaceful then."

"I've never been to those parts."

"Sit down here and I'll fetch us some more coffee. We have all morning to talk." Leona left Aggie in the cabin and returned in a few moments with what was left of the morning coffee. "Living in that wide open valley was the best time of our lives. We were young and in love. We thought we had the world by the tail. It was a beautiful place. But all good things come to an end. When the valley became settled by honest, hardworking folks, our way of life disappeared."

"As it will here, too, someday. When the railroad comes through, the homesteaders will come with it. And with homesteaders come the schools, churches, and the law."

Leona grinned. "By then I'll be too old to care."

"There will be no place for those of us who do as we please. We'll have to change."

"Change? Never," Leona said emphatically.

"I've tried talking my boys into living honest lives and giving up the outlaw ways. Like you, I followed my outlaw husband wherever he went. I raised my two sons on the run.

There were times I'd have liked to have settled down, sent my sons to school, and had a place to call my own. I could have changed after Tom was killed, but I don't know how else to live."

"I'm with you there. I just worry about how I'm going to take care of myself. I'm getting old. One of these days, Murdock will be done with me for good."

"I know my sons won't care for me either someday."

"Do you quilt?" Leona asked.

"I have quilted. When I was in Deadwood, I helped the saloon owner and a few other women make a couple quilts. One was for her man friend who was serving time in the Yankton prison for cattle rustling. Another quilt we made for a needy lady who took in neglected children. We were working on a Chinese Lantern quilt when I left." A stab of guilt jolted Aggie when she reflected upon the pain her sons caused Kat.

"While we're here, we can sew after we do the cooking. I don't have a sewing machine, but I sure could use some help."

"What happens when you have to pull out of here fast? I mean, with all the quilts and materials?"

"The law won't bother an old woman. I can act quite eccentric if I need to. And sometimes I act like I don't know where I am." Leona laughed. "I load up my belongings on my buckboard and head west. The boys always find me later."

"You're never afraid that someday they won't...find you?"

"That might happen when I can't cook anymore. Right now, they need me not only to do the cooking, but doctoring as well."

"See, we're not worthless yet."

Aggie fretted during the two days her sons were gone,

but she noticed Leona didn't have a care in the world while they quilted.

"Do you ever worry that someday one of these men won't come back?" Aggie asked while they worked on yet another quilt.

"You mean killed?"

"That's what I'm saying."

"You have more to lose than I do. Murdock is of no consequence to me, except that I wouldn't have a place to stay if he didn't come back. The gang wouldn't put up with an old woman like me. Maybe they would even split up. Nothing ever stays the same." Leona looked up from her stitching. "What would you do?"

"I don't intend to dwell on the thought of losing my boys, but it's hard in times like these. I suppose if I was left alone, I could find a job cooking somewhere. That's a tiresome job, though."

"Do you think about the future much?" Leona asked.

"I try not to. No use worrying about something we can't control. Why, I could get sick and die tomorrow. Do you have any kind of kin?"

"No. When I left home to follow Murdock, my family disowned me. My parents are gone, and my sister...well, I don't know where she is. I have nobody."

"Where did you learn to quilt, then, if you have no one?"

"I learned from Murdock's mama while he was on the run. I was expecting a baby then, so he told me I had to stay put. To pass the long, cold winter, the two of us made quilts."

"And the baby?"

"Oh, I lost my poor baby to an influenza outbreak when he was just a young fellow. Couldn't have any more babies. Just as well. Spent my life hiding out or on the run. How'd you manage to raise two sons?"

"It wasn't easy. I made a home for them the best I could," Aggie said. "Sometimes we stayed a month or so in the same place. I liked it when we settled for a while. And when Tom wasn't around."

"Murdock told me he was mean. When did you take up smoking?"

"When I worked the gambling halls. Smelled that smoke all day long so I thought I'd try a stogie and found out I liked it."

Aggie heard a rustling in the trees. She got up to have a look. "What would you say if someone found our camp?"

"We'd just say our men folk were out scouting for a homestead. It's not against the law to squat on a piece of land. I don't think they would think we were rustlers, especially with my collection of quilts."

"Yeah, you're right. That would seem odd. Has anyone come up on you like that?"

"They have. A couple lawmen, in fact. I always have a story figured out to tell them. They believe me and ride on. Do you see anything suspicious?"

"No. I think it's deer." Aggie sat back down to work on the quilt. Daylight was fading fast, and it was difficult to see where to place the stitches. Besides, her fingers were getting sore, and her back began to ache. "Shall we call it quits for the night?"

"I suppose. We'll find us something to eat. You can bunk in the cabin with me," Leona said.

Aggie took her up on her offer. She wasn't particularly fond of sleeping alone on the dirt floor of the tent. At least the cabin had a semblance of a wood floor, although a varmint wouldn't have any problem finding a way in.

Leona poked around the fireplace. "Do you think we could make a fire?" It's cold in here."

Aggie looked through the window at the sky. "It's cloudy tonight. Nobody would notice."

"Fine. We can make a hot meal and warm up. I think it's going to be a cool one tonight."

"What are you cooking up?"

"I got a few spuds and some bacon. Peel these here spuds and I'll get the fire going."

Aggie obliged her hostess's request, and soon the two women were sharing a mess of fried potatoes and bacon. "Nothing like a hot meal to warm the innards," Leona said.

"My old bones get to creaking when it's cold out. I'm thinking Texas could be a lot warmer. Ever been there?"

"No. Murdock says it's a long way."

"Me neither. Can't say I'm looking forward to a long trip. Maybe I could find somewhere else for the winter."

"Any ideas?"

"I'd like to go back to Deadwood," Aggie quickly said.

"Deadwood?"

"You'd like it. I've been thinking seriously about returning."

"Are you sure? By the way you came in to this place, it seemed to me you were running away from something."

Aggie shrugged. "My boys were. I'm not guilty of anything."

"Well, I'm not wanted in Deadwood, either. Would you let me tag along?"

"You want to go with me and leave your gang...and Murdock?" Aggie believed Leona thought more of Murdock than she let on.

"Yeah, I could always find them again if it doesn't work out."

"If you earn your way," Aggie warned, "you can come along. It's hard enough to support myself."

"Do you suppose Deadwood can stand two more cooks?" Leona asked. "I'm too old to be a saloon girl. Lost my looks a long time ago." She giggled.

"I think so. There are lots of eating places there." Her time at the Birdcage Saloon flooded her memory. She had tried to put it out of her mind, but she had to encounter Kat.

She held no hard feelings toward Kat. *Surely Kat would have no use for me,* Aggie thought. *She must hate me, too. She probably knows I'm with Rio and Jed.* Aggie wasn't proud of her sons' actions, but she had nothing to do with it.

"Want to play a game of cards?" Aggie said as she lit up her cigar.

Leona laughed, exposing several gaps in her teeth. "Do you cheat?"

Aggie glared at her new companion. "Only when I have to."

"I don't have any money to gamble with, but I have an idea." Leona reached into a sack and lifted out a handful of beans. "How about we use these here beans."

"Good enough for me." Aggie nimbly dealt the cards and discovered that Leona wasn't such a bad dealer either. "You dealt cards professionally?"

"No, not like you. My husband and the gang spent many hours playing cards during the winter when we were holed up in our hideouts. Some days I felt like a badger sealed in a den. I played cards to keep my sanity."

The women played for several hours until Leona suggested they lay some quilts on the makeshift bedsteads and retire for the night. Aggie wrapped herself in one of Leona's star quilts and watched the fire crackle and snap its last embers. The draped quilts took on warm hues in the firelight. She searched the kaleidoscope of patterns in each quilt. For a rare moment, she allowed herself the luxury of imagination, buried deep in quilts on her parents' Kentucky farm.

CHAPTER 8

The next morning, a team of the rustlers rode into the camp, Rio among them. He pounded on the cabin door. "Ma, are you in there?"

Aggie awoke with a start and grabbed the rifle beside her bed. "That you, Rio?"

"Yeah, Ma. Open up."

"Just a minute." Aggie had slept in her clothes. She slid out of bed, accidentally tangled herself in her quilt, and stumbled toward the door. Luckily, the hardwood door was sturdy enough to catch her. She took a moment to compose herself and lifted the bar. "You're around a little early this morning."

Rio leaned against the doorframe. "We finished the job. Some of the boys are driving the cattle east. Jed's with them. We had better be moving out of camp."

Aggie pushed Rio out of the doorway and stepped outside, closing the door behind her. "Rio, I've given it a lot of thought. I don't think I want to go to Texas with you boys."

"Why not? You always go with us."

"I know, but I'm getting too old to be on the run."

"What will you do, then? Where will you go?"

"Back to Deadwood."

"You can't go there. We're wanted men."

"You may be wanted, but I'm not. I didn't do anything wrong, except to feed you and dig a bullet out of Jed's arm."

"But they'll be questioning you about our whereabouts."

"They could. Just don't tell me exactly where you're going, and then I won't have anything to tell them."

Rio shrugged. "Well, if that's the way you want it. Won't you get lonesome by yourself?"

"Leona's going to live with me for a while. We'll see how we get along."

"Do you have any money?"

"Not much. I'll have to find work right away."

Rio pealed a few bills off the wad of money he pulled out of his pocket. "Here. I don't have much, but it will keep you from starving for now."

"Thanks." She patted his hand. "You wouldn't be a bad son if you'd just give up them outlaw ways."

Rio tipped his hat. "Okay, then. I'll look you up when we get back in the country."

"You do that, and say good-bye to Jed for me." Aggie watched Rio walk away before once again closing the door. She had never considered parting from her boys for such a length of time.

"Did you notice if Murdock was out there?" Leona asked, now also awake.

"I think he is. I just talked to Rio about not going with him."

"I need to go tell Murdock I'm not going either." Leona grabbed her shawl from the bed and left the cabin. Aggie watched her through the window. It wasn't long before she was back. "Just as I thought. He don't care a lick."

Aggie folded the quilt on her bed. "Do we stay here, or do we get going?"

"There's no need to stay. I like it here, but we'll surely run out of supplies."

"I suggest we pack up and head to Deadwood. I hope we can get all your quilts in your buckboard. My buggy doesn't hold much."

"I've done it before, and I haven't added much since my last trip." Leona stepped up on a packing crate. "Here, help me take these down off the walls and get them folded and into the wagon."

The women worked at dismantling the quilts that decorated the old cabin. Aggie heard the men outside shouting to one another. It wasn't long before everyone had left. *I hope I've made the right decision,* Aggie thought to herself. She hadn't known Leona for more than a few days, and here she was taking on a roommate for the winter. *Anyone who quilts with such passion can't be all bad,* she decided. She hitched her horse to the buggy and lit a cigar.

"I'm ready," she shouted to Leona who was right behind her with her buckboard.

"Lead the way, and I'll follow," Leona hollered back. "Just make sure and stop for lunch. I hate to miss a meal."

Aren't we a sight, Aggie thought as they hit the westward trail. There was a day when she had a little pride in how she looked. When she was young, her family could afford cleanliness, not glamour. Those habits still affected her today. She had changed her dress for the ride to Deadwood. Glancing back at Leona, Aggie shook her head. Leona was still wearing the same skirt and blouse she had on when Aggie met her. She shuddered when she wondered about the last time Leona had a bath. However, Aggie had noticed that Leona always washed her hands when she cooked or handled her quilts. Leona had once been the Queen of the Rustlers, but she sure didn't look it now. There was no way Leona could get a job looking like a derelict.

What was I thinking, anyway, to invite her along? Aggie thought. *Maybe in my loneliness, I am willing to put up with just about any companion. I do feel a little sorry for Leona. She is such a broken-down woman, living at the mercy of her husband, who has rejected her.*

Aggie hoped she could get her old shack back in Chinatown until she and Leona could afford something better. With two of them working, maybe they could take a step up in the world. But first, she somehow had to get Leona looking better.

I could also use a new dress or two, Aggie pondered. She again pinched the wad of money Rio had pressed into her hands before leaving. He had never done that before, and that gave Aggie hope. He was more like her; he had a little more feeling in him. Jed, on the other hand, was just like his father—mean to the bone. That extra cash could cover dressmaking materials. But then there were the shoes, too. Leona's were full of holes. If they went without eating too much, maybe she could afford a pair.

As Aggie drove the horses, she kept pondering the best approach to Deadwood this second time around. She sure wished she could work for Kat again. She liked that job. She liked Kat, who had treated her fairly. She also missed quilting with those ladies. But since her boys caused that ruckus in the saloon, Kat wouldn't be the least bit interested in Aggie. If she had known what her boys were really up to, maybe she could have stopped them. Kat surely thought she was spying on her. But she would swear on a stack of Bibles that it was not her intent to do any spying. She was bound to run into Kat somewhere in Deadwood, and Aggie dreaded that encounter.

A cloud of dust up ahead nudged Aggie out of her musings. She automatically reached for her rifle beside her, and then looked back to see if Leona had noticed. Leona's head was bobbing with the rhythm of the jolting buckboard. "Guess I'll have to do this alone," Aggie muttered to herself. As the stranger came closer, he signaled for her to stop. The gun in her lap was pointed at the man. He didn't appear willing to do them any harm, but she remained vigilant.

"What you ladies doing out here all by yourselves? Did you run into trouble?"

"Why should we be telling you?"

By then, Leona had awakened and driven up beside Aggie's buggy. "I'm sorry. Guess I should have introduced myself. Name's Ken Hastings. Range detective. I've been out looking for a gang of rustlers. They hit one of the local ranchers a couple of days ago. Have you seen anything suspicious?"

"No, can't say we have."

"So why are you ladies out here all alone?"

When Aggie hesitated, Leona said, "Our husbands are looking for land to homestead. We left them back there a ways. We're going to get some supplies. Heard there's a store nearby."

"There is. Take the trail to the north when you cross the Cheyenne River."

"We'll do that, Mr. Hastings," Leona said. The man tipped his hat and rode to the east.

Aggie's eyes followed him. "Do you suppose he believed us?"

"There's no cause not to. This might be a good place to stop for lunch. I'm hungry."

"Well, all right. Let's take a short rest. I don't want that range detective coming back and asking us more questions." Leona climbed down from her buckboard and threw a quilt on the grass. Aggie brought out a small basket of food they had prepared that morning and joined Leona on the quilt.

"That range detective mentioned that store at the river," Aggie said. "I had forgotten about it."

"What of it?"

"I've been doing some thinking. It might be best if we put our best foot forward, so to speak."

Leona swallowed her biscuit before she spoke. "What do you mean by that?"

"I think we need to clean up and wear a new dress when we go into Deadwood."

"I suppose we could bathe in the river, although I don't know what for. By the time we get to Deadwood, we'll be full of sweat and dust anyway."

"It does sound like a waste of time, but I think we should give it a try."

"You said something about dresses. I don't have a new dress."

"I don't either, but they might sell material at that store, maybe even a dress or two."

"Both are expensive. I don't have any money," Leona said between bites.

"Well, I do. Rio gave me some before he left."

Leona tilted her head and squinted. "Why are you so concerned about how we look?"

"We'd have a better chance of getting decent jobs if we didn't look like a couple of vagrants."

"Well, aren't we?"

"I'm afraid we are. But lately I've been thinking of settling down in one place, and I don't want to be a charity case."

Leona flashed a sly smile. "You're gonna have to give up that cigar of yours, then. It's unladylike."

"I know that. It's going to be hard, kind of like losing an old friend, but I'll do it if I can earn a little respect."

Leona stuck her chin in the air. "Ah, those snooty people in Deadwood will remember who you are anyway. And they'll hold it against you."

"I suppose at first, but at least I'll know I've made an improvement."

"I don't know why you want to change. I'm plumb fine with who I am."

"You once said you were the Queen of the Rustlers. Don't you want to see if you can at least look that part again?"

Leona shrugged. "That was years ago. I had Murdock then. Life was exciting, and I was full of daring."

Hard to imagine, Aggie thought. "So you're telling me you don't have anything to live for?"

"Just my quilts. When I finish one, I feel like I have made something beautiful."

"At least you have that."

"And what about you? What do you have?"

Aggie pursed her lips. "Nothing, I guess. I let my boys go. Guess it was about time, though."

"Sorry, I didn't mean it that way."

"I'm just hoping I can find something in Deadwood."

———

It took the women two days to reach the store near the river. "I for one am looking forward to a few days' rest," Aggie said as she feasted her eyes on the meager attempt at civilization.

"I suppose we'd better find out where we can camp," Leona said as they pulled their rigs near the livery barn. After paying a fee for the horses, Aggie and Leona tramped over to the general store. "By gosh, there's room to stay and even a place to eat," Leona observed.

Aggie pulled off her gloves and yanked the cigar from her mouth, tossing it aside. "All that costs money. Remember, we have to save a wad for Deadwood." She straightened her hair the best she could before they entered the rustic store.

Aggie was surprised by the variety of merchandise. By the look of the shelves, one could imagine this establishment bustling with commerce. It was an oasis, a very refreshing sight after all those days in the wilderness. Aggie grabbed a few bolts of material, just enough to create two different dresses. Leona motioned her over to where full dresses were hanging from hooks. They were plain, but suitable for either woman. "What do you think? Do we sew or buy one ready-made?" Leona asked. "I don't know much about sewing a dress."

"I made dresses for myself all the time," Aggie said. "If we don't want anything fancy, I can sew us up something rather quick. It would be easier if I had a sewing machine. Suppose we'll have to hand stitch everything. Wow, look at this price!"

"I've got scissors and thread with me, so that'll help. By the way, did you notice that sewing machine sitting over there?" Leona said, pointing to a corner of the store.

"It's probably for sale."

"Let's go and have a look." Leona prodded her.

"It doesn't look new. See these signs of wear?" Aggie traced the nicks and mars on the machine with her finger. A young lady emerged from behind the counter just as Aggie was examining the mechanical workings.

"May I help you with something?"

"Oh, we couldn't help but notice this sewing machine. Is it for sale?" Aggie asked.

"Well, I don't really know. Someone left it here a while back. I guess they were lightening their load, although I can't imagine not needing a sewing machine. Would you be interested if it were for sale?"

"Perhaps we could just use it. Me and my friend here want to make us a couple of dresses. We plan on staying around here the next few days."

"I see. Let me go and ask my mother. I'll be right back," the young woman said as she left them.

Leona grinned. "Maybe luck is going our way."

"It sure would save a lot of time if I could sew our dresses on a machine. I'm not sure about buying it. I don't want to get too carried away with spending."

"But just think if we had a sewing machine, we could make lots of quilts and you could sew our clothes." Leona's eyes lit up with an idea. "Have you ever thought about sewing for people?"

"I don't know if I'm that good. Besides, I never stayed in a place long enough to even think about it."

The young lady returned shortly. "Good news. It's for sale."

"How much?" Aggie asked.

"Oh, just a couple of dollars."

"If I buy it, could we use it right where it stands for a few days?"

"Sure, I don't see why not. Do you need material?"

"We do. Cut us each a dress length from these two bolts."

"Great. When do you want to start sewing?" the young lady asked.

"Right after we wash up. You do have a place to take a bath?"

"We sure do. Right next door. We also have an evening meal, if you'd like."

"Thanks, but I think we'll pass this time. I'll pay up, and then we'll start sewing."

"As you wish," she said, leaving them to cut the material.

"Let's at least wash our hands and face before we settle into sewing," Aggie said.

Leona yawned. "Do we have to start today?"

"It's going to cost hanging around here. The sooner we get done, the sooner we can leave. We need to get your sewing supplies from the buckboard. We'll need scissors, thread, pins, needle, and a tape measure. You do have those things, don't you?"

Leona nodded.

After the women washed and retrieved the sewing supplies, they returned to the store and made their purchases. Two dress lengths of material were draped over the sewing machine. "Which do you want?" Aggie asked.

"I don't care."

Aggie held the blue up to Leona. "I think the blue works best for you. I'll take the brown."

Leona shrugged.

"We'll have to measure each other so I know how to cut the material."

"Right here in the store?"

"Well, yes, unless you want to go outside," Aggie said impatiently.

"No, that would even be stranger."

"All right, let's get this over with." Aggie measured Leona first, and then Leona fumbled with the tape while measuring Aggie. After determining the sizes, Aggie looked for a place to lay out the material. The young clerk came to her rescue with a wobbly table from the back room. Before the store closed for the day, Aggie had cut out the dresses that she would begin to sew in the morning.

"Let's save our bath for the day we leave," Aggie said. "By then, you'll have something clean to put on."

"There you go again, insulting the way I look," Leona grumbled.

"I don't mean to, but I really believe it's in our best interest."

"Well, I don't know. I'm thinking I should've gone to Texas."

"Ah, it won't be so bad."

Leona laughed. "We'll see if you change your tune when you give up your stogie." Aggie threw up her hands in disgust, and they set off for their campsite. As they neared the buggy and buckboard along a copse of trees, Leona hollered, "Hey, somebody's been rummaging around in the wagon box!" She quickened her pace until she reached the belongings she had left in the back of her buckboard. "Somebody's been messing with my quilts."

"Why would anyone want to do that?"

Leona hastily sorted through them. "Just as I feared, one is missing."

"Are you sure?"

"Yes, I am. It's the Wandering Foot."

"Well, it didn't just grow legs, did it?" Aggie covered her mouth to keep from laughing.

"That's not funny." Leona fumed.

"Who would take just one quilt?"

"I don't know, but I just bet they're still around. I'm going to look for it."

"It's dark. How will we find anything?"

"We got a lantern. I aim to check every camp until I find it."

"Good luck."

"You're coming with me," Leona demanded as she lit the lantern.

"I hadn't planned on it."

"I'll need your help."

"Oh, all right," Aggie grumbled. "I'll play like a thief in the night."

"I'm not going to bed until I find that quilt. It's one of my favorites," Leona insisted. "I made that one during one of the worst winters in our Utah hideout. There was so much snow; nobody could get in or out of that valley. Murdock liked me then."

Aggie rolled her eyes at the mention of Murdock. She joined Leona and prowled around each campsite trying to be as unobtrusive as possible. "What you want?" one man grumbled from the dark.

"Oh, we're looking for our lost dog," Leona quickly responded.

"A lost dog?" Aggie whispered. "How do you come up with all these lies so fast?"

Leona laughed. "I wasn't called Queen of the Rustlers for nothing."

"Were you lying about that too?"

"Well, maybe just a little."

Aggie scowled. "I thought so."

"Hey, a bunch of men over there is rolled up in blankets," Leona said. "Let's go have a look."

"They're sure to be armed."

"Somebody should be keeping watch."

"Keep holding that lantern high. I want them to see we're women," Aggie ordered.

"Good thing you don't have that stogie in your mouth," Leona chuckled. "They'd think you were a man for sure." She raised the lantern, so as to illuminate their faces.

"Who goes there?" a voice growled from the dark.

"Just a couple of women," Leona answered.

"Whatcha want?"

"One of my quilts has gone missing. Thought maybe one of these fellers borrowed it for the night," Leona said, changing her story about the lost dog.

"I wouldn't know. Come on in and have a look."

As the women neared the camp, they had a better look at least twelve ill-kept men. Some appeared to be sleeping while the others played cards. Aggie halted when she saw them. "I don't think we should get any closer," she whispered to Leona. "They look kind of ornery."

A man stepped toward the lantern's light. "What sort of quilt you looking for?"

"It's a hand-pieced quilt, mostly blue," Leona said. She inched forward to have a better look at the camp.

"Anybody could have a quilt that's blue!"

"If you don't mind, I see something blue over there," Leona said. Aggie took several steps back, but Leona proceeded further into the camp. Her heart began to thump with uncertainty. "I found it!" Leona jerked the quilt off the stranger, who awoke with a start.

"What the—" Staggering to his feet and spitting out curses, the man turned and fixed his bleary eyes on Leona's. "Just who are you?"

"You got my quilt, you thief." Leona berated him. She took her quilt, bunched it up, and stomped out of the camp.

Aggie followed. "He could have killed you," she blurted.

"But he didn't, and I got my quilt."

By the time Aggie and Leona arrived back at their camp, Aggie had decided Leona deserved to be known as the Queen of the Rustlers. *She's either gutsy or has no brains,* Aggie thought. *No way would I have approached a camp full of men in that manner.*

Leona burst through the tent opening with an armload of quilts. "These are staying with me now," she announced.

"There's no room in here for them." Aggie's patience was wearing thin. *What did I get myself into?* she wondered.

"We'll make room. Help me spread them out here on the ground."

"They'll get dirty," Aggie protested.

"Mostly the bottom one. I can wash them. Somebody else is liable to come along and help themselves to one."

Aggie helped her pile layer after layer on the ground floor of their tent. "I guess it will make for soft sleeping," Aggie admitted.

"Sure it will, and I'll sleep better knowing they're right beneath me."

———

During the next two days, Aggie sewed furiously to complete the dresses. After a hot bath, the two women dressed in their new apparel. A few men even tipped their hats to them as they climbed aboard their buckboard and buggy.

"See what a little fixing up will do?" Aggie said more to herself than to Leona. "When we make some money, I'll sew more."

"Yeah, I guess it helps. But we had to go through a lot of trouble."

"Now let's keep clean for a couple of days."

"Hope it doesn't rain before we get to Deadwood, or we'll be done for," Leona said.

It wasn't long after they left the Cheyenne River breaks that they saw the Black Hills in the distance.

"There it is," Aggie pointed excitedly after she stopped the buggy and waited for Leona to pull alongside. "Wait until you see those hills covered with pines. The air is so fresh, and the wind seldom blows. That's what I call paradise."

Leona shaded her eyes with her hands. "How much longer will it take us?"

"A couple of days."

"It better be worth it. I'm getting tired of rattling along this trail," Leona complained.

After another two days on the trail, their new dresses sagged with dust. Leona had become so grumpy that Aggie was glad they didn't share a buggy. But once they reached the edge of the Black Hills, Leona perked up with interest.

The first thing the ladies did when they reached Deadwood was to inquire if Aggie's old shack was still for rent. When they found it unoccupied, they moved into the ramshackle dwelling. The sewing machine, a couple of chairs, a crate of pots and pans, Leona's stack of quilts, and a few articles of clothing were the women's only possessions.

"The shack is the same as when I left it," Aggie commented. "I never did get around to fixing it up much."

"I wouldn't say this was a step up in the world," Leona said after she surveyed the neighborhood and the three-room shack.

"They call this area the badlands," Aggie explained. "We can't afford much right now, but I'm hoping that will change. Maybe curtains at the windows and a few rugs on the floor will help. At least the stove and table are still here."

"And the broken-down bedsteads," Leona added. "The quilts will help to make these four walls cozy and keep some of the wind from blowing through the cracks."

"You're right. This place was hard to heat and keep cool."

"Do we have some money for food? I'm hungry," Leona said after they had settled in and swept the floor.

"We have enough for a month's rent and a little food. We have to look for work."

"Work?" Leona beat the dust off the table with a rag. "I've never been too fond of a steady job."

Aggie stood with her hands on her hips. "You promised, remember? I won't support the both of us."

Leona plopped into a kitchen chair. "Where do we begin?"

"I know some people here. We just drop in and ask if there's anything to do."

Leona scowled. "I guess I don't have a choice."

"No, you don't. That was part of the agreement. With two people working, we can make some headway and share the rent. Come on. Dust yourself off and wash your face."

Leona reluctantly did as Aggie commanded, and then the two left their shack. Aggie led the way to the Miner's Restaurant. Once inside the door, Aggie's eyes searched for the owner and her former employer, Mr. Lockert. She breathed a sigh of relief when she saw him talking to one of the waitresses. She walked over to where he stood. "Hello, Mr. Lockert."

"Aggie? I thought you left town for good."

"I did leave, but not for good. I just want you to know I had nothing to do with that incident with the boys and the Birdcage. This here's a friend of mine, Leona."

Mr. Lockert nodded and dismissed the waitress. "I suppose you are looking for work?"

"We are."

"I don't have much. I could use a dishwasher, but the pay's not much."

"I was hoping to cook."

"Sorry, I already have someone."

"Okay, we'll think on the dishwashing job," Aggie told him before they left.

"I hope you have some more ideas," Leona grumbled as they continued down the street. The ladies spent the entire afternoon inquiring at all the eating establishments in Deadwood with no luck.

"There are the saloons, but I don't want a cleaning job. It pays a little more than dishwashing," Aggie mused. "We aren't good-looking enough to be barmaids."

Leona laughed. "What about that place across the street?" Leona pointed to the Birdcage.

"Oh, Kat put up a new sign. It used to be a saloon. That's where I worked when my boys went in and caused a ruckus."

"You never told me about that."

"No, I guess I didn't." *I suppose she must know now*, Aggie conceded. She led Leona by the arm to a shaded bench nearby. There she revealed the whole story—the rustling, the death of her husband, her sons' attempt at justice. The entire street had fallen under evening shade by the time Aggie finished her story.

"I'm surprised you came back here."

"I know Kat will never forgive me for being Rio and Jed's mother, even though I didn't know anything about what my boys were up to. I can never work there anymore." Aggie's face brightened. "But you might be able to."

"Me? Go in there by myself?"

"Yeah. It's our best hope for now."

"And what are you going to do for a job?"

"I'll take the dishwashing at the Miner's. Someday the cook will get tired of the hassle and quit, and I'll be there to take over."

Leona pointed at the Birdcage. "And you want me to work here?"

"Kat's a good person. And they have a quilting group you could join. Go, give it a try. Just don't mention anything about me."

"Where will you be?"

"Meet me at the Miner's Restaurant when you're finished. And please do your best to get the job."

CHAPTER 9

Kat sat in her quiet home, grimacing at the figures she had written. No matter how she calculated, the restaurant would never yield the profits of her old saloon, even with the onset of spring. On the other hand, she could think of several benefits to such a change. She would open early in the morning for breakfast, and she would close much earlier in the evening. Owning a restaurant, as opposed to a saloon, would elevate her social standing—not that the uppity women in Deadwood ever caused her to lose sleep. Certainly the chances of another gunfight would drastically decrease.

She massaged her temples in frustration when she remembered Jet. She was to go with him to the Bar Double B Ranch for at least the fall and winter. That would mean she would have to leave her business, whatever it might be, to Jake and Clem. If it became a restaurant, she wasn't sure they would stay.

However, a recent development presented Kat with an alternative plan. Several days ago, she received a letter from

Annabelle, her sister. Annabelle wanted to leave Cleveland with her daughter Miranda and move to Deadwood to be near Kat. Kat sensed that Annabelle needed companionship and help raising Miranda. Kat recalled what a handful Miranda was when she took care of her at the mission. Nothing seemed to satisfy that girl.

Kat hadn't replied to her sister's letter yet, but she would have to tell her she was getting married and leaving Deadwood. And that's where Kat's plan would come in. Annabelle would need to find work, perhaps in Kat's new restaurant. Miranda could even help, too. Annabelle did not mention when she might make the move, but perhaps Kat could convince her sister to arrive before she and Jet married and left for the ranch.

With the plan well formulated in her mind, she took out writing paper and a pencil and began the letter to her sister. She wrote several pages before signing her name. She even invited Annabelle and Miranda to stay with her and have the entire house to themselves after Kat leaves for the ranch with Jet.

Kat felt a sense of relief when she dropped the letter into the mailbox before leaving for the Birdcage. She wanted to share her idea with Jet, but he had left for the mine already. Instead, she discussed her idea with Clem. "Would you stay if the business were no longer a saloon?" she asked.

Clem shook his head and frowned. "I wouldn't be satisfied as a waiter or busboy. The bar is all I know. Sorry, Kat, but I would probably look for another job."

"Could you stay until I get the restaurant on its feet?"

"Well, maybe for a little while. How long are you figuring?"

"I'd like to keep you on through the fall and winter while I'm away." She touched his arm lightly. "I feel terrible putting you out of a job."

"Not to worry. Finding another shouldn't be that hard.

Besides, it'll be some time before I have to look for one."

"Okay. I think I'll do some sewing before the noon meal."
Kat sat at the sewing machine to work on the border of an otherwise completed crazy quilt. She overheard a lady ask about her, and she stood when she heard Clem respond.

"How can I help you?" Kat inquired of the approaching woman.

"My name's Leona Price. I...I'm looking for a job."

"Are you new to town?"

"Just got here with...a friend."

Kat gave her full attention. "What's your experience?"

"I've done a lot of cooking. And I make quilts." Leona examined the crazy quilt on the table.

"You do? Now that's interesting. As you can see, a group of us ladies make quilts, too. Most of them we give away to people who need them."

Leona nodded.

"I run a restaurant here, mostly. The saloon is not here to stay. I have a lady who cooks for me, and I expect my sister and my niece to come and help me out soon. Let me think. Jennie waits tables, but she sometimes complains that she needs a couple days off. You could fill in for her on those days. Would you be interested?"

"I expect so. When would you want me here?"

"Let me ask Jennie what she prefers. Stop back again tomorrow and I'll know more."

"I'll do that."

Kat watched Leona leave the Birdcage. She wasn't sure Leona would be right for the job, but the woman looked desperate. *Maybe,* she thought, *I can talk Leona into helping with the quilting projects. That's where she could really help. I'll give her a try, anyway.*

Kat smiled at her good fortune. She was mostly pleased with the restaurant's success. She just wished she could pay these ladies to make quilts.

———

Aggie immediately began her job washing dishes at the Miner's Restaurant. It wasn't the best job, but it would buy groceries. She watched the door, looking for Leona to appear, anxious to hear if she had found a job, too. Aggie had worked her way through the pile of grease-laden dishes when she saw Leona enter. She wiped her hands, stepped through the swinging door, and motioned for Leona to come back where she was.

"You're working already?"

Aggie nodded. "Well, did you get a job?"

"Yeah, I might have a waitress job, but only for two days a week."

"That's okay. It might lead to more. What did you think of the place?"

"Looks all right to me. I won't know until I work there."

"How did Kat seem? Is she okay?"

"You mean the redheaded woman?"

"Yeah, that's Kat."

"She seemed fine to me. She was sewing the binding on a crazy quilt."

"Glad to hear she didn't get hurt. She didn't say who the quilt would be given to?"

"No."

"You're going to need something else to wear. Wearing the same dress everyday won't do."

Leona shrugged. "I'll wear an apron to cover it up."

"Maybe you're right. I'll see if I can buy some of the leftovers here for supper tonight. Trade my work for a meal. You might as well go on back to our house."

"I'd like to try out the sewing machine, if you don't mind."

"Go ahead. Do you have anything to sew with?"

"I got a little material to use up."

Aggie continued her work until the last of the customers had left and the dishes were done. She scooped out the food that was left in the kettles and dumped it into a pot, which she tucked under her cape until she reached the badlands.

"I have supper," she called as she entered the shack. "What...have you been doing?"

"Sewing," Leona said from atop a chair.

"I see. Curtains for the windows. How nice."

"I had material that would work. Also had some string to run through the header. I just pounded nails on either side of the window frame and wound the string around the nails."

"I have to admit it's starting to look like home." The blue and red curtains were mismatched, but they did add some cheer to the place. "What about your quilts? What do you want to do with them?"

"They'll cover up some of these cracks in the walls. Want to help me?"

"Sure." Aggie sorted through the stack of quilts. "Which ones do you want?" She pulled out the Wandering Foot. "This one?"

Leona stood with one hand on her hip. "That's my favorite. Think I'll use it on my bed instead."

"How come you're so partial to this one, other than being with Murdock when you made it? Why is it called that, anyway?"

"I think most people call it Turkey Tracks nowadays. But Murdock's mama called it Wandering Foot. She said she learned it from her mama. It's an old pattern that maybe started during the Oregon Trail days."

Aggie examined the pattern, tracing the design with her finger. "Looks mighty tedious to me."

"It ain't easy to do." Leona studied the pattern, too. "Maybe I shouldn't have even made it."

"Why do you say that?"

"The pattern has a curse. Never thought much about it

until now. The story goes that a young girl making one—or anyone sleeping under one—will get the roving itch for adventure."

Aggie laughed. "Is that what happened to you?"

"I think it did. I've never settled anywhere but here."

Aggie pursed her lips in thought. "Let's just hang it on the wall. I don't want you taking off on me."

Leona's eyes widened. "You believe in the curse?"

"No, of course not. But just the same, let's not tempt it." After they nailed up the Wandering Foot and two of Leona's other quilts, the ladies stepped back to admire their handiwork.

"It does look good," Leona commented. "You're right to suggest hanging up the Wandering Foot. And I like the idea of settling in. What did you bring us for supper? Smells good."

Aggie stirred the pot she had put on the stove and added a few sticks to the fire. "It's leftover stew." The rich aroma drifted through the tiny shack. Aggie placed the bowls of stew on the rickety table, and they sat down to eat. "I hope to bring supper from work most nights. It just gets thrown out anyway."

"That would help our grocery bill."

"I'm thinking we should also sell our horses. It costs too much to board them out."

"That means we would be stuck here with no way to leave," Leona said. "You're not thinking about selling our buggy and buckboard, too?"

Aggie shook her head. "We should keep those, but we can buy another horse if we really want to leave."

"I suppose you're right."

"Do you have extra material for a couple of aprons?"

"I might. You want one, too?"

"Sew yours first," Aggie said. "If you have any left over, sew me one."

Leona scraped the last bit of stew from her bowl. "Do you really think we can make this work, making enough money to live here?"

"We can try. I'd like to have a place of our own someday."

"Now you're really dreaming. I don't think that will happen to us."

Aggie settled back in her chair and closed her eyes. "This is nice. We got supper in our bellies, a bed to sleep on, curtains at the windows, and a fire if we need it. I feel like I've died and gone to heaven." But an odd feeling caused her to sneak a peek at the Wandering Foot on the wall near her bed. She hoped they had thwarted its wayward powers.

CHAPTER 10

Kat, Jennie, Cilla, and Ling Li spent the morning cutting strips for the Chinese Coin Quilt. Ling Li excused herself early to begin preparing lunch.

"These Chinese prints are so beautiful. No wonder the quilts turn out to be a work of art," Cilla commented.

"We're just lucky to be able to buy the material here in Deadwood. The Chinese stores import practically all their stock," Kat told them.

"And what will we do with this quilt when we have finished?" Jennie asked while coordinating the strips she had cut.

"I think we'll have a time letting go of this one," Kat confessed. "We'll have to make a simple patchwork next. Then maybe we can give it away."

Clem scurried around the partition to the sewing room, startling Kat. "Kat, there's someone here looking for you."

Kat's face tightened. "It's not Rio, is it?"

"Oh, no. I would never let him in the place. It's a man

who speaks like he's from Texas and someone younger, maybe his son."

Kat rose from her chair and peered around the corner. "Tex! What are you doing here?" she shouted as she walked toward him.

Tex tipped his hat and bowed low. "Howdy, Kat. Curt and me had to look y'all up since we was in these parts."

"I never expected to see you here. Sit down and tell me everything. Have you been to the mission lately?"

"Yeah, several times. We moved our cattle from the Belle Fourche country to the Cheyenne River. I'm waiting for the leases to open up on the reservations. We had some business in the Black Hills, so we thought we'd stop by and visit."

"How's Minnie and Jeremiah?"

"They're doing good. Minnie still cooks up a storm and Jeremiah helps Elijah whenever he can," Tex said, glancing at the clock.

Kat noticed it was near lunch time. "You can stay and eat if you want. I serve lunch here now. I have a Chinese cook working in the kitchen as we speak. She does a good job."

"We might as well, and then you can tell us how Jet is doing. I still can't believe it was me and the range detective that caught him rustling cattle that day."

"Well, he didn't want to, remember?" Kat motioned Jennie over and asked her to bring out three plates of food. Kat noticed Curt's gaze lingering on Jennie's slight figure. "Jet's out of prison and has found a job in one of the mines. It's hard work, but he's happy to have a job."

Tex placed a pile of dumplings on his plate. "You know I feel bad that I was with the range detective when we came upon Jet and Tom rustling them cattle. I'm not sure whose bullet got old Tom, but I'm sure glad it wasn't Jet in which the bullet lodged, or I would have had a hard time living with myself."

"I'm glad, too. You probably haven't heard about Jed,

Tom's son. He came gunning for Jet right here in the saloon this past winter."

"Well I'll be darned." Tex tipped his hat off his forehead. "Right here? What for?"

"In his twisted mind, Jed thought Jet was responsible for Tom's death."

"Well, that's nonsense. I assume Jet's okay?"

"He was wounded in the leg."

"And what about Jed?"

"Jed escaped along with Rio—his brother, that is. Believe it or not, their mother Aggie worked for me up until that day. She quit right before the brothers came in, and I haven't seen her around since."

"Was she their spy?"

"I'm not sure. She seemed friendly enough. Maybe she didn't know who I was until later. She never said much about herself. In fact, I didn't know she was Rio and Jed's mother until later."

Jennie returned with three plates of homemade apple pie and set one before each of them. A crisp, fruity aroma rose from the steaming pies. Curt smiled at Jennie, and Kat thought she saw Jennie smile back.

"Your saloon seems more like an eating establishment than a saloon," Tex commented. "You got a kitchen and everything."

"I know. That's my intent. I'd like to give up the saloon business and focus on becoming a restaurant. I thought I'd make a gradual transition."

"But ain't there more money in whiskey than in meat and potatoes?"

"There probably is, but I've had a change of heart. Money isn't everything."

"Yeah, I suppose. But it's hard to live without it."

"How long will you be staying in town?" Kat asked.

"Not long. We'll probably leave this afternoon."

Kat waved Jennie over with more coffee. "Too bad! You could stay and talk to Jet."

"I'm not sure he would want to see me, though."

"It wasn't your fault you happened to be riding by with a range detective."

"No, but I did think the worst of Jet at the time."

Kat smiled. "We're getting married soon. Jet promised Ed that he would come back to the Bar Double B to help with the fall roundup."

"Congratulations. Will you be staying at the ranch long?"

"Probably through the winter. Jet prefers the ranch to Deadwood."

Tex patted his mouth with a napkin. "Will you sell your business?"

"No, I intend on returning to Deadwood in the spring."

"We'll probably see you at the mission sometime. We visit whenever we get the chance. Good people there."

"Yes they are. Too bad it's so isolated."

"I take it you prefer town life," Tex said.

"That's all I know."

"You do have a nice place here. Guess I don't blame you. That was a delicious meal. Long time since I had chicken and dumplings. But we'd better get going."

"Thanks for stopping by. Give my best to the mission folks when you see them."

"I'll do that. Hope to see y'all in the fall."

———

Jet and Kat were again eating at the Miner's Restaurant when Kat asked if he knew anyone called Cheng. "Cheng? There are a few Chinese men in our mine, but I guess I never paid attention to names," Jet told her.

"There aren't that many Chinese around Deadwood anymore. He shouldn't be hard to find. Most have gone back to

China or the big cities. Think," she urged him. "He's average size and wears a queue. He speaks some English. Oh, yeah—he spent some time in jail for opium use."

"Now I know who you're talking about. Why are you interested in Cheng?"

"Ling Li likes him. Jennie thought it might be a good idea to get him a different job so that her father might approve of him."

"What kind of job are you thinking about?"

"A houseboy for some prominent Deadwood citizen could be a very good job."

"Ling Li's father owns the laundry. Right?"

"Right. In fact, that would work well for Cheng. He'll need to have his clothes extra clean and well pressed. Ling Li could see to that."

"The way I see it, you ladies have it all figured out."

"Ling Li's father doesn't approve of opium. That could be a problem."

"Well, I thought all Chinese used it."

"Guess not. Anyway, do you know anything about him?"

Jet shrugged. "He does his work. Doesn't get into any trouble...except for the opium incident."

"Well, just keep an eye on him. I want to make sure he's a good match for her."

"Since it's that important to you, I will."

"It is," she said. "Ling Li is a very nice girl. I feel somewhat responsible for her."

"I don't know why you should."

"We all have taken her under our wing, included her with our sewing group, given her a cooking job."

"I see your point, but I always made it a habit to leave people of different customs alone. They have their own ways."

"You might be right, but she loves this guy. Otherwise, she'll have to marry someone her father has chosen for her. I wouldn't put myself in that position. In fact, that's why I left home. My father thought I needed to marry the neighbor's son."

"You didn't like him?"

She frowned. "He was goofy looking and acted the same." Jet laughed and abruptly changed the subject, pushing the empty plates aside. "We need to set a date for our wedding. Fall will be here before you know it."

"I'm waiting to hear from Annabelle. I want her to be here with Miranda for our wedding."

"Your sister is coming here?"

"I haven't had a chance to talk to you, but she sent me a letter. She has decided to leave Cleveland and move here with Miranda."

"What's she going to do here?"

"I have a terrific plan."

"And what's that?"

"As you know, I want to eventually turn the saloon into a restaurant. While we are gone, I will need someone to manage it. I thought about Annabelle. The best part is that she and Miranda could live in our house while we are away. How does that sound to you?"

"Yeah, if you think she is capable of running a business."

"I'm not too sure about that part. I hope she's matured since I last saw her."

"What do you mean by that?"

"Annabelle hasn't been all that good with money. I thought I'd have Jennie look over her shoulder, if you know what I mean."

Jet raised his eyebrows. "I hope you know what you're doing."

"I'm excited to find out when Annabelle's coming. I would like her to be here for the wedding."

"I have a feeling that our wedding is becoming less and less simple."

Kat nodded. "It is. The girls want to be bridesmaids and wear fancy dresses."

"You said girls?"

"Yeah, I know. At first I said just one. I asked Jennie first, but Cilla and Ling Li were disappointed. And then there's Annabelle. She's my sister, and I can't leave her out."

"So who does that leave me with? I don't have many friends here."

"There's Clem and Jake. Oh, gosh, we need two more. I'll have to think on that one."

"Just let me know when you've decided."

"I will. You should see the girls. They're choosing my dress, talking about flowers, cake, and decorating."

"I can just imagine."

"Just bear with it. It'll be over before you know it," she reassured him with pleading eyes. "I had wanted to be a traditional June bride, but time is passing much too quickly. How about August?"

Jet shrugged. "As long as it's before September."

CHAPTER 11

The railroad through Deadwood was barely a decade old. It stretched up from the south, hauling hope. Kat's hope was that her sister would arrive less worn and dusty than if she had come by stagecoach. Waiting at the station on that sweltering, July afternoon, Kat took a deep breath and noted the pungent pine. Although the train was not yet late, she tapped her foot until the machinery groaned and whined to a steamy halt. She stood vigilantly until her only remaining family disembarked, and rushed to them. The whole time, she felt as though she were fighting against waves of heat that seemed to bounce off the buildings.

The fringes of Annabelle's red hair, curling out from beneath her hat, glistened in the sun as she stepped out of the passenger car. She wore an olive green traveling suit with a matching hat. She was stylish like Kat, but not as flamboyant. Miranda followed, dressed in her beige frock. Kat was astonished at how the girl had matured. Her strawberry blonde hair framed the pretty, freckled face. After hugs all around, the sisters prattled on and on. They inquired after each other's health, the train ride, and the decision to leave Cleveland. They finally reached the topic of where they would be living.

"I want you to meet my friends first," Kat said. "Jet should be in from the mine before too long. Oh, and don't worry about your trunks. I already arranged for them to be delivered to my house. I want you to see the Birdcage first."

———

Once inside the doors of the Birdcage, Kat introduced her family to Clem, Jake, Jennie, Cilla, and Ling Li. Ling Li brewed a pot of tea, which they all sipped while enjoying pleasant conversation. The men resumed their duties several minutes later, leaving the women to discuss wedding plans. Kat sighed in relief as soon as they were out of sight. "Annabelle, now that you're here, Jet and I can set a wedding date. I would be honored if you would be one of my bridesmaids."

"Of course. Thank you for asking."

"Jennie has been a big help in planning my wedding. With so many bridesmaids, Jennie is looking for someone to sew the dresses. Have you found anyone yet?"

Jennie shook her head. "Not for all of them. I'll have to find an extra person. That's a lot of dresses to sew. No one wants to take on that many. And maybe someone will sew Kat's too. She was going to order one, but it won't get here in time."

"I wish I could help," Annabelle said. "I can't sew that well."

"I can't either," Kat admitted. "I wonder if Leona could help out. I hired her the other day to fill in for Jennie occasionally. She said she made quilts, so I'll ask her about sewing."

"Actually, you can ask her now," Jennie said. "Clem's just now showing her around."

"If you'll excuse me, I'll go ask her."

Kat found Clem and Leona in the kitchen. He was explaining where everything was stored. "Clem, I'd like to ask Leona something. It will just take a minute."

"I'll be out front," Clem said.

"Leona, you said you made quilts."

Leona avoided her gaze. "I do."

"We need someone to sew some dresses for my wedding. Jennie has found one person, but we need someone else. I would pay you well. Do you think you could sew up a few dresses?"

Leona tugged at her ear. "Sew? When...would you need them?"

"We haven't set an exact date yet, but I would think in about a month."

"Ah, let me think about it tonight."

"Good enough. I'll send Clem back," Kat said, leaving the kitchen.

"Well, what did she say?" Jennie wanted to know.

"She said she'd think about it. Hope she says yes. She could use the extra job."

———

Jet appeared through the door of the Birdcage late into the afternoon, shining like a polished apple. Kat stared at him in wonderment. He smiled back and winked. "Here's my man," Kat announced proudly. She introduced the handsome Jet to Annabelle and eagerly awaited her sister's reaction. Kat could tell Annabelle was impressed. "We haven't been to the house yet," she explained to Jet. "I stopped here first so that Annabelle and Miranda could meet everyone."

Jet pulled up a chair and sat next to Kat. "Shall we have

supper out tonight? Or do you have other plans?"

"No, I don't. Let's stop at the house first to make sure their trunks have been delivered, and then we can find a place to eat. Will that work for you, Annabelle?"

"It will."

"I'll join you ladies in about a half hour," Jet said. "Think I'll have a beer with Clem first."

Kat explained to her sister and niece that they could walk to her house on the hill. "Do you want a fancy meal tonight, or just plain, good food?"

"Good food, rather than fancy, would be my choice," Annabelle said. "Jet is rather good-looking. Polite, too. Hard to believe he was a cattle rustler once."

"It is. He got in with a bad crowd. He's a good man."

"You're lucky. I haven't found anyone since Miranda's father left us."

"Deadwood's full of men...but not many good ones. I think I see your trunks by the door."

"We tried to limit ourselves to two trunks. My, it was hard packing our belongings into so little space. I had to leave the furniture behind with Aunt Ethel. She promised to ship it out if I found a place of my own."

"I don't have a lot of room in the house, but when Jet and I leave in a couple of months, the house will be yours for the winter. And by next spring, you might find a place of your own."

"I do have a little money to get by on."

Kat took a hold of one of the trunk's handles. "Let's see if we can move these trunks onto the porch, at least."

"Thanks for taking us in. After mother and father died, I just had to admit that there wasn't anything there for me in Cleveland anymore. I felt so useless."

"I was going to wait to tell you this. But if you're willing, I have a job at the Birdcage for both you and Miranda when Jet and I leave for the ranch. By then, I hope to have it mostly converted to a restaurant. I will still serve beer, though."

"What exactly do you want us to do?"

"I want you to be my manager and look after my interests."

Annabelle's hand flew to her mouth. "I don't have much business experience."

"Don't worry. I'll fill you in on what to look for...how to keep books and such. I have good help. There's a cook and several waitresses. Clem or Jake might stay on. Jennie is quite sharp with anything to do with the Birdcage, but I still want you to take care of the business and this house. It's all I have."

"I'd say it's more than I have."

"We'll make sure you succeed in Deadwood. I'm sorry I'll have to leave you in a few months, but Jet has made a commitment to Ed and the Bar Double B."

"I know. We'll be fine."

"Also, if you want to learn to quilt, the ladies you met earlier come to the Birdcage for quilting sessions whenever they have the time. They make quilts to give to the needy."

"So you have learned to quilt, I take it?"

"I know it's hard to believe, but yes, I have. And I enjoy it." Kat led them to the extra bedroom that Annabelle and Miranda would share. "This room is quite small, but when we leave, one of you can take my bedroom for the winter."

Annabelle hugged her sister. "This is fine. I'm just so thankful we had a place to go."

Jet yelled from the doorway. "Anyone in here?"

"Be right with you," Kat answered. "Did you want to freshen up before we go?" she asked Annabelle.

"We're fine and ready when you are."

"Jet, I think Annabelle would like the Miner's Restaurant tonight. After all that travel, they're ready for some good food, even if the establishment isn't much to look at," Kat said.

"If that's your wish, we'll give it a go," Jet said. "I borrowed Clem's buggy for the night. We should all fit comfortably." Once they settled in, Jet drove them around Deadwood while spouting a little history of the area. Kat smiled at his thoughtfulness.

"When do you want me to start work, Kat?" Annabelle asked as they were taking their seats at the Miner's Restaurant.

"Take some time to settle in. There's no hurry. Like I said, I have plenty of help now. In a few weeks, I'll show you my bookkeeping system, and then take you by the merchants where I buy produce."

"What about me?" Miranda asked.

"Hmm...I'm not sure. Maybe wash dishes when the cook gets behind. I'm sure we can find something to keep you busy."

"Miranda has never done any chores. She might have to ease into it slowly," Annabelle said.

Kat raised her brow. "We won't overwork her."

"Good. She likes to read and meditate. I don't think we want to interfere with expanding her mind."

———

Aggie wiped her perspiring face with her apron before she tackled another mound of dishes. Business was unusually good that day, and the stove had never cooled once. A little breeze blew in through the back door, but it wasn't enough to do much good. She glanced at the clock, which told her she had another two hours in the sweltering kitchen.

Through the swinging doors that separated the kitchen from the dining area, Aggie could see the largest table in the restaurant. It had been occupied all day by one group or another ever since she had come to work. She recognized some of its occupants, but most were total strangers to her.

She heard voices from a new group that was just sitting down to a meal. She stopped scrubbing the silverware and listened again to a lady's voice. *Why, that sounds like Kat,* she thought. She wiped her hands on the soiled apron Leona had made her and carefully peered through the crack between the swinging doors. Her heart thudded. It *was* Kat! She was with a tall, good-looking man, another red-haired lady who looked very much like Kat, and a young girl. She realized she couldn't avoid Kat forever, but she also couldn't afford to be the cause of a disturbance.

The waitress barged through the kitchen door and swung it wide open; Aggie quickly turned her head away from the dining room. *I can't let her see me,* she thought. *There's no telling what she'd do, even if she doesn't blame me for anything.*

Kat remained with her companions for over an hour, and Aggie was relieved when they finally left. Aggie's stomach was in a knot. She felt like a lump of melted butter by the time she scraped the kettles, keeping a small amount aside for supper.

She gratefully let the mountain air cool her as she walked toward her shack. Lamplight glowed in one of the windows as she approached. At least someone was waiting for her, even if it was just Leona.

"Here's supper," Aggie said as she placed the kettle on the table. "It's still warm, so we won't have to light the stove."

Leona peered in the kettle. "Smells like cabbage."

"Yeah, we served corned beef and cabbage today."

"There's not much in here," Leona complained.

"Go ahead and eat it all. I'm not hungry. All I did today was sweat."

"See, we probably should have gone to Texas with the boys and forgotten about making it on our own. It's just too darn hard."

"We'd be cooking for them right now—and getting no

money. It's hot in Texas, too," Aggie reminded her.

"Yeah, you're right. But that's all we'd have to worry about—cooking, I mean. No rent, no buying food, no working our fingers to the bone. I hardly get time to work on my quilts anymore."

Aggie frowned and went in the bedroom to change clothes. She returned to plop into a chair, took a cigar from her pocket, and lit it.

"I thought you gave them up."

"Only when I'm working or out in public."

"You look tuckered." Leona sat at the table with the salvaged food. "This isn't the best time to ask if you want to take on more work."

Aggie sighed deeply. "More work? Like what?"

Leona coughed and waved away the cigar smoke. "That thing stinks. I don't know how you can stand to smoke cigars," Leona complained. "Kat's looking for someone to sew dresses for her wedding. She asked me, thinking I could do it. I didn't say no. Thought I'd ask you."

"I can't go to the Birdcage." Aggie directed another puff of smoke toward Leona.

"She didn't say I had to stay there and sew. We do have a sewing machine, and I could pretend I'm doing the sewing here at home."

"There would be fittings and such. I suppose I could show you what to do."

"Kat said she'd pay well. Do you think you could do it?"

"I could try one. I'd have to sew at night, though."

"I told Kat I'd let her know tomorrow."

"Make sure you don't have to be there to do the sewing. And keep in mind you'll have to do the measuring and the fittings. Kat can't find out that I'm doing the sewing."

"I'll see what she says."

"By the way, I saw Kat and her companions at the Miner's Restaurant tonight."

"She didn't see you, did she?"

"No, I made sure of that. I was glad when she left. There was another lady with red hair and a young girl."

"That's probably her sister and niece. I heard Kat talking about them coming from Cleveland."

"Guess that explains the red hair."

"Someday, you're going to run into her when you least expect it." Leona placed her empty plate in the dishpan.

"I know, but I want to stall it as long as I can. Bring me the wash pan with some water. I need to soak my feet." Aggie secretly agreed with Leona. Holding down a job was hard on her, but she didn't want Leona to see that she was weakening, too. Somehow she had to make this work, even if it meant taking on sewing. She just hoped she was strong enough to do it all.

———

By the end of the week, Leona brought home the pattern, thread, and material. Aggie looked it over after work. "I've never sewed with such beautiful material. I'm afraid to even cut it. You did measure the lady correctly?"

"I did what you showed me to do."

"Who's this one for?"

"This one's for Cilla."

"She won't use up a lot of material."

"Save the scraps for me," Leona reminded her.

"I bet they'll want them back to use in their quilts."

"Oh, darn. I suppose."

"Help me clean off this table," Aggie said. "We'll lay it out. You might as well learn how to do this, too. I've been thinking of your idea to sew for people. If I can please Kat and her ladies, maybe I'd be good enough to give it a try. It might beat washing dishes."

Leona held the lavender crepe up to her face. "This smells

so new. How do I look?"

"Once upon a time, you might have looked mighty good."

"Ah, you're just jealous."

Aggie smirked. "Hardly." She carefully read the instructions while Leona washed the dishes. After she determined she understood the basic layout, she took the patterns and pinned them in place. "Come here, Leona. I want to show you what I've done." Aggie patiently explained every step. She rechecked what she had done to make sure that she wouldn't ruin the material. "Here goes nothing," Aggie muttered as she made the first cut into the material.

Leona grumbled that it was getting late. But feeling up to the challenge, Aggie continued sewing until past midnight. She was surprised that the pattern went together so well. In her excitement, Aggie woke Leona, who was sleeping in the chair. "Leona! Stop by the Birdcage tomorrow and have Cilla try this on. I basically put the dress together. All that's left is the sleeves, collar, and such. See if it fits her."

"What? Oh, the dress. Can I go to bed now?"

"Did you hear what I said?"

Leona yawned. "I did."

"Go to bed," Aggie said rather harshly. "I should, too. Work starts early tomorrow. I hope I don't sleep in." Yet Aggie knew she was in no danger of sleeping in; Leona's snoring irritated her. Aggie tossed and turned all night, worrying that she had taken on too much. She realized that she wasn't young anymore and was discovering that she just couldn't work like she used to. She detested washing dishes, and it looked like the cook wasn't going to leave anytime soon.

Aggie played Leona's suggestion in her head over and over. Could she start a sewing business? For one thing, her location was all wrong. The proper ladies of the town wouldn't come to the badland section of Deadwood where she lived, except when the Chinese were celebrating their New Year. That was the only time the stores would cater to white trade. She punched her pillow. *It's useless,* she thought. *I could barely hang on the way it was. Leona was right. Perhaps we should have gone to Texas with the men. How am I to move to a better section of town? No, I'll just have to keep the dishwashing job and do a few sewing jobs on the side.*

———

Morning came too soon for Aggie. She had just fallen asleep when the sunlight flooded through the windows of her shack. Wagons began rumbling down the street. With the kindling she extracted from the wood box, she started a fire in the stove to boil a pot of coffee. She quickly stirred up some pancakes. Her head felt like mush this morning. She was glad she didn't have to do much thinking; she only needed to keep up with the dirty dishes and sew on the dress later in the evening. Leona was still snoring when Aggie left her and trudged to the Miner's Restaurant. The usual customers were demanding their breakfasts, but the cook was nowhere to be found. Aggie sliced and fried a slab of bacon and served it with eggs, also fried.

"Aggie, I'm glad you're here," Mr. Lockert said. "The cook sent a message that she was too sick to cook today. Could you fill in for her? Oh, I see you have already taken over."

"What about a dishwasher?"

"I'll see if I can talk one of the customers into filling in for you. There's a few that owe me."

Aggie already knew what the cook had planned to make for the day, and she had no problem finding her way around the kitchen. She felt she could do a better job than the woman the owner had hired. Today, she had a chance to remind Mr. Lockert what she could do with the inferior produce he had a habit of ordering.

Aggie had just finished serving the breakfast rush when she saw Cilla enter the restaurant. *Oh, great,* Aggie thought.

There are other restaurants in town. Why does everyone I know have to congregate here? She couldn't worry about Cilla when she had dinner to prepare. Not much time remained. The dishwasher that Mr. Lockert had cajoled into working wasn't very efficient, causing Aggie to fall behind in her own work. She had just finished peeling a huge kettle of potatoes when Cilla passed by the kitchen, doubled back, and poked her head through the swinging doors.

"Aggie? What you doing here?" Cilla asked in surprise. "I thought you had left town."

Aggie almost dropped the apple pie she had just taken out of the oven. "Cilla?"

"I—I was looking for the cook...to compliment her on the fine breakfast."

Aggie inhaled deeply to calm her nerves. "I'm the cook today. The regular one's sick." Aggie placed the pie on the counter and moved toward the swinging door. "Please don't tell anyone I'm in town."

"But...why not?"

"You know. Everybody probably connects me with the ruckus at the Birdcage. Believe me; I didn't know my boys were planning such a thing."

"We were wondering if you were spying on us."

"Has Kat mentioned me?"

"She had quite a time getting over it. Jet was shot, you know."

"And Kat?"

"She took her gun out of her bag and fainted. Where are your boys? They're not in Deadwood, are they?"

"No. I'm tired of being on the move, so I thought I'd come back to Deadwood. I don't mean anyone any harm. Honest, I don't."

"I believe you. I won't tell anyone you're here, but someone's going to find out soon."

"I know, but I'm...not ready for that yet."

After Cilla left, Aggie sighed with relief. She hoped she could trust Cilla not to say anything because she also didn't want them to find out her association with Leona. She just wanted to finish the sewing project as soon as possible. The extra money and experience would come in handy, especially if their situation were to unravel.

———

Aggie was even more tired than usual when she returned home with the kettle scrapings. "Leona, I'm back with supper. I even have a surprise."

"What is it?" Aggie peeled back a dish towel to reveal two pieces of pie. "Apple pie. Does it have lots of cinnamon in it?" Leona asked. "I just love the smell of cinnamon."

"It does."

"How'd your day go?"

"I got to cook today. The usual cook was sick. I made sure to save enough for our supper. How did the fitting go?"

"Cilla said it fit pretty good."

"She didn't say anything to anyone about seeing me at the restaurant?"

"No, did she see you?"

"Yes, I even talked to her," Aggie said. "I told her not to say anything about it. I didn't give her any more information than I had to."

"Good, because I think you might even have to sew Kat's dress."

"The wedding dress?"

"Yeah."

"I thought you said she was ordering it."

"Kat was going to, but it seems it won't get here in time. She thinks she needs someone to make it. The ladies were impressed that you...I mean that I have Cilla's dress nearly done."

"Right now, I don't know if that's good news or bad news," Aggie said. "I'm so tired."

"Well, sit down and eat. I'll do the dishes, and then maybe we can work some more on Cilla's dress."

"I guess, I'll have to. You know what I was thinking of last night instead of sleeping?"

"What?" Leona said, sliding two steaming helpings of stewed chicken onto their plates.

"Wouldn't it be grand if we would open our own sewing shop one day? We could live there with our business, either in the back of the store or up above."

"You're thinking a little too grand for two over-the-hill women like us. Let's just concentrate on making enough money for food and rent."

"I suppose you're right. We probably shouldn't be dreaming at our age."

Leona nodded. "Eat your supper, Aggie."

———

"But you just have to sew my dress," Kat pleaded with Leona the next day. "All the other dressmakers are too busy, and Jet doesn't want to postpone our wedding."

"Is it complicated? Ag—I mean...I can't do really complicated work."

"I'll tell you what. Let's go and pick out a pattern you think you can sew. Corella keeps a good supply of material. I'm sure I can find something in ivory."

"Go now?" Leona's voice squeaked.

"Yes, the sooner the better. You know you can use the sewing machine here at the Birdcage."

"Thanks, but I'd rather sew at home. I don't like anyone looking over my shoulder."

Kat shrugged and then led Leona to the general store. Much to her consternation, the only one available to help her was Corella.

"What can I do for you?" Corella asked, looking up over the top of her spectacles.

"Just looking for a pattern."

"What kind of pattern?"

"A wedding dress."

"Who's getting married?"

"I am."

"I see. Congratulations. A local man?"

"No, he's not from around here." Kat ignored Corella's inquisitive expression and thumbed through the patterns. "What about this one?" she asked Leona.

"Well, I just don't know. What about all these ruffles and fancy trimmings and such?"

Kat rapped her fingernails on the counter. "I probably should have a little trimming, or it's going to look mighty plain."

"True, true."

"We'll look a little more." Kat and Leona scrutinized a few designs. Although accustomed to pretexts, Leona was beginning to anxiously perspire. But Kat was too focused on the patterns to notice. She clearly preferred the first one, so that's what they decided upon. With the pattern established, Kat turned her attention to the fabric.

"This one's kind of slippery," Leona commented after feeling the silk.

"I like the looks of this one." Kat picked up a bolt of fine cotton. "With some lace, I think this will do nicely."

Corella placed the bolt of fabric on the counter and cut the yardage needed for the dress. "Where are you getting married? A church, perhaps?"

Kat frowned and answered, "We're having a quiet wedding and reception in my backyard."

"I see. Considering all the material I've sold to you lately, you must be having a number of attendants."

"Yes, I didn't want to disappoint anyone."

"Highly unusual to have more than one each."

"It may be, but I don't do things the way everyone else does."

As soon as Corella briskly tied up her purchases, Kat squared her shoulders and left the store with Leona following. "I hate doing business with that uppity woman, but I simply don't have any other choice," Kat said as soon as she was out the door.

"Do you suppose she was hinting at an invitation?" Leona laughed.

"I doubt it, but she wants to know my business for some reason."

"Every town has to have a busybody or two."

Once inside the Birdcage, Kat pushed aside a half-completed crazy quilt and plopped the packages on the table near the sewing machine. "When you finish my dress, why don't you join our quilting group? We're making quilts for the needy."

"I would like that. I'd rather quilt than do anything else."

"I'd say you are one talented lady."

Leona shrugged. "Not really."

"By the way, can you cook?"

"I've done my share."

"I need someone to make food for the reception. Ling Li does most of my cooking now, but she will be a bridesmaid, too. I don't want her to be stuck in the kitchen."

"I'm not a fancy cook," Leona said. "I usually just cook rib-stickin' food for a bunch of men."

"Can you bake a cake and decorate it?"

"Never decorated a cake."

"Hmm. Want to bake and decorate your first cake?"

"You're that desperate?" Leona gathered up the ivory material and pattern.

"You weren't sure that you could sew well enough, and

look what you did! I think you can make my wedding cake, too. I'll pay you."

"Oh. If you don't expect too much, I suppose I can do it. But I don't know if I can prepare all the food, too. That's too much for one person."

"Do you think you can find someone to help you?"

"I might..."

"Go ahead and choose your help. The important thing is that this wedding happens soon."

CHAPTER 12

Kat was surprised when she stepped into her backyard on the morning of her wedding. The ladies had been up early, decorating with brightly colored Chinese lanterns that bobbed from the tree branches.

"I hope you don't mind some Chinese touches," Ling Li said.

"I love your idea. It's so colorful and...different. Thank you all for pitching in to make this day special. Now you all better get in here and pretty up for the wedding. I'm going to check on the cake Leona's baking at the Birdcage."

"Don't take too long," Jennie reminded her. "And don't be late for your own wedding."

Kat laughed. "Don't worry, this won't take too long." She skipped down the set of steps leading from her house to the main street below.

What a beautiful day, she thought. *My wedding day.* She could hardly believe it. She had nearly given up on finding a man worth her attention and had resigned herself to being an old maid for the remainder of her life. She jubilantly pushed aside the swinging doors and entered the Birdcage. She inhaled the aroma of the freshly baked cake. The voices of more than one woman drifted from the kitchen. Leona must have found someone to help, she thought. But before Kat even walked through the kitchen doorway, she froze in panic. Her heart beat wildly against her chest, and she broke into a sweat. Her eyes searched the kitchen and then swept back to Leona and her companion.

"Kat," Aggie said, sounding surprised.

"What are you doing in my kitchen?" Kat demanded.

"Helping Leona."

Kat's head jerked toward Leona. "You know Aggie?"

"Ah, yeah. We met on the trail."

"Are Rio and Jed here, too?"

"No, they're long gone," Aggie said. "Kat, I had nothing to do with that night. I didn't know what my boys were up to."

"Where are they now?" Kat felt her face flush.

"They should be in Texas. They're not going to hurt you or Jet."

"I trusted you, Aggie."

"I know you did, and I felt terrible about what happened."

Kat's gaze intensified into a glare. "I can't believe you'd show yourself around here after what happened."

Aggie's face grew pale. "I thought I explained. I had nothing to do with their attempt on Jet's life. And maybe, just maybe, Jed just wanted to scare him. I can't believe I have a son who would kill someone."

"So why are you in my kitchen?"

"Helping Leona."

"You're making my wedding cake?"

Untying her apron strings, Aggie said, "I can leave."

Kat held up her hand. "No, I need a cake. Maybe I believe you. I'm not sure why I should. The fact that you came back to Deadwood seems to confirm your innocence."

Aggie retied her apron. Her hand shook as she stirred powdered sugar into the icing.

"Why haven't I seen you around Deadwood, Aggie?"

"I stay pretty much near Chinatown."

"You have a job?"

"I work at the Miner's Restaurant."

"I've been in there and didn't see you."

"Probably was washing dishes or cooking."

"Mighty strange, I'd say. I hired Leona and didn't even know you two were friends." Kat shifted her glare to Leona. "Continue with the cake. I'm going back to the house. We'll talk more about this later."

Leona finished the last swirl of icing. "Are you sending someone for the cake?"

"Yeah, tell Clem to bring it," Kat said. "Leona, you ride along just to make sure the cake gets to the house in one piece." Kat left the women to their work. She shook her head at the strange turn of events. She trusted that Aggie had told her the truth, but still felt uneasy thinking about her two sons and the night at the Birdcage.

———

Kat's bridesmaids were already dressed in their lavender wedding frocks when she arrived back at her house. "You had better hurry and get ready, Kat," Annabelle called from the back yard.

"What are you gals doing?" Kat asked.

"Adding a few more decorations," Jennie giggled.

Kat lifted her dress off the bed and wriggled into it. What was that smell? She lifted the fabric to her nose. A pungent odor reached her nostrils. *Aggie's cigar. Oh, great. That woman had something to do with the dresses, too,* she concluded. *I can never get away from her and her boys.* At least the dress fit the way she wanted. Lace accented the low neckline and bodice. A small train, trimmed in lace, flared before cascading down the back of the dress. She picked up the atomizer off her dresser and sprayed a lilac fragrance over the dress. *Thank goodness the wedding will be held outdoors. Maybe no one would notice,* she mused. She touched up her makeup and redid a few curls that she had piled in an upsweep earlier. Then she removed an ivory hat adorned with pale white flowers from a hat box and pinned it on her flaming red hair. A thin veil swept over her face, touching just under her chin.

Annabelle tapped on her bedroom door. "The guests are arriving. Jet's here. Clem just delivered the cake. Can I come in and see what you look like?"

"Yeah, come in."

Annabelle entered her sister's bedroom, lifted her palm to her mouth, and gasped. "Oh, Kat! You look stunning."

"Do you really think so?" Kat asked, slowly pivoting.

"Oh, yes."

"It's a good thing I don't have to walk too far in this dress." Kat waddled like a penguin around her bedroom.

"Is it a little tight?" Annabelle frowned in concern.

"It is. But I like it to be snug, and I think it looks divine. Leona did a terrific job...or maybe it was Aggie who sewed my dress."

"Aggie?"

"I'll tell you later. It's a long story."

Annabelle shrugged.

"You are beautiful in that dress, Annabelle."

"Thank you. So nice of you to say. I'll come and get you when they're ready for us. Oh! The flowers." Annabelle turned toward Kat.

"Where are they?"

"We collected roses from the gardens around town. Cilla put them in a bouquet. I'll go and fetch them."

"I hope you asked first."

Annabelle laughed. "Don't worry. We did."

Kat shook her head. *Too many details to keep straight. I just want to get married! But I can't begrudge them their fun. They're so excited to make this day extra special.*

Soon Annabelle returned with a bouquet of red and white roses.

Kat took them and held them to her face. "They smell wonderful."

"They don't exactly go with lavender, but it's the best we could do. We're ready," she announced to Kat.

Kat watched with pride as the girls flounced about the house in their beautiful lavender dresses. They assumed their positions for the processional march. Miranda handed out finely painted Chinese fans, which they each carried instead of flowers. The sweet strains of an accordion initiated their march. As Kat emerged behind her bridesmaids from her little house, she could barely contain her pleasure at the backyard transformation. But it was Jet who took her breath away. Wearing a black suit, she had never seen him look so elegant. Beside him were Clem, Jake, Cheng, and another miner friend.

Jet smiled warmly as Kat's eyes met his. He slipped his hand into hers and faced the minister who had agreed to marry them under an arbor that her friends had brought in earlier. They had draped the altar table with the Chinese Lantern quilt that she and her friends had made. Nothing could distract Kat from the moment; not the noises of the town, the pesky flies, or the dog barking next door. Her only focus was Jet. After the recital of vows, he slipped a plain wedding band on her finger. They were man and wife, ready to build a life together—but not in Deadwood. That thought scalded Kat.

CHAPTER 13

Kat slipped out of bed, unable to sleep. It was early; the sun had not yet crested the horizon. Jet slumbered peacefully while she padded to the kitchen to make coffee. They were to leave that afternoon on a stagecoach for the mission and the Bar Double B. She had packed a trunk with her necessities, agonizing over what to leave behind. She kindled a blaze in her cook stove and brewed coffee. Having Annabelle and Miranda care for the house and cat would ease her mind.

Kat had filled Minnie in on the details since she had left them a year earlier, writing that she and Jet had married and that they were coming to the Bar Double B Ranch in the fall so Jet could help Ed with the roundup. She had also asked if she could stay with them at the mission until Jet had time to build them a small house. Kat lit a stumpy candle and reread Minnie's response:

Dear Kat,

Of course you can stay with us as long as you want. We enjoyed your company and miss having you in our midst.

We are so excited that you will be living near us, and even more excited that you married Jet. The ladies and I have been planning a reception for you at the mission. We'll decorate the gazebo just like a wedding. We'll even have a wedding cake!

There have been many changes since you left.

Evangeline and Willow won't be here when you arrive. There's been some trouble with funding the new dormitory. Evangeline has left with her father and mother to return to Boston and tend to legal matters. We miss them terribly.

I have a helper in the kitchen. Her name is Bea. We also have a young teacher named Ethel. Sara is filling in during Evangeline's absence. But it seems we are always shorthanded.

Elijah's father Ben is with us, too. He is painting murals and helping us with the rodeos.

We see Tex and his son Curt every once in a while, since they have moved their cattle closer to the reservation. Tater, their former cook, has opened a store here. He may even apply to have a post office here, too. Seems we got a little more civilization around here. Oh, yes, and we even have ourselves a doctor. You'll like the changes.

Can't wait to see you. Have a safe trip.

Minnie

Kat took a deep breath. Everything had been arranged. She wanted to see Minnie again, but she still didn't want to leave Deadwood. She would just have to endure the fall season—perhaps the winter as well—away from the Birdcage and her little house on the hill, just so Jet wouldn't feel that he was letting Ed down by missing the roundup.

Jet arose with the sun and shuffled into the kitchen, rumpling his hair. "Coffee sure smells good. Anything to go with it?"

"Sure, I can stir up some pancakes and fry a few eggs. I was just rereading the letter from Minnie. Here, I don't know if you read it." She handed Jet the letter and turned to her cabinets. After rustling up a bowl and a frying pan, she began to measure the ingredients for pancakes.

Jet glanced up from the letter. "Minnie's looking forward to seeing you."

"Seems that way. It would have been difficult for me out on the Deadwood trail without her help. I was just a teenager then. Had no idea what I got myself into. The freighter I hooked up with wasn't exactly concerned if I ate or not."

"I'm glad she was there for you, too." Jet continued reading the letter. "I see that the mission has a store, maybe a post office. Staying at the mission might not be so bad." Jet winked.

"Maybe not."

"I know you don't want to leave. Thanks for giving up your comforts for a while." He drew her on his lap and hugged her tightly.

"Stop it. I'll burn the pancakes." She peeled his arms from her and dashed to the stove to flip the last of the flapjacks. Kat had just placed breakfast on the table when Annabelle rapped on the door, carrying a big box. "Just in time for breakfast," Kat invited. "Here, let me help you with that. You didn't carry this all the way over from the Birdcage, did you?"

"No, Clem gave me a ride. Thought I'd bring this over. Miranda and I will move in today, if you don't mind. Living above your saloon has been nice, but I sure do miss a house. Thanks so much for letting us live here for a time."

"You're doing me a big favor. I won't have to worry about the house or the business."

"Sounds like an even trade for both of us," Annabelle said.

"I think so, too." Kat said. *There! She said it,* she thought to herself. *But did she really mean it?*

———

Elijah dipped his paintbrush into the pail and slapped on several swaths of the white paint onto the latticed gazebo in the church yard. His heart wasn't in the project, but he had to help prepare for the reception the women had been planning for Kat and Jet. He told himself he should be praying for the success of Jet and Kat's marriage, but all he could think about was himself. A sense of melancholy had been nagging him all morning. *Why did I volunteer for this project?* he asked himself.

The gazebo held too many memories. It was a reminder of better days for him and Evangeline. It was his idea to surprise Evangeline on their wedding day. He had recruited the men to construct the gazebo at Swift Bear's old camp, and they had brought it over to the mission on the morning of the wedding without Evangeline knowing. He smiled when he remembered how touched Evangeline was when she saw it for the first time. That look of surprise and love on her face would never leave him. What a happy day that was.

Drawing the brush over the lattice, Elijah's mind filled with the same questions he had been asking since she left. *What had happened between us since that happy day? Is our marriage doomed? Could it be that we weren't meant for each other? If Evangeline would have used common sense and paid the bills in a timely manner, we might not have found ourselves in this predicament.*

The creditors had depleted the Collier estate, Evangeline's hefty inheritance from the death of her first husband. Yet Evangeline had also credited that estate toward building the mission's dormitory. Frederick, Evangeline's father and a savvy businessman, had suggested that the creditors were not solely to blame; he felt that something didn't ring true. So he had advised Evangeline to return to Boston and look into the matter. Taking her father's advice, Evangeline had left Elijah and the mission to return to Boston with her parents and daughter, Willow.

In the weeks since his wife and daughter had been gone, Elijah was in turmoil. *I didn't even try to stop her,* Elijah thought. *All that was on my mind was the mission. What's the matter with me, anyway?* He continued to berate himself as he slapped paint over the boards. Ben approached him and jolted him out of self-pity.

"Need some help?"

"Oh, no. Save yourself for real painting. Have you finished a masterpiece, yet?"

"Not really. Haven't been in the mood."

"I know what you mean," Elijah mumbled.

"I shouldn't interfere. I'll speak my mind anyway," Ben warned. "You've brought your sadness down on yourself."

Elijah stopped painting and stiffened. "You think I'm sad?"

"It's hard to miss. You mope and work yourself to a frazzle."

"I brought this on myself? What do you mean? You're saying that the possibility of bankruptcy is my fault?"

"Is that the only reason you're unhappy? No, I'm not talking about the dormitory."

"What, then?"

"I let your mother go because I thought I had a greater cause than my family." Before Elijah could respond, Ben turned and walked away, leaving Elijah alone once again at the gazebo.

"Now my father is against me, too," Elijah said to himself. Cassandra had been giving him the cold shoulder since Evangeline had left with her grandchild.

"What were you thinking?" she had asked him. "You

may have jeopardized your family." Now Ben's words cut even deeper, and Elijah was soaked in regret. He knew the mission had been his first priority for so long that he had forgotten himself and taken those close to him for granted. He wondered what he would do if Evangeline decided not to return to him. He feared that his daughter would have no memory of him.

Elijah dipped his brush in the pail again and beat the boards. Evangeline hadn't written him. He hadn't written either, but he had determined that she would be the first. *That way,* he figured, *I'll know that she still cares.*

"I've never seen someone tackle a project with such zeal." Jeremiah interrupted Elijah's thoughts. "Coming to lunch today?"

"I'll skip lunch and finish this. Besides, I have to wash up before I eat. Can't eat covered in paint."

"I think you're looking for an excuse."

"Excuse?"

"You've been avoiding everyone around here. Any special reason?"

"It should be obvious to you. Everyone thinks I treated Evangeline badly, that I blame her for the predicament we're in."

"Is that true?"

"I suppose so. But why does everyone blame me—even you?"

Jeremiah knelt down beside him. "Think about it. How have you behaved?"

"God should be first in my life. The mission is my commitment."

"True. But your family is a commitment, too. You can admit you were wrong. A change of attitude could make things right again."

"So you think confessing my wrongs before everyone would help the way they feel about me?"

"I do. You're not going to be an effective minister until you make this right again. We still want to be your friends and support you like we always have."

Elijah put the paintbrush in the pail. "What you say is true, Jeremiah. I'll take your advice and talk to the staff at our next meeting to clear the air about my behavior."

"That's all well and good, but don't forget Evangeline. She needs to know, too. I'm sure she is having a difficult time of it."

"You're right. I wasn't a supportive husband at all. I shouldn't even be a pastor. I can't even be a good husband or father."

"Don't be so hard on yourself. Pride can lead us down a very wrong road. We all make mistakes. It's difficult to admit you were wrong, but you've already done that—with me, just now. Own up to your mistakes and ask for forgiveness. Now, come on. Let's eat lunch."

Elijah placed the lid back on the pail and scrubbed the stubborn paint drips from his hands. As he walked with his trusted mentor, he envisioned himself confessing to the mission staff, admitting he wasn't the pastor he thought he was. But could he admit that he had failed as a husband?

———

The sun-bleached grasses danced as Jet and Kat made their way over the prairie to the mission. She disliked the landscape when it withered under the fall heat and wind, but she knew she must tolerate it for Jet's sake.

The wind constantly whipped up dust from the worn trail. Debris flung against the stage and into the faces of the disgruntled passengers. Kat finally stopped applying powder and lipstick that only mingled with the dust and accumulated in gritty layers. At several points along the trail, the passengers had lowered the thick, black window flaps to keep out both the heat and wind. But when they began to suffocate from lack of air, they opened them again.

To Kat's relief, the long and uncomfortable trip across western Dakota seemed shorter with Jet. Even though they were unable to have a private conversation for hours on end, Jet squeezed her hand in assurance that they were one for the rest of their lives. The emotional distance that Kat had noticed when Jet first came to Deadwood was beginning to diminish. She had assessed his mood correctly; he needed a great deal of space and freedom. She hoped that once he saddled up again and rode the endless range, he would heal from his imprisonment.

The voyage on the river from Fort Pierre to the mission was also more pleasant than usual. The waves chopped against the sternwheeler, but Kat didn't feel much difference between its motion and that of the stagecoach. She turned her face toward the breeze gliding across the water, which brought misty cool air without the dirt.

Jet closed his eyes, uttered a sigh and stretched out his long legs. "Ah, it feels good not to be cramped." He patted her hand again. "It won't be long before we're there."

Kat pursed her lips for a rebuttal. "But you will be leaving me once we get there."

"It won't be for long, a few weeks at the most," Jet said gently.

"Then what will we do?" she asked, quickly realizing she sounded more accusatory than she had intended.

"I'll have to talk to Ed and see if we can build a house of our own somewhere."

"Hmm." She couldn't keep herself from reviewing the long list of comforts she would have to live without. Then she remembered her grandmother's advice. The woman had told her years ago to take one day at a time and not to worry about something that might never happen. She had lived this philosophy and it had gotten her by.

Jet spoke from under his tilted hat. "Are you anxious to see Minnie and the rest of them?"

"They're well-meaning people. I just don't want them pressuring me too much about religion."

"What do you mean?"

"I was never brought up that way." She turned her full attention to him. "Were you?"

"My mama took me to church when I was a little guy. I remember some of the hymns we sang—and the church bell, too."

"Did you believe?"

"I was too small to know what was going on. But I liked going to church. It gave me a warm feeling. Can't explain anymore than that."

"Minnie's a good woman. I don't think she'd push me into something I didn't want to do. Since you're working for Ed, I suppose we'll be coming to the mission church?"

Jet pushed himself up straight and clasped his hands together around his knees. "We'll probably be too far away during the roundup, but I don't see any harm in going to church every now and then." Kat shrugged. "Elijah's a good sort, too. They all are." Jet yawned. "Now how about we both close our eyes and soak up this peacefulness before we get there?"

"I'm tired, too. The movement of the water makes me drowsy." Kat mimicked Jet's yawn and then attempted to put her head on his shoulder, but her hat whacked him in the face. They both laughed and were slightly embarrassed, so she leaned back against a support post instead.

———

The stern wheeler's engines droned and conversation hummed in the background for a few hours until they reached the landing. The first thing they saw was a buggy decorated with paper streamers and a string of cans tied to the back. Kat laughed in surprise when Jet helped her into the buggy seat. "Look, Jet," she said as she picked up a fall bouquet of handmade paper flowers. A young boy at the landing heard her amusement and came over to the buggy before they departed.

"Are the flowers all right?"

"Yes, they're beautiful," she said, holding them up to her nose.

"I was told to put them in the buggy after the horses were hitched and to put on the streamers, too."

"Imagine, all of you going to all this trouble." She nudged Jet, "give him a little something."

Jet deposited a coin in his hand. "Thank you now." After he climbed in the buggy, he affectionately kissed her cheek. "Do you feel like a new bride?"

She smiled. "Yes, I do, once again."

"Then I guess their plan worked," he said, snapping the reins.

Once they adjusted themselves to the well-worn trail, Jet flashed a concerned glance at Kat. "What are you going do while I'm away?"

"Gosh, I don't really know. Minnie and Cassandra are always sewing. Maybe I can help them with a project or something. I'm sure they'll find something for me to do." During their long buggy ride to the mission, Kat noticed Jet relaxing more than he had before. She realized he truly loved this desolate country.

Jet pulled into the mission some time later. He remarked, "Wow, has this place changed! It's beginning to look like a town." Both of them sat in the buggy, dumbfounded, scrutinizing the new store, doctor's office, and dormitory.

"And there's even a post office. I can at least send and receive mail. I like that." Suddenly, Kat felt better about the prairie.

Minnie came scurrying out of the kitchen door and was in the process of wiping her hands on her apron when she rushed over to meet them. "Congratulations!" Minnie gushed. "I just love it when true love makes a match."

Kat laughed at her sunny personality and her obvious happiness.

"Hope you don't mind me leaving Kat with you. Ed needs me at the fall roundup."

Minnie winked at Kat. "You go right on ahead. We ladies have a reception to plan."

"Now don't go to any trouble on account of us," Kat pleaded.

"Oh, we want to. Just find out when you can be here, Jet."

"You'd better give me some time to finish up the round-up first."

"Oh, we will." Minnie beamed at the couple and then frowned apologetically. "I'd better get back to the kitchen. Supper will be ready in about an hour. Join us at the dormitory dining room. In the meantime, search out the others. They're looking forward to seeing you."

"I like the changes," Kat remarked to Jet.

"Change is even coming here. Hard to believe, isn't it?"

CHAPTER 14

When Jet had finished helping with the fall roundup, he promptly came back to the mission. Kat and Jet seemed to spend every waking moment together. One morning, they lay in bed much later than usual, catching up on what they had missed of each other's lives during the roundup. Snuggling in his arms, Kat eventually asked, "What are we going to do after the reception today?"

Jet sighed. "I know you won't be excited about this, but Ed says he could use help during the winter. If we decide to stay, I'll build us a small house on the ranch."

"The winter?"

"Would you mind?" Jet croaked. "Being back at the ranch was just like coming home, riding the range with no one to bother you. What a feeling."

"I don't know." The scenario Kat had prepared herself for over the past few months had finally arrived. *Can I do this for my husband? After all, he's so happy to be back on the ranch.* "Can we afford a house?"

"I saved up money from my work at the mine, but we'll have to make a decision soon. Winter will be here before we know it."

Kat gathered her courage. "I'm concerned about being the only woman on the ranch. I don't know if I can handle being that far away from civilization."

"I'll take you to church every Sunday, weather permitting. We'll spend the whole day at the mission if you'd like."

"That'd help." She left their bed and began to brush her long, glistening hair while she settled on her decision. "I'll tell you what. I'm willing to give it a try, but I can't say that living on a ranch will be a permanent situation."

"That sounds fair enough."

"Are you going to start on the house after the reception?"

"I plan to." He propped himself up on his elbow.

"So that means you'll leave today?"

"I'll leave in the morning. Cheer up. We'll have the entire day together before I go."

Kat knew this, but it didn't help the attack of loneliness. "Church services start in an hour. We'd better get moving. I'll need to wash my hair and hope it dries in time. Want to go to the dormitory and bring our breakfast back over here?"

"Sure." Jet threw off the cover and pulled on his clothes.

"Maybe we can eat outside. I'll have to spend some time in the wind in order to dry this hair."

By the time Jet returned with two covered plates and two cups of coffee, Kat had washed her hair and prepared their breakfast site on the porch. "The dining room's a mass of confusion this morning. You'd think everyone was planning a wedding instead of a reception," Jet said.

"I'm certain that Minnie wants everything perfect for us. She really didn't have to go to all that trouble."

Kat and Jet arrived at the service just before Elijah greeted his parishioners. Kat had done her hair in an upsweep, still slightly damp from the morning wash. For the reception, she had purchased a yellow dress as well as a yellow hat accented with white daisies. The color complemented her red hair. She did her best to concentrate on Elijah's sermon. She had to admit he had his congregation's attention. But he seemed to lack the passion that he once had. *Perhaps he's missing Evangeline,* she thought.

After the church service, the crowd moved to the gazebo where the women laid out a scrumptious lunch of roast beef, potatoes, gravy, and the last of the vegetables from the garden. The guests filled their plates and found a place to picnic in the churchyard. When the guests had eaten their fill, Cassandra and Minnie carried the cake and placed it in the middle of the table for Jet and Kat to cut. Using autumn colors, Cassandra, Minnie, and Bea baked and decorated a four-layer cake, the most elaborate they had ever attempted. A cluster of orange, brown, and yellow paper flowers adorned the top.

"It's too pretty to cut," Kat remarked as Jet coaxed her into making the first swipe with the knife. The crowd cheered the couple and lined up when Bea began to distribute the cake slices.

While the crowd brought out their wedding gifts, the mission women gathered together and whispered among themselves. Kat knew they were up to something. Before the musicians began to entertain the crowd, Minnie gathered up a bundled quilt and walked over to Jet and Kat. "We have a gift for the newlyweds," she announced loudly to the gathering. "We made this quilt over the winter, and we all agreed that we would give it as a wedding gift to Jet and Kat." The crowd clapped their pleasure as she unfolded the quilt with Kat's help. "This is a quilt is called Flying Geese. The female students made this one in their sewing classes last winter."

Blue and green triangles tripped across the quilt like geese in flight.

Kat opened the other gifts which had collected beneath the table. Most were from the mission staff. Cassandra and Minnie had embroidered pillowcases, Bea and Ethel had embroidered dresser scarves, and some of the parishioners had canned vegetables, jams, and jellies to stock their larder.

Kat smiled appreciatively, and Jet cleared his throat and then spoke of their appreciation and gratitude for such a wonderful reception. "I have news. We will be your neighbors awhile longer. I'm going to build us a house on the Bar Double B where I'll be working. Kat will visit you from time to time, I'm sure."

The musicians, including Doc on the fiddle and several men from the Bar Double B, struck up their newly formed band. "Can we dance?" Jet whispered to Kat.

"Yes, I think so. I overheard Jeremiah talking to Elijah about dancing. He said dance is a way to express joy, and that the Israelites danced in praise to God."

"Well, we're not the Israelites. Not the last time I checked, anyway."

Kat punched his arm playfully. "You don't even know what an Israelite is. Neither do I, for that matter." She giggled.

He shrugged, then hugged her. "Guess I have a lot to learn."

Jeremiah stood, and the guests riveted on his glowing face. "The Bible says there is a time for everything—even a time to dance. This is it! Let's all dance in celebration." The guests cheered and clapped until Jet and Kat danced the waltz the musicians were playing in celebration of their marriage. Other couples soon joined them. Jeremiah blushed as he took Minnie in his arms. Curt—Tex's son—bashfully took Sara's hand, and Lily and Sol held Howey between them as they swayed to the tune.

At first, the newly formed orchestra sounded like a fox in the mission's henhouse, but as time went on, they became more accustomed to each other. Doc took on a new personality as he drew his bow across the strings. Newfound confidence played across his face.

"Why, Jet, I didn't know you could dance so well!" Kat said as he box stepped his way around the gazebo.

"There's a lot you don't know about me," he teased.

"Is it all good?"

"I think you'll approve."

———

Jet's kiss lingered on Kat's moist lips when he left the next morning for the Bar Double B Ranch. Ed and his men hadn't stayed long at the reception. They had returned to the ranch after the dance last evening. "Now, don't fret. I'll talk some of the men into helping me out with the house. As soon as I get the roof on, I'll come for you," he said as he waved her out of sight.

Minnie came and settled beside Kat as she watched her husband leave. "I'll get you to sewing for your house. You'll see that the days will pass so fast."

"Sew for the house?"

"Sure. You'll need curtains, aprons, tablecloths, towels, linens, and whatever else we can think up. Tater has enough material in his store to keep us sewing for months."

"You'll never believe me, Minnie, but I organized a quilting group when I returned to Deadwood."

"You did? Well, I declare."

Kat laughed. "A few of the saloon girls met at the Birdcage. We made quilts to give to the needy. We even tried a few Chinese patterns that a Chinese girl by the name of Ling Li taught us. The girls gave us the Chinese Lantern quilt for a wedding present. Now I have two quilts to start off my married life."

"Do you suppose they'll keep on sewing now that you're away?"

"I hope so. My sister and Miranda moved to Deadwood, so I put her in charge of the restaurant. I'm trying to turn my saloon into an eating establishment."

Minnie lifted her brow. "You are? Why?"

"Selling alcohol probably isn't the best way to make a living. Maybe Elijah's sermons were getting to me."

"I like how you're thinking." Minnie winked.

Kat laughed at her good nature. "You probably should teach me about cooking, too."

"See there. We have lots to keep us busy." Minnie patted her on the arm as she would a child.

Minnie is right, Kat thought. *She has enough ideas to sew from dawn to dusk.* In a few days' time, she and Minnie visited the general store and chose red checked fabric for her curtains and tablecloth. "But I don't know how many windows our house will have," Kat realized.

"Probably not too many. The fewer the windows, the snugger the house."

When Kat wasn't sewing, she helped Minnie with the meals. "Let me write this down," she said to Minnie as she patted out the dough. "How many cups of flour did you say?"

Minnie rolled her eyes. "I never think to measure."

"I've noticed that Elijah seems less enthusiastic than what I remember. And Sara isn't nearly as bubbly as she used to be."

"They're missing Evangeline and Willow. And Cassandra misses her granddaughter something horribly."

"Evangeline is coming back, isn't she?"

"I certainly hope so." Minnie formed the dough into buns. "I haven't wanted to interfere where I'm not wanted, although once in a while I ask Cassandra if she's heard anything."

"Has she?"

"It seems that something illegal is going on, and a detective is working with Evangeline's father to find out just what it is."

"I have to confess, Evangeline and I haven't really found out what we have in common. But the mission doesn't seem to be right without her."

"I agree. She put a spark in it somehow. I pray she comes back soon and that everything returns to normal."

———

Much to Kat's surprise, the weeks passed swiftly. By the end of the month when Jet came for her, she had accumulated a stack of recipes and a few bushels of sewing. He smiled at her accomplishments and packed the wagon with her belongings. "Please come for a visit, Minnie," Kat said in earnest as she climbed into the wagon.

Minnie promised, "We'll come as soon as we can. I'll bring some quilt patterns along that you can work on for the winter."

"I'm one step ahead of you, Minnie," Cassandra said, handing Kat a box tied with string.

"What's this?"

"They're quilt templates and patterns you can work on over the winter. I chose the easier designs for you to begin with."

"You trust me to sew them on my own?"

She nodded. "Minnie told me about your quilting group in Deadwood."

"Then I guess I won't be able to act like I can't sew. We'll try to come to church when we can."

Minnie smiled with an idea. "Cassandra, perhaps we should plan the sewing circle for Sunday afternoon."

"But what would Jet do while he waited for me?"

"Oh, we'll find him something to do," Minnie promised, still smiling.

"I'll need a sewing machine. I forgot all about arranging for one," Kat realized.

"We'll lend you a machine. Evangeline wanted to order more anyway." Cassandra offered.

"That's very kind of you. I hope it won't cause you any trouble."

"Oh no, we order items for the mission all the time. I'll just add a sewing machine to the list."

"Why don't you load it up now?" Minnie suggested. "There's no point in waiting."

"As long as you're sure you can get by without it."

"Oh, yes. I'll get the order in right away," Cassandra said.

Jet followed Cassandra to the sewing room and helped her carry the machine to the buckboard. In no time at all, they had it loaded and secured for the trip to the ranch. Minnie hugged Kat, and Cassandra waved her away with shouts of good cheer. Perched on the wagon seat, Kat waved back one last time to her women friends. She realized it would be a long time before she saw them again. She squeezed Jet in happiness. "I can't wait to see the house."

"Don't expect much. It's something to keep the rain off our heads for a time. Someday I'll build you something much better. But first we'll have to decide where we're going to permanently live."

"While I waited for you, I sewed up all kinds of things for the house to help make it our home. And while I was sewing, cooking, and baking, I had a lot of time to think about us."

"And what did you decide?" he asked as he tweaked her nose.

"That I'm one lucky woman."

CHAPTER 15

"Ah, boss, I just don't feel right about this," Tater protested as he stacked canned goods on the shelf behind the counter at his store. He liked his shelves neat, tidy, and full of merchandise. Curt stepped into the room with a large box of cans to unpack.

"It ain't that big of a deal. I'm not asking you to murder anyone or rob a bank," Tex countered. "I don't want to do anything illegal either, but the land laws favor the homesteader, not the open range. Besides, everyone is doing it."

"I'm not claiming that I've always been a saint, but I don't want to get throwed in jail," Tater said earnestly.

"You won't. I've enough money to pay the perjury charges if I have to."

Tater turned from his task. "Perjury? What's that?" The can he held slipped from his fingers, dropped, and hit the floor with a thud. Tater frowned at the dent in the can.

"You have to file on 160 acres in good faith. You know—that you're going to live on it, improve the land, put up a house, and all that. And you have to promise you're not filing for the benefit of another person."

Tater glared. "So I'd be lying because I'm not doing it with the intention of making it my home. I'm doing it for another person—you."

Tex laughed. "Tater, you've been known to tell a yarn or two. What's one more?"

"But they weren't meant to hurt anybody," Tater said. "This time I'd be lying to the government. Fibbing to the government is another story."

"Like I said, don't worry. It's been done before."

"But I got a business here. I don't want to homestead. And what about the filing fee? I put all my money into this here building." Tater rubbed his whiskered chin with his hand.

"I'll help you with the fee. When you meet the requirements, I'll buy it or lease it from you if you want to keep the land."

"I don't want any land. Nor do I want to break my back plowing up the sod," Tater protested. "Any fool knows you can't grow anything out here."

"The government sure thinks 160 acres and a strong back will make a living. Well, I doubt that, too. Don't worry. All you have to do is file on land adjacent to our range. I'll fence the alternate sections and that will keep the homesteaders from getting to my land."

"Yeah, but I can't file on enough land to protect your interests."

"Maybe not, but I'll find someone else to file. If I can find enough willing people, eventually my grazing land will be protected from them homesteaders."

"But it ain't your land."

"I know it's public domain," Tex said, becoming irritated. "But I've a right to it just like anyone else, even though the government doesn't think so. Us cattlemen can't get title to the land." Color came to Tex's face as he continued. "Them congressmen think we're asking for too much—that we're going to control the entire state or something. Don't those brainless politicians know this is cattle country?" Tex lowered his voice, smiled, and then gazed at Tater from under his hat brim. "I've another proposition for you."

"I think I got enough." Tater turned his back to him and continued stocking shelves.

"I'll pay you good for this one."

Tater growled back, "What are you cooking up now?"

"How would y'all like to be a land locator? You could run the business out of your store here."

"What would I want to do that for? Remember, my store's on the reservation."

"But the land you would locate for land seekers would surround my grazing pasture off the reservation. Of course, I'd prefer entries that I might be able to buy or lease."

Tater scratched his head. "Oh, I get it. Then you could legally fence what you think is yours."

"That's right. Homesteaders who'll get title to land can fence it, but the cattlemen can't fence the public domain. How's a cattleman supposed to improve his herd with good Hereford bulls if he can't fence out his pasture?"

"And how are we to put up hay and keep drifting cattle from eating and trampling it?" Curt, who had been silent to this point, added.

Tater turned from his task. "How am I supposed to talk homesteaders into filing and then relinquish or lease their claim?"

"They'll come by your store. As a locator, you can advertise. You'll collect a locating fee. Oh, I'd say about seven to ten dollars—and I'll pay you a little extra. And no agreements on paper. I'll pay good money for their relinquishment and pay a fair amount for a lease, too."

"Yeah, but maybe they'll prove up and want to keep their land."

"I doubt most will make it. It hardly ever rains here—not enough to raise much, anyway. I'll make it worth their while to sell out and move on."

Tater shook his head. "Sounds a little shady to me. This is more than I bargained for, and I can't be away from the store that long. Why, sometimes it would take days to find a claim they'd like."

"Curt can mind the store while you're gone."

"Me?" Curt asked, nearly exploding with the new revelation. "Who's going to take care of the ranch?"

"I will," Tex said. "I'm going to hang around awhile before I go back to Texas. Tater just has to do this until all the land surrounding my ranch is filed on. Then he can taper off. He'll say his store is taking up all his time. I'll make it worth your while, Tater."

"Ah, I don't think so."

"There's nothing illegal about helping homesteaders find land," Tex coaxed. "The land would just happen to be close to my ranching headquarters."

"I'm not interested," Tater said, raising his voice.

"I said I'd make it worth your while."

"How?"

"When we get those reservation leases, the money will pour in. I'll give you a third of our first-year profits."

Tater scratched his head. "But there's no guarantee there will be profits. What about the Dakota blizzards? Those storms can wipe out a herd in no time. No. I want cash on the barrel if I'm going to help you with your scheming."

Tex fixed his eyes on Curt, and Curt shrugged.

"Well, okay then. Would a thousand dollars do?"

Tater puckered up his mouth and nodded. "I'll give it a try." Tater knew Tex would hound him until he agreed. Tex had treated him fairly over the years, but asking him to do something illegal was a new development. He hoped he wouldn't lose his store on account of it. He liked not having to answer to anyone but himself.

———

"Good morning Sara," Curt said with a grin when she entered the store.

Startled, Sara abruptly stopped her advance to the counter where Curt stood. "Oh! Good morning." She fumbled over her words. "I...I was expecting to see Tater." She fingered the fringe on her shawl. After collecting herself, she noticed Curt's gray clerk's apron and stifled a grin. She thought he looked rather silly—a cowboy reduced to a store clerk.

He blushed at her glance. "I'm minding the store while Tater's away," he explained. "He's taken on the job of land locator. I've never clerked before. Hope you know where to find what you're looking for."

She slipped her shopping basket on the counter. "I think I know my way around." Her footsteps echoed over the wood floor to the bolts of fabric arranged on a long, narrow table. *No longer did the women have to wait for the Christmas barrels containing handouts from the East,* she thought. She was appreciative that Tater kept a well-stocked assortment of fabric on hand.

While Sara looked over the material, Curt picked up a broom and began sweeping. She sneezed at the dust he stirred up and shook her head at his bumbling. After a time, she found what she wanted and carried a bolt of blue and white calico to the counter. She slyly watched him out of the corner of her eye as Curt propped the broom up behind the counter, picked up the fabric bolt and turned it end over end, looking for the price. "I don't know what this here sells for."

"I'm not buying the whole bolt. Why, that contains yards and yards of material. I just want a yard."

Curt lifted his brows. "A yard?"

"Yes, three feet of it."

Curt stood motionless while Sara yanked the bolt out of his hand, unrolled a length of fabric, and measured it with the tape measure she found on the counter. Then she snatched the closest pair of scissors and cut the amount she wanted off the bolt. "There," she said, self-satisfied. "That's how it's done."

"I see. Thanks for the lesson." He grinned sheepishly.

"Oh, I about forgot." She reached into the pocket of her brown skirt and produced a list and handed it to him. "These are things that Minnie sent me for."

As he filled the order, he asked her, "How's your first year of teaching?"

"It's just fine. Evangeline was able to return to Boston."

Curt pushed the full, wicker basket toward her. "I think I put in everything Minnie asked for."

Sara searched for the coin purse in her pocket and handed him the exact amount. "Are you going to be working here every day?"

"No, just on days Tater's taking settlers around the country." He paused. "Ah...would you be interested in a buggy ride with me some evening?"

Sara quickly brushed an imaginary spot off her skirt. "I think Evangeline would think I'm too young."

"But she's not here."

"Elijah is. I wouldn't want to do anything behind Evangeline's back."

"I bet she's too busy to worry about what you're doing."

Sara stiffened. "I don't know if I like your attitude."

Before Curt could respond, Doc came bursting through the door. "Sara, I've been searching for you. I need your help."

She turned her full attention to the doctor. "What happened?"

"A woman a few miles out in the country is having trouble with her delivery. I need your help."

165

"I'll hurry this basket to Minnie, and then I'll meet you at the buggy." Sara noticed Curt's puzzled look before she rushed out of the store with Doc, leaving Curt alone.

"Sorry to bother you," Doc apologized to Sara. "I hope I didn't interrupt anything. I mean, you and Curt."

"Oh, don't worry about Curt. I think he has his eye on me," she said, surprised at her explanation.

"I see." Doc cleared his throat. "Thanks for coming with me. My patients accept me better when you're along. Besides, you speak their language. I'm just learning."

"I remember when I first started learning English. It was very frustrating at first, but I eventually learned it. Though sometimes, I still want to speak Lakota. It's still easier."

"You can when you're with me. Maybe I would learn it faster that way."

"I guess we could give it a try."

"I have been meaning to ask how you are faring without Evangeline and Willow. I know you are very close to them."

Sara searched her heart for the right words. It had been very painful for her to see Elijah and Evangeline separate. They had been her only chance for a family. Willow was the sister she never had. She missed them desperately and wished they would come home soon. Pushing aside the lump welling in her throat, she simply replied, "I miss them."

Doc nodded. "I'm sure you do."

The two lapsed into silence during the ride across the brown prairie. *Any day now, the weather will turn cold,* Sara thought. *Surely Evangeline and Willow will be home for Christmas. They just have to be. Christmas would be so empty without them.* Evangeline had been gone for two months. Sara had only heard from her once, even though Sara had written her several times. Still, every day she looked for a letter. She knew they were making progress with James's estate. Elijah had told her that. She was grateful because that meant Evangeline would come home soon. In the meantime, Willow was growing by leaps and bounds, and Sara was missing each precious moment.

Realizing that Doc was left out of her thoughts, she pulled herself back to the moment. "Are you happy here, Doc?" surprising herself that she had asked about a personal matter.

Doc started at her abrupt question. "I...guess so."

Doc's face doesn't say so. He looks plain miserable, Sara thought. *He must be lonely. He's so far from his life back East.* She wondered about his family, but couldn't bring herself to ask. *Did he leave someone special behind? No matter.* Sara decided to help him adjust to his new life here with her people. The Lakota would accept him if she showed them he was trustworthy. *Or would they? They are slow to change and cling fast to the old ways.* Since she was young, she had been around Evangeline's people more than her own. Her confidence began to fade.

CHAPTER 16

The autumn leaves had reached their peak hues by the time Frederick, Maud, Evangeline, and Willow reached Boston by train. The golds, the russets, and the oranges were as vibrant as any tapestry displayed in the Dumont mansion. "This is what I miss most," Evangeline remarked to her mother as she stood on the doorstep of her parents' home, waiting for Frederick to let them in. He jiggled the key into the lock while the women breathed the crisp air, redolent of dying foliage.

"I could never live in that drab landscape you call home," Maud told her daughter.

Evangeline shifted Willow to her other arm. "We do have color, but not as dazzling as this."

"Ah, finally!" Frederick cried as the door lock clicked.

"My beautiful home," Maud gushed as soon as she entered. "How I have missed you!" She crooned to it as if it was an old friend she had left behind. She caressed the furniture, the draperies, and her favorite chair.

168

Frederick pocketed his key. "I have to agree. It's good to be home. I did enjoy our trip, but I also like my comforts."

"Oh, so do I." Maud plopped in her chair, leaned back, closed her eyes, and stretched her legs as though she would never leave again.

"We'll have to let the staff know we're back," he called over his shoulder as he opened the door to his study.

Maud's eyes flew open as if in sudden thought. "The staff? How will we manage until they arrive?"

"Mama, how do you forget so quickly?" Evangeline reminded her. "I can care for us until they get here."

"I doubt there is anything to cook with. We've been gone so long." Maud's lids closed again.

"Mabel must have received our letter by now. She knew we were coming," Evangeline reminded her. She handed Willow to her mother and turned toward the kitchen. Inside the icebox she found fresh milk, eggs, and meat. A search through the cupboards revealed assorted ingredients, and there was even fresh bread in the bread box. "Mabel didn't forget us after all. There's food here. I can fix us supper and even breakfast before Mabel comes."

"Wonderful," Maud replied groggily from the next room. "I momentarily forgot you can cook."

Evangeline laughed. She was proud of her cooking. Alice from the Missionary Society advised her to learn to cook before she went West to serve as a missionary. Mabel had taught her the rudiments in the short time she had to prepare, and Minnie and Cassandra had rounded out her skills at the mission. There was always a group of people to cook for. How she enjoyed merriment at the table.

She glanced through the doorway to see that Maud and Willow were nodding off in the chair, both weary from the long train ride. She heard Frederick in the study. *Probably lighting up his cigar and sipping brandy,* she thought. Careful not to disturb them, Evangeline snatched a couple of valises and trotted up the stairs to her old room.

She opened the red velvet curtains to let in the fading afternoon light, and then plopped down in her favorite, faded red chair. She had to admit she was weary, too. The train trip was long and tedious.

Her eyes roamed over her old room. Mother kept it the same way as the day she left for the mission the second time. Everything had been left just as she had remembered it. She had spent many depressing days mourning the loss of James in this room. *What would James and I be doing today if he hadn't died at sea? My life would be so different. But there's no use thinking so morbidly,* she told herself. She simply didn't want to let herself slide back into her old depression.

She pushed herself out of the chair and began to unpack her trunk. She hung her clothes in the wardrobe and draped the Job's Tears quilt across the foot of the bed. She wondered why she was so desperate to bring that quilt. She slumped on the edge of the bed, stroking the quilt, once again in deep thought. It was supposed to signify the end of tears for her, Sara, and Cassandra upon her return to the mission. But her tears hadn't ended.

She realized she was foolish to think returning to the mission would solve everything. Instead, the mission presented her with bigger problems. She and Elijah had suffered a rift in their relationship all because the money she was going to use for the new dormitory wasn't in James's estate settlement after all. It was simply ridiculous to think that after all this time, she and Elijah would separate over something that they had both wanted.

Evangeline stepped out in the hall to the adjoining room. Surprised at its transformation, she opened the curtains there, too, to let the light's soft glow rest on the white wicker furniture from her own baby years. Maud must have instructed the staff to retrieve the furniture from storage for her granddaughter's use.

What a beautiful room, she thought. She retrieved Willow's suitcase and unpacked Willow's things. She draped the quilt she had made for her over the crib and placed her clothes in the low, three-drawer wicker chest. Soon she heard the padding of footsteps on the stairs. "Oh, what a surprise. Mabel and the help took my suggestion to heart. The room is ready for Willow," Maud said. "Do you like it?"

"Very much, Mama."

"I just couldn't part with your baby things," she explained to Evangeline. "And I will look for a nanny tomorrow. That will give you the freedom to consult with lawyers and such without having to worry about Willow's care."

"You really shouldn't be going to all this trouble. I don't plan on being here any longer than I have to."

"Nonsense. You might as well be comfortable while you're here. Besides, I'd love to see this beautiful wicker used again."

Evangeline had learned long ago that she could hardly ever win an argument with her mother. "We'll be quite comfortable. Thank you, Mama." Evangeline took Willow from her mother's arms. "You didn't nap very long."

"No, Willow woke me up, or else I think I would have slept there all night." Maud laughed. "I...I hope you're able to stay for a long time."

Evangeline touched her mother's shoulder. "Now, don't go getting any ideas."

"I know. I just can't get used to the idea of you being so far away from us. And now there's Willow."

"Willow belongs to Elijah, too, Mama."

"I know." Her mother lifted her brows. "Frederick tells me to stay out of your business, but I noticed that Elijah wasn't exactly attentive to you before we left."

"He's very upset with me."

"For what? How could you know that there were problems with James's estate?"

"I...shouldn't have been so quick to depend on the money and I could have checked into it a little more. I put the mission in danger."

Maud frowned and shook her head. "What's done is done. Frederick will know what to do. He always has."

"Father is a rock. I don't know what I would do without him. I'm eager to talk to some lawyers. Now, let's see about making something to eat. Are you hungry?"

Her mother nodded as the two linked arms with Willow supported in between them. They descended the stairs.

Evangeline scrambled eggs and fried sausage for supper while her parents and Willow joined her in the kitchen. She buttered toast and placed it on the kitchen table they hardly ever used. They usually sat at the table in the dining room, where they were waited on by the house staff. After Evangeline dished up the eggs and sausage, she sat down and joined them.

"Evangeline, I made some contacts this afternoon," Frederick said. "Our family lawyer will see us tomorrow, late morning."

"The sooner the better. I have to get to the bottom of this."

Frederick's face grew serious. "I agree. We've waited too long as it is. I just hope it's not too late."

———

Evangeline slept poorly that first night at her parent's home. She couldn't get the mission's financial predicament out of her mind. If only she could go back and handle matters differently. She played the scenario over and over again in her mind. She had offered to finance the house in which she and Elijah were living, the mission's new dormitory, and even the rodeo grounds—all with the money from James's estate. She had paid some of the bills without any problems, but later she had been notified that creditors had drained the remaining funds. It just didn't ring true. How could all that money be gone?

Willow awoke early the next morning. Evangeline heard her whimpering and went in to change her diaper. She then took her downstairs. While she snuggled with her baby in the parlor chair, Frederick came downstairs and sat across from her. "You look tired, Evangeline."

"I didn't sleep well. Too much thinking."

"Try not to worry. We have a good lawyer. He will have some angles. I can promise you that."

"It's my fault the mission's in jeopardy."

"Nonsense. The matter was out of your control. I truly believe it."

"I hope you're right."

"I know I'm right. How about some coffee?" He rubbed his hands together in anticipation.

"I haven't made any yet."

"I'll make it."

"You know how?"

He laughed. "I haven't been rich all my life."

Soon, Evangeline joined her father in the kitchen. "If you hold Willow, I'll make us breakfast."

Frederick cradled Willow in his arms while Evangeline stirred up pancakes. "It sure is nice to have you and Willow here."

"Now don't you start on me, too."

"Too? I simply made a comment."

"Mama made a similar remark."

"You know your mother. She'll never give up wanting you near." Frederick cleared his throat. "I noticed the strain between you and Elijah. I'm sorry for that."

"I'm sorry, too." Evangeline poured batter in the skillet and searched for the butter and syrup. "I believe when I clear up this financial matter, things will go better between us."

"I hope so."

Maud entered with a yawn. "There you are. I'm not used to finding you in the kitchen." She reached for a coffee cup. "Aren't we becoming efficient? Making our own coffee and meals."

"Shall we just keep it this way?" Frederick laughed.

"Not on your life. In fact, I'm going to hire a baby nurse to take the load off Evangeline. She'll have enough on her mind without caring for Willow."

Evangeline placed the pancakes on the table. "Would you be able to watch her when I go with Father to the lawyer this morning?"

"I can manage. You won't be gone too long, will you?"

Evangeline turned to her father.

"A couple of hours."

"I can manage that," Maud agreed.

Evangeline placed Willow in the high chair and sat at the table with her coffee. "Very well, then. After we finish eating, I'll make myself presentable and we'll be off."

Maud helped herself to two pancakes and smeared them with butter. "I do hope the lawyers have an encouraging angle. This entire thing is simply dreadful. And you think something underhanded is going on, Frederick?"

"I do. Call it a gut feeling, but it merits looking into."

Maud passed the pancakes to Evangeline, but she waved them away. "You're not eating?"

"My stomach feels a bit queasy today. Guess I'm nervous about the meeting."

"Nervous?" Maud asked.

"Of what we'll find out."

Frederick glanced up at her. "Are you worried about James's reputation?"

Evangeline nodded. "I'm concerned he was connected in some way."

After breakfast, Evangeline washed the dishes. Frederick

and Maud entertained Willow while Evangeline went upstairs to dress for their outing. "I'm ready," she announced to her Father an hour later.

"I'll hitch up the horses, and we'll be off. One of these days, I'm going to look into buying one of these motorcars I see darting about. At first, I thought they were a nuisance to those of us still driving carriages. But the more I see, the more I like."

"That would be something." Maud took the baby from Frederick. "I think you should wait until after winter."

Evangeline smiled at the notion, too. "Willow should be ready for a nap," Evangeline said to her mother as she pulled on her black gloves. She watched through the window as Frederick brought the carriage around to the front door. "Have a good morning, Mama." She kissed Willow and scampered down the steps to the awaiting carriage, pulling her cape close around her.

It took only a short time before they pulled up in front of the offices of Hector McMan and Son. "Here we are," Frederick announced.

Evangeline nodded, hoping with all her might that this visit would be helpful.

After the introductions and small talk, the elderly Hector McMan sat across the desk from them. He opened a folder and studied its contents before speaking. "Everything I see here appears to be in order. The creditors seem to be legitimate—"

"Seem?" Frederick loudly questioned. "You have yet to examine their credentials thoroughly, I assume."

"Certainly. If they are making legitimate claims, I see no recourse." Mr. McMan pushed the folder across the desk to Frederick and Evangeline, and Frederick passed it over to Evangeline.

"Look this over, Evangeline, and see if you recognize these names."

Evangeline carefully studied the creditors' names and their claims. *Oh, if only I knew more about James's affairs, I might not have found myself in this predicament!*

"Well?" her father asked.

"I know this one." She pointed to the document. "James often bought horses from him. In fact, the horses were delivered a few days before James left for England. I would have thought James would have paid him when they were delivered."

"And the others?"

"I don't recognize these names. This one from England claims James bought four horses. I was under the impression that James was only interested in bringing back one. And, again, why wouldn't James have paid for them on the spot?"

"Good question," the lawyer agreed.

Frederick stirred in his chair. "This can be verified, can it not?"

"Paperwork can verify some of it, but maybe not all. For example, the ship's manifest can be secured to verify the number of horses James was bringing home."

"Would hiring a detective help?"

"If you feel a conspiracy is being perpetrated, yes; a detective may be able to uncover the truth."

Evangeline eyes widened. "A conspiracy, father? Who would do this to me?"

"I don't know, but I have felt all along that the judgments filed against James's estate are bogus. Where do we begin, Hector?"

"I'll do what I can to establish if these creditors and their claims are authentic. A detective would be able to do the footwork and actually visit their addresses."

"Would you be able to recommend a good detective?"

Hector nodded, wrote a name, and handed the paper to Frederick. "He is one of the best."

Frederick accepted the suggestion. "I'll contact him today. The sooner the better."

———

A menacing blizzard was encroaching upon Boston. Evangeline peered outside at the steel gray sky. She shivered at the thought of early snow. Evangeline paced the floor in helpless anticipation. A storm could keep her cooped up for days. She had little to do since the baby nurse had practically taken over Willow's care.

"What's the matter, Evangeline?" Maud asked when she entered the parlor. "You look like a caged bird."

"I need to go out before the storm hits. I'm so used to being busy. I've had too much time on my hands these days."

"Visit some of your old friends. You haven't seen anyone since you returned. I'm sure they'd love to see you."

"I'd like to see how Gertrude is getting along."

"What? That weird woman who sewed the same quilt pattern all the time? What was that called, anyway?"

"The Storm at Sea."

"Yes, that one. Do you think it's wise to dredge up those memories?"

"We did share some good times."

"Yes, as well as both losing husbands to the sea. You do have that in common. You'll just get depressed all over again. Wouldn't it be better to visit Ida?"

"I will, later. Today I think I'll see Gertrude. I'll ask John to drive me over."

Maud shrugged. "You're making a mistake."

"Don't worry, Mama, I know what I'm doing."

Evangeline brought out her warmest black coat and winter hat from the closet and wrapped a white scarf around her neck. She briefly visited Willow in the nursery before leaving in the carriage. The low clouds skirted across the sky.

A snowflake spat against the carriage window. *This must be a brief visit,* she thought. Gertrude's address led them to a flat in a modest section of Boston. The driver, John, waited until Gertrude answered the door before departing.

"Evangeline, what on earth are you doing here?" Gertrude asked when she opened the door to her.

"I came to see you, Gertrude."

Gertrude remained expressionless for a few moments before she opened the door wider and invited Evangeline to enter. Evangeline couldn't help but stare at her old friend. She hadn't changed much since she had last seen her. Her hair was still disheveled; her eyes still held a hint of wildness.

"You know I married?"

"Yes, the lighthouse keeper. Ethan Halloway."

Gertrude nodded.

"Is he still the lighthouse keeper?"

"He is."

"And your house by the sea?"

"Ethan stays there sometimes."

"You're alone today?"

"I am. Take off your coat. Hang it on the coat tree by the door. I'll make us some tea."

Evangeline unwrapped her scarf, unbuttoned her coat, and hung them on the hook. In her effort, the coat brushed against the umbrella stand and the threads became tangled upon it. As she bent to release its hold, an umbrella handle drew her attention. She reached for it. Initials were carved into the handle—"JC." *It couldn't be. Could it?* Her heart slammed into her throat. *What would James's umbrella be doing here?* Evangeline jerked her head toward Gertrude as she entered the room from the kitchen.

"Tea is ready. Shall I bring it out here?"

"What...whatever you wish," Evangeline managed to say.

"Come into the kitchen. It isn't fancy, but it's convenient."

Evangeline joined her, wondering what she was doing

with a woman who seemed not especially happy to see her. But now that she had seen James's umbrella, she had to learn why it was there.

Gertrude's kitchen wasn't any larger than the one in her former home. Evangeline also noticed the walls in the new house weren't covered with quilts as they were in that small, seaside house. "Do you still quilt?" she asked timidly.

Gertrude sighed deeply with a far-off look in her eyes. "Not much anymore. I don't seem to be interested in anything these days."

Evangeline did her best to keep from shaking as she held the teacup. The discovery of James's umbrella had given her a jolt. While she sipped her tea, she searched her thoughts for something appropriate to say. Gertrude seemed even sadder than the day she had left her in that cottage on the coast near their horse farm. She had expected her to be happier with her new husband, freer from the haunting memories of losing her husband to the ocean depths. Dare she pry? She knew it was not her business, but she pitied her. Besides, she felt she needed to investigate James's umbrella. Finally, Evangeline said, "Would you like to begin a quilt? I could help you."

"I gave all my quilts away. Ethan insisted."

"But why?"

Gertrude shrugged. "He thought I spent too much time sewing."

Evangeline frowned. She didn't like what she was hearing. Ethan didn't sound like he had helped Gertrude at all. In fact, Gertrude seemed more depressed than ever. *How can I help her?* she wondered. *Quilting is the only way I know to cheer her up!* They had spent many hours together when they were neighbors by the sea.

"Maybe if I worked with you, Ethan wouldn't mind so much. Besides, you must have something to do while he's away. Surely he would want you to be happy."

Gertrude shrugged dispassionately, and Evangeline felt a twinge of guilt. Quilting would be the excuse she needed to visit Gertrude more often, and it may also help lift Gertrude's spirits.

"What do you suggest?" Gertrude asked without enthusiasm.

"Are there any quilt patterns you have wanted to do?"

"I haven't given it much thought lately."

"I'll give it some thought, then. Next time I come to visit, I'll bring patterns. Do you have material?"

"No. I gave that away, too."

"What have you been doing with your time?"

"I don't know. I sit in my chair. I sleep a lot."

"Are you happy here?"

"I miss the ocean and my house by the sea. I won't be there when Norman comes home."

Evangeline's heart sank. Gertrude truly hadn't improved. In fact, Evangeline suspected she might have worsened. "When is Ethan home with you?"

"Not too often. Sometimes on Sunday. He comes by for his clean clothes."

"That's it? In other words, you live alone?"

"Yes. That's true."

"Why did Ethan marry you, then?" The question popped out of her mouth before she had time to think.

"I...don't know."

"Don't worry. I'll be back for another visit." Evangeline patted her on the shoulder. "I don't know how much longer I'll be in Boston, but I should be able to come back next week." Evangeline placed her empty cup and saucer on the sideboard and retrieved her coat and hat from the clothes tree before taking one more glance at the umbrella. She was certain it had belonged to James. She was sure, for she had given it to him for Christmas on the second year of their marriage.

———

Several days after Evangeline and Frederick visited Hector the lawyer, Frederick hired the recommended detective. Middle-aged Henry C. Knox appeared at the Dumont's door in a long, black coat that reminded Evangeline of the Civil War era. A hat covered wiry, salt-and-pepper hair. Henry Knox didn't seem like any detective Evangeline had envisioned. She had never seen one before, but she wasn't expecting their man to be so unkempt. She guessed he didn't have a wife, or else he worked around the clock and took advantage of catnaps wherever he could and slept in his clothes. He insisted that the family call him Henry.

Frederick invited Henry into the sitting room to join Evangeline and Maud. Mabel brought in tea and finger sandwiches for them to eat while they planned Henry's assignment. When offered the square plate of sandwiches, Henry swept up several in his hand, plopped them onto a matching plate, and devoured them within seconds. Maud appeared uneasy and whispered to Mabel to bring in a few cookies and another pot of tea.

Frederick opened the conversation. "Mr. Knox. As I have already briefed you on our predicament, I'll fill you in on what we have discovered on our own. Then I hope we can arrive at what we need investigated."

Henry gulped the last of his tea and held out his cup for Maud to fill. "I'm listening."

"You go first, Father," Evangeline invited.

Frederick nodded and began. "I have done my best to find the manifest for the ship that James boarded to come home from England. It's hard to find out anything from such a distant place as London. You see, the creditors—if they are indeed legitimate creditors—are claiming James bought four horses in England, which he hadn't paid for before his departure. Evangeline understood he was only interested in one, two at the most. Evangeline also feels that he would have paid for them before returning. I feel the only way to get to the bottom of this is for someone to go to England."

"You have a point there." Henry stretched back in his chair and munched on a cookie.

"I've discovered something unusual, too," Evangeline spoke up. "I went to visit Gertrude Halloway the other day. She is currently married to Ethan Halloway, the lighthouse keeper on the coast outside of Boston. I knew of Gertrude when James and I lived on our horse farm. She lived in a small dwelling, a cottage, really, on the coast near the lighthouse. When I returned to the mission over a year ago, I heard she had married Ethan and moved to Boston. I was anxious about her, so I went to visit her in Boston just a few days ago. When I went to hang up my coat and hat at her flat, I saw the very umbrella I had given James as a Christmas present in her umbrella stand. His initials are on the handle. I have no idea how Gertrude came by the umbrella."

Henry sat up straight in his chair. His eyes twinkled with curiosity. "Now this is beginning to get interesting. Did Gertrude know your husband?"

"As far as I can tell, they didn't know each other personally, other than to offer a good morning and such. She was our neighbor when we owned the horse farm."

"Perhaps your husband visited her once and left his umbrella there."

"I suppose he could have, but he would have missed it."

"Anything else I should know?"

"I found it strange that Gertrude's husband doesn't really live with her anymore. I think a search into Ethan Halloway's past might be worthwhile," Evangeline suggested.

"And what about your friend Gertrude? How much do you really know about her?" Henry asked.

"I...really don't know anything about her, other than she

lost a husband at sea and has been negatively affected because of it."

"In what way?"

"I believe she's unstable. I expected her to have improved since I left, but I think she's even worse."

"Why do you make that assessment?" Henry probed.

"When I first met her, she was obsessed with making the same quilt—the Storm at Sea quilt—over and over again. She had them hung all over her walls. I suppose it had something to do with her husband's death."

"Maybe she just liked the pattern."

"She is also convinced that Norman, her late husband, is coming back to her. She is afraid to leave in case he does."

Henry stroked his chin. "Odd. Do you plan to see her again?"

"Oh, yes. Next week. I offered to make a quilt with her. She seems so lost and lonely."

"Have you asked her about the umbrella?"

"No, I haven't, but I will when the time is right."

"Frederick, who did you have in mind to send to England?" Henry asked.

"I've been thinking of going myself. I feel that this is something we have to pursue. Someone is trying to dupe us. I would send you, Henry, but you're needed here to do your sleuthing." Frederick rose, and Henry did the same. They shook hands. "Thanks for coming by."

"I'll be going, then." Henry reached for another cookie. "Shall I report to Evangeline?"

"Yes. If I discover something, I'll wire Evangeline, and she can discuss it with you." Frederick walked Henry to the door. Evangeline and Maud remained in the sitting room.

"This sounds all too sinister," Maud whispered when Frederick and Henry were out of sight.

"It does. Father is quite serious about all this." Evangeline shivered.

Frederick returned and joined the women. "Well, what

do you think?"

Maud's eyes widened. "We were just saying how sinister all this sounds."

"You will be safe, won't you father?" Evangeline asked.

"Oh, yes. We're not dealing with assassins." Father's laugh faded quickly. "It's a matter of greed and duplicity."

Frederick joined his wife on the settee.

"When will you be leaving us?" Maud asked.

"Soon. I'll have to find the ship's manifest and then visit Kenington Farms where the horses were allegedly purchased."

"I wonder if your trip will all be in vain. Maybe James did purchase four horses and didn't pay for them," Evangeline said.

"Highly unlikely. I can't ignore this sense that something doesn't ring true. I have to do this, even if it means a long trip across the ocean."

Across the ocean. Evangeline didn't want to think of her father risking a trip to England, although she knew he must go if they were to save the mission. She trusted him and knew his instincts were usually right.

Maud quietly left the room. Evangeline suspected that her mother was about to weep.

"Oh, do be careful, Father."

Her father appeared rather grim when Evangeline hugged him. Then she mumbled that she was going upstairs to be with Willow. The nurse had put Willow down for a nap, but Evangeline still liked to sit in the room with the sleeping child. But before she settled into the rocking chair, she tiptoed to her room for paper and pencil. It had been some time since she had left Elijah. She felt she must write him and tell him their plans. She wrote about her father suspecting fraudulent creditors, about his impending trip to England, and about hiring a detective. Her words smacked of stiff formality, of staunch duty. She paused, reflecting on the tension in their relationship...the debacle she had caused. A knot stuck in her throat. She once again placed pencil to paper and wrote, "Willow and I miss you. Hope to be home soon."

CHAPTER 17

Frederick departed for England on the day Evangeline was to visit Gertrude for the second time. The send-off was difficult for both Evangeline and her mother despite the calm conditions. He appeared especially strong and capable in his hat and tweed coat, waving his final farewell from the gangway.

Evangeline suspected he would rather have stayed home with his dear Maud. She depended on him so much. Evangeline envied their intimacy. They always seemed to be there for each other. Evangeline, on the other hand, learned to be independent when she had journeyed to the mission. Her experiences in the wilderness had prepared her for the sometimes distant relationship with James, and now Elijah.

Before Evangeline had made the trip to visit Gertrude, she had gathered scraps of fabric and found a simple pattern called running squares that the two of them could work on without too many difficulties. Evangeline felt somewhat like a traitor when she knocked on her friend's door. After all,

Detective Knox was being paid by her father to look into Gertrude's affairs. When Gertrude answered the door, she seemed surprised to see Evangeline.

"Oh, I didn't think you would return so quickly."

"Why yes," Evangeline answered. "I told you I would be back within the following week."

"Very well, then. Come in."

Evangeline quickly glanced at the umbrella stand to see that James's umbrella was still there. It was, and she picked it up. "I like this umbrella. Where did you get it?"

Gertrude turned around to look. "Let me see. Oh, I don't rightly remember. I think it belongs to one of Ethan's friends."

"Which one? I might know him."

"I guess I don't know for sure. He has so many."

Evangeline hid her disappointment. Gertrude's answer didn't help her at all, but she couldn't help wondering if more of James's belongings were kept in the house. "I brought a simple pattern and some material." Evangeline began to empty out her bag on the table.

Gertrude pulled a chair toward the sewing machine, which was partially hidden in the corner of the living area. "I'll get the machine ready. Hope it still works."

While Evangeline arranged the templates she had made earlier and the fabric scraps she had collected from the seamstress, she kept thinking about James. *What had been his connection with Gertrude and Ethan? Had James given them his umbrella before he died? Or did they simply buy it at the estate sale? Did I even put it in the sale?*

"I'm not sure how we should put this pattern together," Evangeline said. "But I was planning to make the inverted squares from light fabric and cut the triangles out of darks. Together, the dark triangles will make a square of their own. What do you think?"

"Whatever you believe is best," Gertrude said absently.

Evangeline's heart sank. Gertrude didn't seem the least bit interested in quilting, but perhaps she would perk up after sewing awhile. Gertrude joined Evangeline at the table and helped her cut out the large squares and smaller triangles. Evangeline waited for Gertrude to rekindle the conversation as she always had. Instead, Gertrude sat quietly and snipped the fabric in small strokes. "Have you seen Ethan lately?" Evangeline began.

"Ethan? Oh, he came by on Sunday for a few hours. Said he had to get back to the lighthouse."

"Gertrude, I feel terrible that you are left alone so much. Does Ethan take you anywhere?"

"No. I would like to see my old house by the sea again. I miss it so much. At least I got to look at the ocean and smell the sea air. Here I have nothing."

"Why don't you just move back?"

"Ethan won't let me. Says it's not good for me."

Evangeline had to agree with some of what Gertrude was saying. The sea seemed to contribute to her imbalance, but Evangeline could perceive that she wasn't getting well in this flat, either. Should she volunteer to take her to her old house? Evangeline had never been back to the horse farm after it had sold, and she knew she lacked the constitution to return now.

After an hour of cutting, some of the blocks were ready to be sewn together. "Want to try your hand at it, Gertrude?"

"No. You sew first, and then I might give it a try. I'll put on some tea while you're sewing." Gertrude left for the kitchen, and Evangeline zipped through the first two blocks. She had pulled out the pins holding the pieces together but couldn't find the pin cushion. Finally, she opened the drawer in the sewing machine cabinet to look for one. Inside, she found several warped photographs. She picked up one of them, holding it closer to her face. She knew this man. It was James, younger than she had ever seen him before. *Ger-*

trude didn't buy this at the estate sale. She heard Gertrude returning with the tray of clinking cups and saucers. She shoved the photograph into the drawer and closed it. Her hands trembled as she took the scissors to cut the thread from the quilt block.

"Quit for now. We'll have a cup of tea."

Evangeline did as she was told. *Who is this woman who has a picture of my late husband in—of all places—a sewing machine drawer?* She wasn't sure how she should react or what she should say. She was more determined than ever to discover how Gertrude and James were connected.

———

Evangeline parted the lacy curtains at the window to watch for Henry. He had contacted her the day before to notify her that he would stop by the following morning and share what he had learned. She was more than eager to hear what he had to say. She had been away from the mission for more than a month, but she most desperately wanted to return home to Elijah. She missed him, and she could tell Willow did, too. Willow had been especially cranky this last week.

A motorcar pulled up in front of the house and stopped with a jolt. Out jumped the befuddled detective who kicked the left front tire in passing. She ran to the door when she saw him approach the portico. Before he could push the chimes, she jerked the door open, startling him. He stepped back and smoothed his wrinkled coat, the same one he had worn before.

"I'm sorry," she said, slightly embarrassed.

"Quite all right. I usually don't have beautiful women rushing to open doors for me." He laughed, and Evangeline blushed. "Excuse me if I appear overwrought. I've been trying to learn to drive this contraption they call a car."

"Father would like one," she said. She took his coat and hung it in the closet, briefly thinking Mabel might press it for him while he was there.

"Hope he's more patient than I am, although I have to say it has its advantages."

Evangeline led him into the study. "Well, what have you learned?"

"This case gets more interesting by the day." Henry rubbed his stomach. "I haven't even had time for breakfast today. A pot of tea would be nice."

Evangeline rang for Mabel, asking her to bring in a pot of tea and some sandwiches. Henry seemed pleased as he nestled in the wing chair. He remained rather silent until Mabel plied him with tea and sandwiches. After gulping down several of the delicacies and drinking two small cups of tea, he rubbed his hands together. Evangeline sat expectantly, but her patience began to wane. Henry tediously wiped the last traces of sandwich from his fingers with a napkin. "I decided to visit your horse farm and the cottage in which Gertrude lived. Saw the lighthouse, too."

"Did you talk with anyone?"

"No. I saw no purpose in visiting with the current owners of the horse farm. Looks like everything is kept in tip-top shape." Henry paused.

"What else? What have you found out?"

Henry held up his hand. "Patience, Evangeline. I'm getting to it. I stopped at the cottage by the sea. Nobody was there, and the door was locked. I tried peeking through the window, but the panes were so grimy I couldn't really see anything."

"Gertrude tells me Ethan stays there."

"Really? It looks deserted to me." Another pause.

Evangeline ground her teeth, annoyed by his slow, methodical mannerisms. "And the lighthouse?"

"I strode over to it. It looked deserted, too."

"But that can't be. Where is Ethan?"

"Good question." Henry tapped his temple. "I searched all afternoon at the proper facilities for any kind of record bearing his name and Gertrude's."

Evangeline held her breath. A few seconds passed, and she asked, "Well? Did you find anything?"

"No. I didn't."

"But I thought you said you had found out something?"

"I did, didn't I? Maybe you know this already."

"What, what is it?" She leaned forward in her chair.

"The cottage in which Gertrude lived was on your land. It would have been part of your horse farm."

"On our land? James never said anything about that. Are you sure?"

"I checked into the deeds and abstracts. The lighthouse was on your farm, too."

"But I don't understand. James told me he never knew much about Gertrude. Could he have rented the cottage to her?"

"That's a possibility. But I have a feeling there wouldn't be any records to confirm that she was a renter."

"Why do you say that?"

"Just a hunch. I get them a lot in my line of work."

Evangeline's skin prickled with anticipation. "What kind of a hunch?"

"I think your husband knew Gertrude much better than he let on."

"In what way?"

"That's what I need to find out. It's going to be difficult without knowing their legal names."

"I can't believe Gertrude would lie about who she is."

"Maybe she doesn't remember who she is. Have you thought about that? After all, you told me she's close to crazy."

"I wouldn't use that word. But she does have some kind

of problem."

"I'd suggest you keep paying her visits and see if you can find out more."

"I feel guilty using her for information."

"It might be the best chance we have. How was your last visit with her?"

"You'll be pleased that I did find out something rather disturbing."

Henry smiled and wagged his finger at her. "Don't keep me in suspense."

Like you have, she thought. "I found an old photograph of James in her sewing machine drawer."

Henry whistled. "Did you ask her about it?"

"No. I didn't know what to say."

"Well, think of something. Like I said, she may be our only hope." Henry stood and paced the room. "What do you know about James's family?"

"Not much. I asked about them many times, but he told me they were dead. I didn't pry, thinking it must have been too painful for him to talk about."

"Have you seen any photographs of them?"

"I haven't."

"There were none in his personal effects?" He turned to face her.

"Strange to say, none."

"And their first names?"

"Gene and Emily. I believe he told me that once."

Henry sat back down, took out a pad and pencil from his pocket, and began scrawling. "Do you know where his parents lived while James was growing up?"

Evangeline sighed, realizing she should have persisted when asking James questions about his past. "James always waved toward the coast and said he grew up near the sea."

"Strange, wouldn't you say?"

Evangeline nodded. "Wait a minute. I just thought of

something! James hired a cook when we were first married. She was about to tell me about his parents when James walked into the kitchen. She never finished what she was about to tell me. I wanted to do my own cooking, and I never saw her again."

Henry's face brightened. "Let's see if we can find her. Do you remember her name?"

"Her first name was Doris, and that's all I know."

Henry slapped his hands together. "By golly, that's a start. If we can find her, perhaps she can shed some light on James's past."

Evangeline shivered. "You talk like James might be guilty of something."

"He was guilty of not telling you who his parents were and what really happened to them."

Just then, Maud peeked into the study. "Evangeline. There you are. Oh! Henry, I didn't know you were here, too. I would have been here with you, Evangeline. I had a headache and took to my bed."

Evangeline smiled sympathetically at her mother. She was missing father dreadfully. "Come in, Mama. Henry came by to tell me what he found out." Maud sat near Evangeline while she explained Henry's progress in the investigation.

"This is all so mysterious," Maud commented.

"Have you heard from Frederick, yet?" Henry asked.

"Just that he arrived safely. I do detest all this waiting," Maud wailed.

"Don't worry, ladies. I'm quite confident we'll get to the bottom of this," Henry said as he turned to leave. "No need to let me out."

After the door closed behind Henry, Maud faced her daughter. "So, do you think this detective is any good?"

Evangeline tightened a pin in her upswept hair before she answered. "A little unorthodox, but I think he's on the right track. He was suggesting that our answer may be with

James's past. I know nothing about his early years."

"I wish your father were home. I worry about him so."

Evangeline patted her hand. "I know you do. We'll just have to keep ourselves busy while we wait."

———

Evangeline awoke to the first major snow of the winter. She padded over to the window and pulled the red velvet draperies aside to see the magic of a new snowfall. The fluffy, pure, white flakes reminded her of her childhood innocence. How she had enjoyed romping in the snow with her father, building snowmen, and making snow angels. Evangeline sighed deeply. Those days were so much simpler. What she would give to go back in time for a visit.

She eased onto her window seat and folded her legs under her. She had hoped to return to the mission any day now, but the investigation was taking much longer than she had predicted. Willow was growing by leaps and bounds, and Elijah was missing these moments. She was sorrowful that he wasn't there to share in their daily life, those joyous little moments that could never be replaced. She had heard from Elijah once since leaving. He said he was doing his best to work out a payment schedule with their own creditors. At least he admitted to missing Evangeline and the baby. She had written him about the latest developments in the investigation, including the news that her father would be home in the next week.

Evangeline had intended to visit Gertrude today, but the snowfall changed her plans. Besides, she wasn't getting anywhere with the old lady. The last time she was there, Gertrude didn't seem the least bit interested in sewing. Just before she had left, Evangeline had taken the photographs out the sewing machine drawer and asked Gertrude about them. She had looked at them without the slightest hint of recognition and simply said that she didn't know the people in the photographs or where the photographs had come from. Gertrude wasn't going to be any help in the investigation, and Evangeline was becoming increasingly uncomfortable around her.

Evangeline's musings were broken by Maud. She yelled up the stairway. "Henry's going to be coming by in an hour."

"I'll be down shortly," Evangeline called. "Make sure Mabel has something ready for Henry to eat." Evangeline dressed quickly and scampered down the stairs to the aroma of freshly baked cinnamon rolls. She poked her head in the kitchen. "Oh, Mabel, my favorite. I'm sure Henry will approve, too."

She laughed. "What is it with this poor man? Doesn't he ever eat, besides here?" Mabel complained.

"He isn't married. I feel sorry for him."

"You feel sorry for everyone." Mabel smiled.

Evangeline poured herself coffee from the pot in the kitchen and joined her mother at the dining room table. "I wonder what Henry has up his sleeve today?"

Maud frowned and put down the morning paper. "I'm almost afraid to find out."

Henry arrived famished, just as Evangeline predicted. He ate two of Mabel's fragrant perfections and licked the frosting off his fingers before he began to talk business. "I have found Doris, the cook James had hired when you were first married. It took me several days, but I've got her full name and address."

"Have you talked to her?"

"No. It would be best if you come along. She might open up to you a little better."

"When are you planning a visit?"

"Today, provided that she's available."

"But it's snowing. I wasn't planning on going out."

"Wouldn't it be better to resolve this as soon as possible?"

"You're right. Where we going?"

"A retirement home."

Evangeline raised her eyebrows. "She's in a retirement home?"

Henry nodded. "It's possible that she may not remember much, but we have to try. Do you think John could drive us? I don't trust my motorcar in this snow. In fact, I think it would certainly hang up on even a piece of chewing gum."

Maud took the initiative. She left to locate John, leaving Evangeline and Henry to their discussion. Henry eyed another cinnamon roll. Evangeline accommodated by dishing one up for him.

"Have you visited Gertrude lately?" Henry asked. His eyes danced with pleasure as he chewed.

"I haven't. I don't think she's going to be any help to us. She needs to be placed in an institution where she can get care. But I can't do that; I'm not her family. What can I do? What about Ethan?"

"Since that isn't his real name, my hands are tied, too. I have one recourse left, and that is to follow him—if I ever see him."

"Gertrude told me he comes on Sundays."

"Then Sunday will be the stakeout."

Maud returned with John, and Henry helped Evangeline with her coat.

"Thank you, Maud, for your hospitality," Henry called out.

Once inside the carriage, Evangeline continued the conversation concerning Gertrude. "Will following Ethan be dangerous?"

"It could be."

"Have you followed dangerous criminals before?"

"I have. Even had a few close calls. Don't worry; I can take care of myself."

"You're not carrying a gun, are you?" Evangeline's blood

ran cold as Henry nodded and patted his coat pocket matter-of-factly. She didn't like where the investigation was taking them. She would feel so much better when her father returned home. Even though he had such a practical and insightful nature about him, the potential for danger was now all too real to Evangeline.

The snow had let up some when John pulled the carriage in front of the retirement home. John opened the door for Evangeline and Henry and commented that he would wait inside for them. At the reception table, Henry inquired about Doris. A lady in a white uniform led them to the somber solarium. The nurse introduced both Evangeline and Henry to Doris before excusing herself. Evangeline wasn't sure that Doris recognized her. "Do you remember me, Doris?"

Doris squinted as though bright sunlight were pouring through the glass panels. "I'm not quite sure. Am I supposed to know you?"

"We met only one time. James and I were newly married and living at the horse farm near the coast. He brought me out there right after our wedding reception and you prepared our first meal together."

Doris sat in silence for a moment. "James?"

"James Collier. You said you knew his family."

"Oh, that was so long ago."

Evangeline flashed a look of hope at Henry. Henry nodded toward Evangeline, encouraging her. "I never knew James's parents," Evangeline said. "Could you tell me something about them?"

"I wasn't with them very long. Cooked for them awhile. James was a very young boy then, very handsome and very blonde."

Evangeline's eyes softened at the image. "Where did they live?"

"I don't remember exactly, but it was near the sea.

James's father was a fisherman."

"And his mother, Emily?"

"A very pretty young thing. Loved her little boy. Sewed for him in her spare time."

"What happened to them after you left?"

"I don't rightly remember. I moved to Maine to be with my sister and lost all contact with Boston until I moved back. I didn't see James until he hired me shortly before he married. Actually, he didn't even know who I was until I told him."

"You didn't ask him about his parents at that time?"

"I guess not."

Evangeline waited, agonizing over the conversation. *So much depends on Doris's memory. If she could just remember!*

"I do believe something happened...something tragic. Yes, that's it. But I don't remember what."

"Oh, please try," Evangeline begged.

Doris shook her head. "I'm sorry, but I just can't remember anymore."

The nurse entered then and stepped over to Doris's side. "I think she has expended herself. You may come back another time."

"Thank you," Evangeline said, graciously. Henry took her arm and led her through fresh snow to the carriage. Evangeline shoulders sagged in disappointment.

"You've done all you could, but that doesn't mean the end. I have an idea."

Evangeline reached in her pocket for a handkerchief and dabbed at her eyes. "What is it?"

"Tragedies are for newspapers. That's our next step." Henry signaled to John that they were ready.

———

Evangeline slept fitfully the night before the excursion to search the newspapers. That morning, Maud insisted she come along. Henry agreed an extra pair of eyes would be helpful. "Maud may remember something about a tragedy once she gets to looking," he said to Evangeline while Maud had left them momentarily to discuss the day's menu with Mabel.

"And it will get her mind off of Father," Evangeline said confidentially. "She's constantly watching and waiting for him at the window. Actually, I'm surprised she's going to leave the house. He may even arrive home today."

Evangeline cast a glance at Henry from the corner of her eye. "Have you ever been married, Henry?"

"Me?" he sputtered. "Oh, no, no. I don't have time for a wife in my line of work. Besides, she would always be worrying about me."

Once they entered the doors of the news office, Henry explained to an employee what they were looking for. The employee led them to a room filled with back issues. Henry pulled a piece of paper out of his pocket and explained to Evangeline and Maud that he had narrowed the date of the tragedy within a window of several years, based on James's age at the time. After a short discussion, each decided to search through a separate year. Maud sneezed at the dust that had accumulated on the stack of newspapers before her, but she made no complaint. She tackled the assignment with enthusiasm. They spent the entire day sifting through the back issues breaking only for a short lunch, which they ate at a nearby diner.

"Perhaps the tragedy occurred somewhere outside Boston and the newspapers didn't write about it," Evangeline said, closing the last issue of her stack late that afternoon.

"Well, it was worth a try anyway," Henry commiserated.

Maud had two more issues in her mound and handed one to Evangeline. "Here, help me out." She sneezed again and rubbed her red nose with a handkerchief. "I have certainly had enough of these smelly old newspapers."

"We're about done, Mama." Evangeline rubbed her weary eyes as she unfolded the issue Maud had handed her. Large, bold type assaulted her senses. "Oh, my! Look, I think this is what we've been looking for!"

Maud and Henry stood and peered over her shoulder. "What does it say?" Maud asked.

Evangeline read the story. A fishing boat belonging to Gene and Emily Collier had disappeared in a storm off the coast of Boston. Gene had drowned. Emily had regained consciousness and survived, though with little memory of the incident or of her former life. "Where's the rest of the story?" Evangeline rifled through the fragile newspaper.

"Let's check the following issues," Henry suggested, handing Evangeline and Maud more papers. They searched months' worth of issues, but no further information was to be found.

"Now we'll never know what happened," Evangeline wailed. "It's still a mystery."

"But we know more than when we first started," Henry reminded them.

Evangeline thought she detected a hit of disillusionment on his face, too. She stood and dusted off her skirt. "Please tell me you have another idea."

"I do." He scratched his head. "I'll have to check the records of hospitals and mental wards. Perhaps Emily was admitted somewhere for a period of time."

Evangeline sparked. "Could Emily still be alive?"

Henry nodded. "Yes, it's possible. But wouldn't James have said something to you?"

"Now I'm not so sure. I can't believe James kept his early life such a secret. It must have been very painful for him."

"I agree."

"And who took care of him if she was hospitalized?"

Evangeline asked. "I want to know these things."

"In due time. Trust me. We'll get to the bottom of this," Henry promised. "Let's call it a day. We can do no more here at this time."

Evangeline heaved a sigh. "I'm sure we can talk Mabel into making a pot of tea. Would you care to join us, Henry?"

"Good idea!" Maud applauded.

Henry excused himself from the tea invitation. "I have a lot to work to do tonight. Tomorrow, I intend to go through old hospital and mental ward records."

"And what shall I do?" Evangeline asked before they parted company.

"Visit Gertrude."

"But why? She is not cooperating one bit."

"Keep at it. She might say something to help us out."

"If you say so."

"We must know more about her. See if you can jog her memory about her childhood, where she grew up—something, anything about her life. She must remember."

"I'll do my best."

"You might inquire as to how long she lived in the cottage by the ocean, what her husband did for a living, and such."

Evangeline stared at Henry. "Do you suspect Gertrude is involved? How could she be?"

"At the moment, I don't know. It's one of my hunches. I think she has a great deal to do with this case. I haven't deduced exactly how...yet."

Evangeline couldn't shake her disappointment with the day's results. She had been married to James for five years, but knew very little about him. She was amazed at how profoundly his past was affecting her present.

CHAPTER 18

Back at the Dumont mansion, Evangeline joined Maud in the sitting room for tea. "I feel like I'm living one of my mystery books. The plot thickens!"

"It's simply dreadful. I wish Frederick were home with us. We haven't heard anything from him for quite some time, and I'm beginning to worry."

"I know what you mean Mama. I wish Elijah were here, too."

"You do? After the way he treated you?"

Evangeline shrugged. "I forgive him. I knew all along that the mission is more important to him than I am."

"Well, I just don't understand that kind of marriage. I'm first in Frederick's life, and I know that for a fact. He tells me that all the time."

Evangeline smiled. "You are one lucky woman, Mama. Thank your lucky stars for such a devoted man."

Maud's eyes began to tear, and she reached into her pocket for a handkerchief. Evangeline poured the tea, and

Maud changed the subject. "Why is Henry concentrating on Gertrude?"

"He feels she might be the key in this investigation."

"I don't see how."

"I don't know either, but I'll trust his instincts. Do you want to help me make a list of questions to ask her when I see her next? It's highly doubtful she'll remember anything, but I must give it a try."

———

Evangeline chose a cold, windy day for her next visit to Gertrude. She had Mabel bake scones to take along. She figured Gertrude probably wasn't eating properly and that it was always nice to have something to go along with coffee or tea. John agreed to drive her there and come back in about three hours to give Evangeline time to work on the quilt and put Gertrude at ease. But just as John pulled the carriage to a stop in front of the flat, a burly man rushed out of the building. He wore a dark overcoat with a hat jammed on his head. He thrust his hands into his pockets.

"I wonder if that's Ethan," Evangeline remarked.

"Who's Ethan?"

"Gertrude's husband."

"Have you ever seen him before?"

"No, I haven't, but I don't know who else it would be. Can we follow him?"

"We can, but we won't be very inconspicuous in this large carriage."

Evangeline stared ahead. "Give it a try." John swung the carriage out into the street and followed Ethan's motorcar for a few blocks. It was difficult to keep up with the car as it darted down streets and around corners. Soon, Evangeline realized that they were driving into Boston's financial district. Ethan abruptly parked in front of a prestigious bank.

"What do we do now?" John called down to her.

"I don't know. Perhaps I should go in and have a look around. He doesn't know who I am."

"Is that safe?"

"It should be. It's not like I'm meeting him in a dark alley."

"I'll be right here. Be careful," John reminded her.

Evangeline impulsively pulled her coat collar up around her neck and stepped from the carriage. Her heart raced uncontrollably as she approached. She hadn't much time. Before she knew it, she was stepping over the threshold of the bank. She knew her father did his banking there, but she didn't want to be recognized just yet. The bank was fairly crowded with patrons. She scanned the throng for the burly man, and it took only a few seconds to catch sight of him. He had removed his hat, exposing a stern and hardened face. He was talking to a banking executive. She moved closer in order to see the banker's nameplate on his desk. Bernard Mullens. At that moment, she noticed both men looking her way. She shrank inwardly. The men turned their heads to continue the discussion. Evangeline took advantage of the opportunity to retreat to the door and exit the bank. Climbing back into the carriage, she said, "Let's go, John. To Gertrude's."

When John left her at Gertrude's door, Evangeline waved John on his way and knocked several times before Gertrude answered. "I hope I haven't come at an inconvenient time," Evangeline said emphatically.

"No," she hesitated, appearing rattled. "Come on in."

"I think I saw Ethan leave here. Did he come by for a visit?"

Gertrude wrung her hands. "Ethan? Why, yes he did."

Evangeline unwrapped the fragrant scones and placed them on her table. "I brought some scones to go with our coffee this morning." She pushed aside the clutter of papers on the table.

"The coffee is ready. Sit down." Gertrude poured them each a cup and placed two plates beside them. Evangeline placed a scone on each plate and settled in for conversation. While Gertrude shakily buttered her scone, Evangeline's glance fell on a large envelope partially concealing a legal document. *Ethan must have brought that to her,* she thought. She resisted the urge to uncover it. "Gertrude, I have some questions to ask you. It's probably none of my business, but I realize I know practically nothing about you."

Gertrude shrugged. "I don't remember a lot about my life. I suffered an injury some years ago. Once in a while, something comes back to me. Most of the time I live in a... fog."

"What happened to you?"

"I don't remember."

"You must have family that could tell you. What about your husband?"

"He was lost at sea. I don't recall much before that."

"So you don't remember anything?"

"The sea. I have always lived by the sea." Gertrude peered deeply into Evangeline's eyes. "I want to move from this place and go back to my cottage by the sea. My soul is dying here."

"Would you like to see your old place again?"

"I would."

Evangeline's mind whirled with ideas. Perhaps she and Henry could take Gertrude back. Maybe that would jog her memory. Clearly, Gertrude was not thriving here. "I have an idea. Before the weather becomes too miserable, I'll take you there. What day would work for you?"

"Any day."

"Perhaps we will go the day after tomorrow. Now let's get to work on the quilt before the day is done." Evangeline helped Gertrude clear the dishes from the table and lay out the quilt scraps they had been working with. The quilt was well under way, but Evangeline knew Gertrude wouldn't finish if she left before it was completed. Evangeline intentionally placed an incomplete block near the partially hidden document. She detested spying, but it was vital to her own predicament that she have a peek at the document. Evangeline had maneuvered Gertrude to the sewing machine while she cut a few more pieces to be sewn. When Gertrude seemed preoccupied, Evangeline slid the envelope off the paper and turned it toward her. It appeared to be from the Probate Court, a court date to determine if Gertrude was mentally competent. Before she had a chance to read any more, Gertrude left the sewing machine and came to the table to get another block to sew. Evangeline handed her the pieces and then sat motionlessly, trying to make sense out of what she had just read. *Ethan is declaring Gertrude legally incompetent. But why would a husband do such a thing? Gertrude doesn't have money or an estate—or does she?*

After John came for her, she asked him to drive her by Henry's office. Luckily, Henry had just returned from the hospital and mental wards. He was shuffling files on his desk when she entered. A cursory glance revealed an office like Henry's outdated coat; the furniture, the drapes, the books—everything was shabby. "Henry, do you have time to talk?"

"Why, sure. You look like you've seen a ghost."

"I just came from visiting Gertrude."

"And you discovered something?"

"Several things, in fact."

Henry pulled up a tattered chair for her. "Coffee?"

"No thanks," she said after glancing toward his stained utensils. "Did you uncover any information today?"

He plopped down in a rickety chair across from her and rubbed his bleary eyes. "No, I didn't. But I have more records to go through. Go ahead and tell me what you've found out."

"First of all, I trailed Ethan."

Henry lifted his brows. "You trailed Ethan? I haven't even had that opportunity yet."

"I saw a man coming out of Gertrude's flat. Before I got out of the carriage, I had John follow him. He stopped at the bank, and I went in. He was with Bernard Mullens, the banker. They noticed me, so I made a hasty retreat."

"Very impressive."

"I can't believe I had the courage." Evangeline shivered. "But how are we going to find out what he is up to?"

Henry tugged at his ear. "That's a tough one. Confidentially and all."

"It might have something to do with a letter I saw on Gertrude's table. I know I shouldn't have been snooping, but I had to know."

Henry laughed. "Welcome to detective work. We're all snoops."

She smiled. "I can see why. Anyway, this letter was about a court date with the intention of declaring Gertrude mentally incompetent."

"I see." Henry rubbed his chin. "Gertrude has something Ethan wants. We have to find out what it is."

"But I feel like a spy."

Henry grinned. "You are. Get used to it."

"I promised Gertrude we'd take her to her cottage by the sea. She's so homesick."

"That might be a good idea. Perhaps she'll remember something. We must protect Gertrude from Ethan. He may be planning on putting Gertrude away. I have a feeling he has been using her for some greedy purpose, and now he wants her out of the way."

———

Within two days, Henry and Evangeline had made plans

to take Gertrude on a jaunt to her house by the ocean. Evangeline had insisted that Gertrude bundle up warmly for their excursion. John drove them in the carriage and waited for them while they explored.

Evangeline anxiously stepped down from the carriage and took a deep breath, inhaling the sea air. She then closed her eyes and listened to the gulls circling above. She had missed the ocean since the day she left the horse farm. The pungent air and the gulls' calls brought an image of James into sharp focus. She shook her head. *He's dead,* she reminded herself. *He will be no more.* She pushed her memory of him aside and closed her eyes again, searching for Elijah. Once again, she was torn by them both.

Gertrude produced the key to open the door. She had told Evangeline that Ethan stayed here periodically, but Evangeline didn't believe it once she stepped inside and looked around. Dust and cobwebs had taken up residency. Gertrude had taken all her personal items with her when she left for Boston, except for a rickety rocker by the fireplace and two heavy chests in her former sleeping quarters. The Storm at Sea quilts were no longer lining the walls. A few pots and pans and chipped dishes occupied the kitchen shelves. Otherwise, it didn't look like anyone but the spiders and mice had stayed here since Gertrude had left. But Gertrude didn't seem to notice the place was in shambles or that the drawers of the chests looked like they had been ransacked. She smiled as she walked from room to room.

The interior startled Evangeline and prompted her to ask, "Had you known Ethan for very long before you married him?"

Gertrude looked at Evangeline with a blank expression before she answered. "Ethan was the lighthouse keeper. He stopped to check on me from time to time. He brought me groceries and took me to Boston when I needed."

"So you knew him for a time?"

Gertrude nodded.

"He was kind to you?"

"He was. He's different now. I see him so seldom, but he makes sure I have food and everything I need."

Henry lifted his brow at the open drawers. "Let's look around outside. Maybe Ethan's at the lighthouse."

The outdoors offered a brisk, cold wind from the ocean. Waves crashed against the jagged rocks on the shore. The three trudged against the gale to the cylindrical, granite tower perched on the craggy shore. The lighthouse wasn't as picturesque as some Evangeline had seen, but nevertheless she respected its sound construction. She gazed to the very top until she began to feel dizzy while Henry unlatched the warped door and pushed it inward.

"Doesn't appear anyone is here," Henry said. "I'll have a look around."

The women followed him through the musty interior, up the spiraling metal staircase to the small living quarters, which contained a cot, a cookstove, an icebox, and a cupboard. Henry inspected the stove for warm coals, opened the cupboards and icebox for signs of food, and then shook his head. "It doesn't appear that anyone has stayed here lately." Henry proceeded alone to the very top where the lighthouse apparatus was located. He called from the top. "Great view from up here! I believe someone does man the lighthouse. I wonder if it's Ethan." Henry descended and joined the women in the living quarters. "Do you see anything belonging to Ethan here?" he asked Gertrude.

She shook her head. "Nothing."

Henry inspected the quarters one more time before they left the lighthouse. Henry closed and latched the door. He chose a different path to the cottage. It was quite rocky, and Evangeline stumbled, lurching forward. Henry caught her just before she fell. Henry's discerning eye retraced their steps. "What do we have here?"

"I must have caught my toe on a rock," she muttered.

"It's not a rock. It looks like a foundation."

Gertrude followed to where Henry pointed. "It's the barn."

"Barn?" Henry questioned.

"The barn where we kept the horses." Gertrude said.

"You and your husband?"

"Yes. Norman liked horses. We lived on a horse farm."

Henry knitted his eyebrows. "How long did you and your husband live here?"

"Ever since we were married."

"And when was that?" Henry asked.

"I don't remember."

Henry glanced at Evangeline with a quizzical expression. "You owned a horse farm, but then your husband died at sea?"

Gertrude nodded.

"Tell me more about your life here," Henry prompted.

"That's...all I remember."

"Did you have any children?" Henry asked.

Gertrude's gaze swept the ocean, the lighthouse, and her cottage. "I don't know where he is."

"Where who is?" Henry persisted.

"Someone I know."

"What's his name?"

Evangeline and Henry leaned toward Gertrude. *At last, we might be getting somewhere,* Evangeline thought. But Gertrude shook her head.

"Do you mean Norman?" Evangeline prompted.

"No. Someone else."

"If it isn't Norman, who is it?"

"I don't know."

Evangeline expelled her breath in frustration.

Henry's shoulders slumped. "You ladies wait in the carriage. I'm going to look around some more."

Evangeline agreed and escorted Gertrude to the carriage. "Anything else you want to see, Gertrude?"

"No. It's cold and lonely here. I don't have my quilts to keep me warm." Her voice trailed off and she became silent.

When Henry returned, Evangeline descended from the carriage to meet him. "Today's happenings point toward deeds," he said in a husky whisper. "Our theory that Gertrude rented from James may not prove true. I'm thinking she's a landowner."

Evangeline spoke quietly. "You believe she owns the cottage and a portion of the land?"

"I think so. Maybe the lighthouse, too. Ethan may have discovered this, even after marrying Gertrude."

"So that would mean he wants it, and would be entitled to it if she is declared incompetent. He could gain quite a profit from that property."

Henry nodded. "Looks that way to me. Do you know who owned the farm before James bought it?"

Evangeline hesitated. "No, I guess I never asked." They walked back to the carriage where Gertrude was waiting. Evangeline saw a chill run through the elderly lady. She suddenly regretted leaving her to sit in alone the cold for so long. "Would you want to live here again?" Evangeline asked Gertrude.

"It's not the same. My quilts are gone."

Evangeline agreed. It wasn't the same. She had ridden her horse over this very coastline many times. Sometimes James had even accompanied her. She had enjoyed pleasant afternoons sewing with Gertrude in her cottage, but the cottage didn't welcome her this time. Nothing welcomed her. It was strange and disconnected. For some reason, she too felt that she wouldn't have been able to come back and pick up where she had left off. That part of her life was over, forever.

Frederick returned home just before another winter storm. The biting wind pushed him through the open door and into Maud's awaiting arms. Evangeline also embraced him, relieved to see him home safe. But when they released their embrace, she took a step back and realized he appeared weary and thinner than before. "Summon Henry," Frederick said. "I'm too exhausted to repeat my adventures and discoveries."

Henry arrived within the hour and joined them for afternoon tea in the library. The family was discussing Frederick's trip. Maud could barely contain her emotions. Frederick had donned his smoking jacket and was puffing on his cigar. He waved away the tea and poured a glass of brandy for himself and Henry.

"It's good to be home. I enjoy England, but not when I'm playing detective. I would rather have been sightseeing or partaking in afternoon tea."

Henry lifted his glass to Frederick and downed the contents. "What did you find? Was it worth the trip?"

"Most definitely. It took a long time to get the information I needed, but I persevered. Evangeline, you were right. James left England with just one horse. The ship's manifest clearly showed it."

"What about Kenington Farms?" Henry asked.

"Kenington Farms exists only on paper; there is no such place. James bought the one horse from a small farm outside London. He paid for the horse on the spot."

"And you investigated Halloway?" Henry asked.

Evangeline set down her teacup. "As in, Ethan and Gertrude Halloway?"

Henry nodded. "I had a hunch for Frederick to explore. I wired him after you told me about following Ethan. The creditors are from England. Ethan was talking to a banker. I just thought it was strange."

"Indeed, the reason we haven't been able to find anything on Ethan is because he's from England," Frederick announced proudly. "Good instinct, I'd say," he added. "The Halloways are a lawyer family from London. Ethan, his two brothers, and their father are lawyers."

Evangeline shook her head. "Why ever would such a man marry Gertrude and work in a lighthouse?"

Henry smiled. "My guess is to get close to Gertrude and her money."

"Money. You're saying Gertrude has enough money for an English lawyer to envy?"

Henry then shifted so close to the edge of his seat that he nearly fell over. "I spent two days going over patient records and deeds, and I've come across something very interesting that might enhance what Frederick has just told us. Brace yourself. This might come as a shock."

Evangeline couldn't imagine what Henry was about to reveal. She unconsciously gripped the arm of her chair, waiting for more news about her late husband's family estate.

"I searched and searched and searched for anything confirming that Gertrude had been in a mental institution." Henry paused to look at Evangeline, who was nodding impatiently. "Well, it's now clear to me why I had such difficulty. I finally found her name on a patient list, but it was only listed once. That is, she was checked out of a mental ward. I didn't find her name checking in." He looked around the room.

Evangeline, Frederick, and Maud hung on his every word, their eyes transfixed.

He continued, "I found that Emily Collier had checked into the same ward the year before, as expected. But she was never checked out, does not live on the ward, and lacks death records."

Evangeline heart raced. "What are you saying?"

Henry nodded. "I believe Emily, the mother of James, is alive. Furthermore, she's not using the name Emily."

"Gertrude. Gertrude!" Evangeline covered her mouth with her hand. She grew pale and felt nauseous. "Did James know?"

"He must have known. Why he permitted her to change her name still puzzles me, though," Henry mused.

"He must have visited her during the five years we were married, but he didn't give me any clue that she was his mother or that he even visited Gertrude. Did she know James was her son?"

"Probably not. According to that newspaper we read, Emily apparently didn't remember the boat accident or much of anything before that. It seems that her only consistent memory is losing her husband to the sea."

"Now I know why I was drawn to her. James's mother." A flood of emotion arose in Evangeline's throat, and she took a handkerchief from her pocket.

Frederick moved closer to Evangeline and patted her hand. "James apparently took care of her."

"She doesn't even realize her son died at sea, too," Evangeline said softly. "I suppose it's better that way. Poor, poor woman. But what of Ethan?"

"I believe Ethan wants Emily's estate, which includes the cottage, the lighthouse and a great deal of that land. It's worth a fair amount of money," Henry reasoned. "He is associated with the fraudulent creditors in England. Being a lawyer gives him certain advantages in that regard."

"As well as being Gertrude's...Emily's husband," Evangeline added.

Maud, who had been in a quiet state of shock, finally took part in the conversation. "Why did Ethan Holloway choose James Collier's estate?"

"Good question. Ethan somehow possessed inside information," Henry explained. "He was aware of the estate. He was aware that Gertrude was, in fact, Emily. He may also have been aware that Evangeline, the primary heir, was miles and miles away."

"But how do we protect Emily from being declared incompetent?" Evangeline asked.

"Or worse," Henry added, making Evangeline squirm in her seat. "You are still her daughter-in-law," Henry said, stroking his chin. "However, Gertrude's husband would take precedence as power of attorney unless we can rule him incompetent as well. We'll have to expose his scheme. And that might take months."

Evangeline shifted in her chair. "But I need to get home to Elijah and the mission. Will we be able to expose the fraudulent creditors?"

"My work is about done here," Henry said. "From now on, I suggest you hire a good lawyer to take your case. We have evidence. As far as settling the estate and recouping your money, it will take some time."

"Like I said earlier, Evangeline, your mother and I will lend you the money to pay off the building expenses. You can pay us when you win the case." Frederick's eyes softened.

"Henry, I would like to go home. I realize I will have to testify at some point. But I can return to Boston when it's necessary. There's just one thing that bothers me."

"And what's that?" Henry turned to her.

"Gertrude. Who is going to care for her? I would like to, but I simply must be going home. I've been away far too long as it is."

"We have no idea what Ethan Halloway is capable of. Before you leave, perhaps we can find a nice, safe home with people to look after her."

Evangeline agreed. "I would feel better about leaving if she were safely settled."

"Actually, she can come and live with us," Frederick said.

Maud nodded. "We can hire a private nurse for her. She is James's mother. He would want us to give her a home."

"Oh Mama! Father! How generous of you!"

"It might be temporary. But for now, I think this is the best we can do for her," Frederick said.

"Evangeline and I will visit her tomorrow and see if we can get her moved before nightfall," Henry said. "We certainly don't want Ethan to know what we know before she is safely transferred."

CHAPTER 19

Now that the investigation into James's estate had concluded for the time being, Evangeline could only think of returning to the mission. She had been away for five months, and she was most anxious be home for Christmas with Elijah and the mission staff. Besides, their correspondence had ceased. She was worried. Her marriage had undoubtedly suffered during their separation. She only hoped they could repair it once she got back.

While she had been in Boston, James had been in her thoughts constantly, though mostly out of necessity because of the investigation. That old feeling had returned. She once again felt torn between James and Elijah. She felt as though she had just relived her five-year marriage to James, and she could once again sense the loss. She kept reminding herself that all this had been dredged up against her will. Until now, she believed she had coped successfully. Now that the time had come to push that part of her life into the recesses of her memory, she rediscovered how difficult it could be to do so.

Guilt had overtaken her. Guilt for having deliberately pushed Elijah aside so that she could focus on the matters at hand. Guilt for withholding so much of Willow's growth from Elijah. *Willow won't even remember him,* she thought. She kept telling herself over and over again that these sad circumstances would further the mission and that once she and Elijah were reunited, their relationship would mend somehow. But there were a few things left to settle before she and Willow boarded the westward train.

Evangeline and her father made an appointment to see Frederick's lawyer to discuss the proposed lawsuit against Ethan Halloway. Henry offered to drive them so that Frederick could ride in the motorcar. Evangeline had already been on one of his rides, and she hadn't really enjoyed the new sensation. This time she wore a hat she could tie down firmly to keep the wind from wrecking her hairdo.

Frederick laughed the entire way to the lawyer's office. "Oh, I must have one of these. Does it take long to learn to drive?" he asked Henry.

"Oh, not really," Henry said. He turned his head as they passed the bank, and the horn of an oncoming motorcar honked as they approached one another. Henry steered hard to the right to just avoid a head-on collision. For the remainder of their journey, he kept his attention strictly to the road.

Henry delivered them safely to the lawyer's office, but not without honking the car's horn more times than necessary, Evangeline decided. She silently vowed she would never ride with Henry again. She wondered if she could even ride with father, should he take leave of his senses and purchase one of these dangerous contraptions.

"I'll be back in about an hour to pick you up. If you wish, I'll take you automobile shopping." Henry grinned at Frederick as he and Evangeline stepped out of the car.

Evangeline brushed the wrinkles from her beige suit, secretly relieved that she had arranged to go shopping with her mother after meeting with McMan. The look on Frederick's face gave her the feeling that he would accept Henry's offer. She took her father's arm and entered Hector McMan's office. A lemony fragrance lingered in his highly polished office.

"Pleased to see you again." Hector extended his hand across the gleaming, marble-topped desk to Frederick. "I am most eager to see what you have for me. I'm looking forward to a winning prosecution." His eyes gleamed with the challenge.

"We trust you will win this one, but you may have your work cut out for you." Frederick opened his briefcase and removed the stack of documents that he and Henry had collected.

Hector shuffled through them, expressing delight at particular findings. "Now, summarize what I have here in my hand." Hector leaned back in his chair as Frederick and Evangeline explained the events they uncovered with the help of the shabby detective. By the time they finished their accounts, the lawyer's elbows were perched on the desk. "Fascinating. Absolutely fascinating. The case against Ethan looks promising." Hector squinted at the documents. "We may require a little more investigation to build a stronger case. For example, does Ethan have a prior record? And how did he discover this woman's true identity? With all the pieces in place, I can't see how we could lose. We should have enough evidence against him to sue for damages."

Frederick smiled. "How soon would we be able to start proceedings?"

"I'll get to this right away, but I wouldn't expect any substantial developments until after Christmas."

"Wonderful. It is very important to my daughter, Evangeline, to settle this matter as soon as possible."

"I understand."

Evangeline spoke softly. "I'd like to return home until the court proceedings commence." She trusted her father, Hector, and Henry to tend to all legal matters in her absence. She wished she could avoid returning to Boston to delve into the past once more. However, she knew she must.

After exchanging salutations with Hector McMan, Henry and Frederick dropped Evangeline off at Maud's favorite store. Evangeline had accepted Maud's invitation to go shopping for a winter traveling suit for herself and for Willow. Evangeline had not intended to stay through November, so she had not packed anything suitable for the freezing temperatures. Also, Willow had outgrown nearly all of her clothing.

"We haven't had any time to do something fun," Maud complained. "I'm so glad we decided to go shopping. There's nothing like a new purchase to lift one's spirits."

"I'm going to agree with you today." Evangeline kissed her on the cheek. "I'm ready for some fun, too. You have been such a blessing, Mama. What would I do without you?"

Maud smiled. "How did it go with the lawyer?"

"He seemed confident that we have a good case against Ethan and his crooks. I asked if it would be alright if I returned to the mission while they're building their case. It won't really begin until after Christmas"

"So soon?"

"Mama, I've been here much too long." Evangeline threw up her hands. "It's time for me to go home to my husband. That is, if I still have one."

Her mother shook her head. "I hate to see you leave again. I've just gotten used to having you and Willow with me and your father." Her smile drooped into a frown.

"You know I have to go."

"Well, if Elijah is not happy to have you back, you just get back on that train and come home," Maud said.

Evangeline nodded to indicate she had heard her, but did

not look her in the eyes. After lunch, the mother and daughter spent the day finding the perfect traveling suits. Finally, they settled on a deep green tweed trimmed in fur for Evangeline and a pink suit with a fur muff for Willow.

"You two will look adorable. If Elijah doesn't appreciate you, there's something wrong with him," Maud said rather gruffly.

Evangeline admitted to herself that she did not know how Elijah was going to react to their reunion. In fact, she didn't know how was she was going to react, either. *Perhaps,* she mused, *neither of us will know until that moment.*

———

Evangeline noticed a change in Henry's appearance when he came to the door to pick her up and drive her to Emily's flat. He had exchanged his rumpled, black coat for a stylish, brown Norfolk jacket. To top it off, a silk cravat caressed his throat. She had to admit he looked a tad handsome when he doffed his new derby hat as she answered the door.

"Is that a new jacket?" she asked unabashedly. She wondered if he was trying to impress a lady.

"It is. I thought I needed an update to go along with my motorcar."

"Very wise of you. I like the new look." She smiled to herself, realizing she would miss Henry. He was an odd fellow, but very entertaining and a talented detective. He held the door for her as she broke her silent vow by climbing into his shiny motorcar. She hoped he wouldn't notice her firm grip on the seat as he ferreted them through the streets of Boston. During the entire trip, she envisioned her mother's reaction to the motorcar Frederick had just purchased.

When they arrived at Gertrude's flat, Evangeline rapped on the door several times before the door opened. Evangeline stepped back and gasped. The woman's lower arms revealed purple, yellow, and black bruises where someone apparently had grabbed her too tightly. "Gertrude, who did this to you?" Evangeline demanded as soon as she pushed her way into the flat. The room reeked of stale cigar smoke, and she wondered about the recent visitor.

Gertrude broke down in tears, shaking her head. "Ethan. I don't understand why he's so cross with me."

Evangeline gently took hold of her and escorted her to a chair. Evangeline waved her hand toward Henry. "This is Henry, a...friend of mine." Gertrude made no response that she had heard. "When was Ethan here?"

"I think it was...yesterday. I'm so confused. So tired."

"What did he want?" Henry asked abruptly.

Gertrude looked at him strangely and then at Evangeline. "A piece of paper. He was looking for a piece of paper. He emptied everything."

"Was it the paper you had on the table several weeks ago?" Evangeline asked after Henry prompted her.

"I don't know."

"Did he find what he was looking for?"

"No. That's why he grabbed me. He wanted to know where it was."

"You didn't remember?"

"No."

"Do you know that you are quite a wealthy woman?" Henry broke in.

Gertrude stared at him but seemed oblivious to what he had just said.

Henry ignored Evangeline's irritated expression, saying, "You own the cottage by the sea, the lighthouse, and even the land surrounding it."

Gertrude shook her head.

"Gertrude, look at me." Evangeline said softly. "Does the name Emily Collier mean anything to you?"

Gertrude stared blankly at her.

"Don't be discouraged, Evangeline," Henry consoled. "It may take time. She might never remember."

Evangeline nodded in resignation. "Gertrude, we're going to move you to my parent's home. You're going to stay with them. You'll be safe there. Ethan won't be able to hurt you anymore. Someone will care for you, cook your meals, and attend to your every need. Won't that be lovely?"

"Move? I'm too tired to move."

"We're here to help you. Tell us what's most important to you, and we'll pack it up."

Gertrude's eyes roved over her flat. "I don't need anything. Maybe something to wear."

Evangeline sensed that Gertrude wasn't going to be of any help. She looked helplessly at Henry, who just shrugged.

"Pack what looks wearable. Look for keepsakes, jewelry, photos, and other valuables. I'll see if there are any documents lying around. I'm sure Ethan found them all by now."

Evangeline began with the quilt she and Gertrude had begun together. It hadn't been finished yet and maybe Gertrude would still want to sew. Evangeline folded it neatly, planning to instruct the seamstress to assist Gertrude in finishing the quilt for her bed. That woman did love her quilts.

Gertrude sat silently gazing off into space as Evangeline and Henry searched the flat. It wasn't long before they filled the motorcar. Gertrude didn't seem to notice the new mode of transportation as they whisked her away to the Dumont residence. Maud was waiting for them when they arrived. Evangeline and Maud had already designated a room for Gertrude, a bright and sunny space that overlooked the gardens. They had wanted Gertrude to be as comfortable as possible.

When Evangeline opened the door to Gertrude's new home, Gertrude reeled back from the unfamiliar house. Evangeline reassured Gertrude that the move was for the best. She led her through the parlor. The elderly woman's eyes seemed to take in every detail of the Dumont mansion. "Such beautiful things," she whispered. "I had nice furniture once." Evangeline flinched and shot a knowing look at Maud. Gertrude did have some memories after all.

Before Evangeline gave Gertrude a tour of the house, she escorted Gertrude to her bedroom. After Gertrude ran her hands over the fine furniture and tested the softness of the bed, she smiled weakly. *At least she will live in comfort,* Evangeline thought upon observing that hint of approval. *I wonder if she's remembering the early times again,* she thought.

Evangeline had salvaged the few photographs she had found in the sewing machine drawer. While Gertrude sat in thought, Evangeline lifted the photos out of the box and set them on top of Gertrude's dresser. She knew one photograph showed James. The other two she suspected were of Gertrude's husband. "I brought these pictures for you to enjoy. Can you tell me who these people are?" Evangeline asked with a hint of hope.

Gertrude glanced over at them and shook her head. "I don't know. I've never seen them before."

Evangeline sighed. "Maybe you'll remember later. I'll just unpack a few of your things." The only items she had found worth taking were a few hairpins and a broach. She assumed Ethan would have taken everything else of value. Evangeline hung Gertrude's clothing in the wardrobe and seated Gertrude by the window. "Sit here and enjoy the view."

Evangeline had just hung the last garment in the wardrobe when Maud signaled to Evangeline to come out in the hall. "I'll be right back," Evangeline told Gertrude before she scurried away. "What, what is it, Mama?"

"I want you to meet Alexia, the nurse I hired for Gertrude. I thought you might want to speak with her before we introduce her to Gertrude." Maud led Evangeline to a nearby sitting room where they could talk privately. After the preliminary introductions, Evangeline briefed Alexia on Gertrude's present condition and on her run-in with Ethan. "We all are concerned about Gertrude's memory loss," Evangeline said. "Father mentioned that she should be taken to a doctor for more tests. It's probably been years since she has seen a doctor. Perhaps they can do something for her. Do you have any recommendations, Alexia?"

Alexia pursed her pencil thin lips. "I do know of several doctors who deal with memory loss. I can give you their names."

"Yes, we would appreciate whatever direction you can give us," Maud said.

Alexia jotted down several names and handed the list to Maud. "Have you tried calling her Emily?"

"I did mention the name Emily, but there was no reaction," Evangeline said.

"I think we should try it again and see how she reacts. It may jog her memory. She probably hasn't heard her given name for some time."

"I will be leaving in a few days," Evangeline reminded her.

"Don't worry about her. I'll do all I can," Alexia reassured them.

Evangeline stood and straightened her skirt. "Are you ready to meet Gertrude?" Evangeline asked.

Alexia nodded. She followed Evangeline to meet Gertrude, who hadn't moved from where Evangeline had left her. Alexia did her best to strike up a conversation, but Gertrude had little to say.

After Alexia left, Gertrude turned her attention to the window.

Evangeline spoke softly. "Do you like the view?"

"Pretty. But I cannot see the ocean. I want to live by the sea. Where is it?"

"I know you do, but you can't live there alone. Perhaps someday you can return to your cottage. But for now, you will be staying with my mother and father." Evangeline took hold of Gertrude's hands. "I will be going back to my husband. It's a long way from here, and I won't see you for a long time."

Gertrude's eyes filled with tears. "I can't stay here."

"You'll be safe and comfortable. Alexia will be with you when I leave."

"But I need to be near the sea when Norman comes home."

"Norman, your husband?"

"Yes."

"But, I thought his name was Gene, Gene Collier?"

"Gene Collier?" Gertrude said. She assumed a trancelike state, momentarily lost in the past.

"Emily," Evangeline said softly. "Do you hear me, Emily?"

The woman remained motionless, and then lifted her eyes to Evangeline. "Emily?"

"Yes, Emily. Your parents gave you the name Emily, not Gertrude." Evangeline sat quietly on the window seat, waiting for her to internalize what she had heard. "Your husband's name was Gene."

"It's Norman," Gertrude said firmly.

Evangeline frowned at the regression but persisted. "Emily, do you remember a little boy, little James?"

"James?" Gertrude seemed to savor the sound of that name rolling from her lips.

"He had blonde hair and a little, crooked smile. He loved horses."

Gertrude knitted her eyebrows, deep in thought. "I do remember a pony. But not a little boy. And why are you calling me Emily?"

Evangeline knew it was time to end the questioning. Gertrude sighed deeply with irritation and gazed out the window. Evangeline was also irritated. There were so many unanswered questions! She prayed that the doctors would have some success. Somehow, they had to reach into this woman and unlock her past. Evangeline saw Gertrude differently since it was revealed to her that Gertrude was Emily, James's mother, and her mother-in-law. She desired to know the woman she could feel was somewhere deep inside.

CHAPTER 20

"How long is this frigid weather going to last?" Kat complained as she added more wood to the kitchen stove. She then broke the ice in the water bucket for the morning coffee. Lately, it had been cold enough for ice to form in the water pail every night.

"We need coal to bank the fire for the night," Jet answered. "Maybe we can get some when the railroad crosses the Missouri river."

"Well, until then, what would you like for breakfast?" She stood shivering next to the stove.

"Flapjacks," he said, pulling on his warmest socks.

"But we have them every morning. Besides, we're out of eggs. The hens quit laying."

"Oatmeal, then. If we get to church Sunday, we'll stock up on supplies at Tater's store." Jet pulled on his boots.

Kat placed a pan of water to boil and added some salt. While she waited, she opened the bread box. *We're about out of bread, too,* she said to herself as she sliced what was left.

Guess I'll have to set some bread dough again. She heaved a deep sigh. She placed the sliced bread in the oven to toast. Soon the aroma of crisp bread rose from the oven. "What's happening with Tater? Is he going to be brought up on land fraud charges along with Curt and Tex?"

"Ed doesn't say much. I suppose he can't, since he's going to represent them. I get the impression there's not much he can do to get them off. They're guilty of land fraud the way I see it. I suppose he'll do his best to keep them out of prison. He'll be really lucky if they just have to pay a fine."

Kat stirred the oats into the boiling water and stared at the gruel as it bubbled. "What exactly did they do?"

"Talked people into filing on homesteads around his ranch headquarters. Then he bought their homesteads from them. That way he eventually would own the lands around his range."

"That's illegal?"

"Most didn't file on land in good faith."

"What do you mean by that?"

"Their intent should have been to live on the land and homestead, not speculate. The government views such action as land fraud."

"Tex never struck me as dishonest."

"And what about me?"

"Are you saying I'm not a good judge of character? You didn't strike me as a bad sort either. Though I have to admit, you were kind of suspicious."

"It's hard to tell what a man will do when greed grabs hold of him."

Kat removed the toast from the oven and set the kettle of oatmeal to the side. "Ed sure is amazing. I wonder why he's out here when he could be practicing law in a big city. Don't you find that odd?"

"No, he just likes cattle and open land, like me."

"Do you think he's after the Indian leases like Tex?" She

dished the oatmeal into bowls and placed them on the table. "Oh, just listen to that wind," she commented as the snow slapped against the window and a gust shook the clapboard house.

Jet reached for the toast. "The Bar Double B will make that decision, I expect."

"Have you met any of the stockholders?"

Jet picked up a knife and scraped a pat of stubborn butter across a piece of toasted bread. "Not yet. But Ed's expecting a visit from them this summer."

"They're from England? Or is it Scotland?"

"England, I think he said."

"I'm curious. What do the figures stand for in their Bar Double B brand? Is it somebody's name?"

Jet squinted and pursed his lips. "I don't rightly know. I'll ask Ed. Maybe he knows."

"Oh, it's not important. Just wondering." Kat gazed out the window at the spitting snow. "Summer seems so far away."

Jet glanced over his spoon at her. "Would you like to spend a week at the mission with the ladies?"

She sat in thought for a minute. "Yes, I would. I could go to their sewing meeting. I have some questions about this one block I'm sewing. Would you miss me?"

"Of course I would! But I know the days get long for you."

"I could use more cooking lessons from Minnie, too." She watched the expression on Jet's face, but she didn't know what to think when it didn't change. "I'm so glad I paid attention to learning to bake bread—'the staff of life,' they say."

Jet popped the last spoonful of oatmeal into his mouth, rose from his chair, and kissed Kat on the top of her head. "I'm off to chop ice for the cattle and then see if I can gather some firewood. I'll look forward to your fresh bread." He winked.

Kat cleared the dishes from the table, placed them in the

dishpan, and then began baking bread. Stirring in the flour and kneading the dough took all the arm strength she could muster. "Oh, this is hard work," she muttered. She scooped up the massive lump of dough that had accumulated from her efforts and plopped it into a large pan where it would swell to twice its size. She covered it with a dishtowel and then moved it closer to the stove so it could rise.

Moving over to her unmade bed, Kat smoothed the wedding quilt the Deadwood sewing ladies had given her. She ran her hand over the Chinese Lantern quilt. It had slipped to the foot of the bed. Somehow it looked out of place in her shack on the prairie, but to her it was the only pretty thing she had to gaze on this winter. She sighed and wondered if she would ever get used to such barrenness. She felt that the land sucked the life out of everything. She hoped she was strong enough not to be consumed, too.

Snow continued to pelt the window in her kitchen. Now when she looked out onto the landscape, she could barely see any of the outbuildings. She shook her head in resignation. There was no way she would be able to spend time at the mission through this precarious weather. She wouldn't be able to buy any more supplies either. Luckily, she had several sacks of flour in reserve. She took the beans she had been soaking overnight, rinsed them, dumped them in a pan with bacon, and set them on the stove to simmer. Then, wringing her hands, she paced back and forth from window to window peering at the storm. *I have to find something to keep my mind off my situation*, she told herself. She opened the parcel that Minnie had sent with her, removed the patterns, and arranged them on the table. She traced the templates on the fabric with a pencil and began cutting them out. After placing the bread in the oven to bake, she continued her quilt project until Jet came in for dinner, stomping the accumulated snow off his boots.

"Looks like another doozy out there," he announced.

"Smells good in here, though."

"We'll eat as soon as the bread's done. I'll let the crust get a little browner," she said after opening the oven door.

"I'm hungry." He removed his coat and boots, shedding hard cakes of ice with them. "What are you doing there?" he asked, glancing down at the sewing machine.

"I decided to tackle the quilt blocks by myself. There's no way I'm going to get to the mission."

"Suppose not. Seems like one storm follows another. Now how about some of your dinner? My stomach sure is growling. By the way, I asked Ed about the symbols. He told me he didn't know."

"It seems strange that he wouldn't know."

"I suppose he's got more important things on his mind."

Kat shrugged and then dished up his beans, placing a slab of hot bread across them.

"Ah, you're turning into quite the cook," he said as he inhaled the fragrances of the hot meal.

"You aren't hard to please, are you?" she said, nuzzling his neck before she sat down across from him.

"I count my blessings these days. I'm not running from the law. I have a beautiful, red-headed wife who cooks and sews and takes the best care of me. What else could I want?"

"I guess I should do the same."

"The same what?" he asked, wiping the bean broth from his lips.

"Count my blessings."

———

When the weather broke, Jet drove to the mission for supplies and mail. Even though he would be gone all day, Kat remained home. She detested the cold and wasn't about to endure the long trip, even though a chat with Minnie was awfully tempting.

THE BIRDCAGE QUILTS

She watched Jet drive out of sight. She then sat at the table and picked up her cards, shuffled them, and began a game of solitaire. Her mind drifted to her friends at the Birdcage. She missed their familiar presence, but it would be some time before she would see them again. After a half hour of solitaire, she wandered over to her sewing.

The sun, which had been absent for so long, streamed in through the windows and warmed her spirits. She smiled thinking the sewing machine and her quilt projects had become her best friends during these dreary days. She moved over to the machine and assembled a block from the pieces she had cut out the night before. The first block went together well, so she continued to sew the rest of the day away, stopping long enough to eat leftovers for lunch. Darkness began to pull across the horizon like a curtain around four o'clock, and she began to look out the windows for Jet. She carried the kerosene lamp to a table near the kitchen window to illuminate his way. In the meantime, she fried venison steaks with the few potatoes she had left in the gunnysack. "Ouch!" Kat dropped the hot lid on the stove. "Oh, how I hate to cook," she ranted aloud as she jammed it back on the pan.

The wind had picked up. It whistled under the door. Kat kicked a rug up against the threshold, stifling it. She was just beginning to fret about Jet out in the storm when she heard the clomping approach of the sleigh and team. Pulling the pans to the side of the stove, she rushed to the door and opened it for him. "What a load you have there," she shouted in competition with the wind's fury. "Oh, my, I didn't realize it had started to snow again." Wet flakes settled in her hair.

Jet unloaded the supplies and handed them to her. "I stocked up. Had a feeling the weather was about to turn bad again."

She stepped aside to let Jet hoist the large sacks of flour and beans into the kitchen. The smaller sacks and boxes she

233

piled on the table, peeking in to determine the contents.

When Jet had unloaded everything, he handed her the bundle of mail. "I'm going to unhitch the team and take care of the horses."

"Supper's ready when you are," she told him.

"Be in shortly."

Kat sat at the table and sorted through the mail, her only connection to the outside world. Delighted to find a few letters for her, she wasted no time in opening the first. It was from her sister. Excited to hear how they were doing with her business, she had begun reading before she had completely unfolded the four-page letter. Annabelle began by assuring Kat that they were in good health and doing well. It wasn't until the third page that Annabelle conveyed the bad news:

"I am so grateful for the opportunity to manage your business, but I am running into problems. Ling Li is leaving for China with her fiancé. That leaves me with only Leona for a cook. She won't work seven days a week. And of course you know about my cooking skills. I can help, but there's no way I can carry on by myself. Jennie is a gem, but she won't cook either."

Kat dropped the letter into her lap. How was she going to deal with this problem so far from Deadwood? The bar-to-restaurant transformation hinged upon a capable cook. She really didn't want to give up her restaurant idea. *The world doesn't need any more saloons, and I sure don't want to raise my family in one,* she thought. *But it's still the best way to make money if you ask me. Maybe I should reconsider my plans.*

She said little as she dished up Jet's meal. After he had washed up, he sat at the table and rubbed his stomach. "A meal fit for a king." He looked up at the ceiling as she kissed him on the cheek. When he looked back down at the table, he saw nothing but the plate of steaming steak in front of him. "What did you do to pass the day?"

"Oh, I sewed most of the day, played solitaire, cooked. I just read the letter from Annabelle that you brought."

Jet glanced up from his food. "What's she got to say?"

"Ling Li is going back to China. I can't expect Leona to handle it all herself. That means I'm out a cook for most days."

Jet shook his head. "Any ideas for a replacement?"

"No. There aren't that many good cooks around."

"What about Aggie?"

"Aggie? Your head must still be numb from the cold. She's Rio's and Jed's mother."

"I know. I think she's harmless. She's a good cook."

"She is, but I'm sure she works at the Miner's restaurant."

"Offer her a better deal," Jet said.

"That's kind of underhanded, isn't it?"

"Yeah, I guess so. Forget I said anything."

Kat couldn't forget Aggie. She was a good cook. And maybe she wouldn't even want to work for Kat anyway, after all they had been through. She pushed those thoughts to the back of her mind for a moment. "So how's everyone at the mission?"

"Tater's shelves at the store are getting kind of bare. Hard to get the supplies delivered since the snow is so deep. These storms keep coming in, one right after the other. He's got good mail service. Hired some tough cuss to deliver the mail when he can."

"Did you see anyone else?"

"Talked to Minnie awhile. She was in the store buying supplies for the dormitory. I think she's kind of worried that they'll run out of food. She said they convinced Ben Noisy Hawk to move into the dormitory for the winter. He's been painting murals on the walls in the dining room."

"I hope everyone will be okay. Do you think they'll run out of food?"

"I wouldn't worry about them. They're resourceful."

She frowned. "I still haven't solved my problem about a cook."

"Run an ad in the newspaper and see who answers. You might be surprised."

"You're right. That's about all I can do until spring. I suppose I'll need to go back to Deadwood for a spell in the spring."

"We'll be busy for sure, branding and all. Might be a good time for you to get away. With all this snow, the grass will grow and the water holes will be full." Jet closed his eyes and inhaled. "I can just smell that new grass."

"You do love this land, don't you?"

He placed his hand over hers. "I do. I know you're not convinced."

"I'm working at it. We'll see what the spring and summer bring. How about after supper we play a game of cards? I'll let you win," she promised.

———

Since Evangeline had telegraphed Elijah the day she and Willow would be arriving in Pierre, the weather had turned miserably cold and snow was threatening to block the railroad tracks. While the train rolled down the tracks, Evangeline had plenty of time to recount the previous train trips she had taken. As a naïve nineteen-year-old, she had made the trip alone to the mission. Convinced that this was her life's work, she tolerated the primitive conditions and isolation. Little did she know how complicated her life would become.

She prayed with all her might that their trip home would not be delayed. She couldn't bear to be away from home any longer. She missed Elijah very much and hoped he felt the same about her. What if he didn't? What would she do?

A blizzard raged the afternoon they arrived in Pierre. Blinding snow had drastically reduced visibility, and Evangeline's heart sank. She could hardly see the depot when they came to a full stop. It would be impossible for Elijah to meet them there.

She bundled Willow in her pink coat, draped a blanket over Willow's head, and held her in her arms as she carefully made her way down the iced-over steps of the passenger car. The forceful wind stole her breath and burned her throat. Her eyes stung as she gasped for air. She hurried as best she could, pushing her way into the depot. She caught her breath and sat Willow down, brushing the powdery snow off of them both.

Evangeline's head began to swim, and she felt weak. The resolve she had maintained for all these months was beginning to fail her. She was so looking forward to Elijah meeting them. His presence would make everything alright. Tears welled up in her eyes. She swiped them away with her gloved hand, resisting the urge to crumble in a heap right there in the depot. She knew she had to be strong for Willow. Suddenly, she felt a hand on her shoulder. She turned with a forced smile and faced—Elijah! "Oh, Elijah, I was sure you wouldn't be here." Her eyes brimmed with tears. She unabashedly let them fall.

"Nothing could keep me away," he said, pulling her close. "Not even a blizzard. I'm so sorry, Evangeline. I treated you very badly. I don't know what I was thinking."

She sobbed against his chest, and then heard Willow crying. "Willow! We forgot Willow," she said between muffled sobs. She reached for the whimpering child.

"I can't believe how she has grown," he said as he coaxed Willow to his arms. "I've missed you both so much." Bundled in pink to match her rosy cheeks, Willow quieted as she studied his face. "She hasn't quite forgotten me," Elijah said with pleasure. "Now, let's find your baggage and a hotel room for the night." She sensed his reluctance to release his hold on her hand.

Evangeline sunk into a depot chair with Willow while Elijah made the necessary arrangements. It wasn't long before he came with the luggage and kneeled beside them. "The two of you look so wonderful to me. I was afraid I would forget what Willow looked like."

"It's so good to be back. I was gone for far too long," Evangeline admitted, still wiping tears as they fell.

Elijah nodded. "I arranged for a hack to take us to a hotel where we can wait out the storm."

"I'm looking forward to some rest. I worried the entire way that we would be delayed or derailed by the storm."

Elijah enveloped his family once more with his strong, capable arms. "I'll take care of you now." Evangeline melted under his touch. The weight of all their problems seemed to slip away. Once at the hotel, Evangeline immediately tucked Willow into bed. She and Elijah talked late into the night. She didn't even notice that the room was drab and reeked of cigar smoke.

"At first, I threw myself into my work. I simply couldn't face the fact that we were separated by distance and emotion," Elijah admitted. "My mother became very angry with me. So did my father, and he usually never interferes. In fact, the entire staff ostracized me."

"Dear, I'm sorry. It must have been lonely for you."

"It was. It gave me a lot of time to think."

She crossed the room to sit beside Elijah on the carpet, tucking her legs under her. "You only wrote me twice. I was worried."

Elijah stroked her blonde tresses. "Forgive me. It took me awhile to come to my senses. I shouldn't have doubted you."

"As you see, it wasn't my doing. There are still unanswered questions regarding James's family."

"I had no idea his estate was so complicated."

"Father will lend us the money we need to pay off our creditors. We can pay him back when the lawsuit is settled. The lawyers are confident we can recoup the money."

"I suppose you will have to be there in court?"

"I will. I am not looking forward to returning to Boston. But this must be resolved and the proper people punished. James's mother is living with my parents for now. When Ethan is put away, she will be safe in a home." Evangeline paused. "I feel responsible for her. She has no one to watch out for her."

"Of course you do. I would, too."

"I have to admit that I thought a lot about James lately." Evangeline dropped her gaze. "Actually, I discovered that I never really knew him."

"I wonder if we actually know anyone like we think we do."

Evangeline nodded. "So much mystery surrounds him, though not all of it was his fault. A victim of circumstances. His father died when he was young, and his mother lost her memory. I can't imagine what that would be like."

Elijah drew her close. "You've been through a lot. Once again, I'm sorry for not being there for you. I never seem to be. What's wrong with me?"

She gazed into his sad eyes. "You're too independent. You never needed to lean on anyone."

"And you?"

"I need you. I don't want to be alone, ever again."

Elijah reached for her. At first, his kisses sprinkled her lips like summer rain, then more amorously drenched her parched, dry soul.

CHAPTER 21

Back at the mission, Evangeline finished the last of her unpacking. She draped the Job's Tears quilt over her blanket chest, stroked it smooth, and stepped back to admire it. *How could I think my tears would end when I returned to the mission? The mission isn't a place to escape from the world. The mission is life, and life will always hold both tears and happiness. At this moment, it holds happiness—but for how long?* She could not know, but she was determined to enjoy every moment of it.

The marriage had endured the test of separation, and both had learned from it. Elijah became much more attentive to her and Willow. She practically had to throw him out the door most mornings. And the mission was humming along like a well-oiled sewing machine now that the two were together again.

Evangeline heard Sara clattering the morning dishes in the wash pan. "I don't want to teach today," Sara confided to Evangeline when she came to the kitchen. "I'd rather stay here with you and Willow."

Evangeline laughed. "You sound just like Elijah. In a few weeks, you'll take us for granted, just like the old days. Besides, we'll be here at the end of the day," Evangeline reassured her.

"I know, but I don't want to miss another minute of Willow's growing up."

"She sure is doing that. Come and sit with me before you rush off to school. We really haven't had time to talk since I got back."

Sara draped the cotton towel over the washed dishes and joined Evangeline at the table. Evangeline tilted her head. "You are growing, too, you know. Any beaus I don't know of?"

Sara blushed. "No, I don't have time for beaus."

"Someday you will. How's Doc doing?"

"Doc? Oh, poor Doc," Sara said.

"What do you mean by that?"

"He has such a difficult time getting people to trust him as a doctor."

"That he does. He tries too hard, I think. Besides, Lakota people aren't going to easily give up the medical practices they have used for hundreds of years."

"Doc has this nervous habit of fumbling with his spectacles. He gives himself away every time."

"We shouldn't talk about him this way. What he needs is our help."

"He doesn't accomplish much on his rounds, either. The people ignore his suggestions and follow the Old Ways. But we sure do appreciate him at our boarding school."

"Elijah went with him once," Evangeline reminded her. "It helped at the time, but Elijah has his own work to do."

Sara lifted Willow off the floor and cuddled her. "I'd like to go with him more and help him out. I know most of the families. They trust me. I try to convince them to trust him."

"I'm sure he'd appreciate that."

"I'll stop by his office after school and see how he's doing.

"Don't run off just yet. I want you to meet Tex. You know, the cattleman we met on the stage."

"I remember you telling me about him."

"I invited him and his son, Curt, over for coffee and cinnamon rolls. In fact, I'd better put them in the oven." She poked the inflated dough in pans on the table.

"Could I take a cinnamon roll over to Doc?"

"Sure, that would be a nice gesture."

Willow began to fuss. Her face wrinkled into a glower.

"I think Willow needs a nap," Sara said, kissing her cheek.

"Try sitting in the chair and rocking her. Maybe she'll go to sleep before our guests arrive."

Sara rocked only a few minutes before Willow fell asleep. Sara carried her to bed in the next room, just as Tex and Curt appeared at the door.

"Something sure smells good in here," Tex commented when he entered the cinnamon-scented kitchen. "This here's my son, Curt."

Curt quickly removed his hat and nodded to the women, unable to remove his gaze from Sara.

"Come in! Please sit with us. Elijah should be coming along soon." Evangeline placed her hands on Sara's shoulders. "This is Sara."

"Pleased to meet you, Sara," Tex said in his booming voice.

Evangeline scrunched her shoulders into her neck and grimaced, hoping he didn't wake Willow with his loud voice. She felt a spark of electricity in the air and noticed Curt's immediate fixation on Sara. Startled, Evangeline spilled the coffee she was pouring and then quickly asked, "Are you here visiting Tater?"

"We are. We miss the old coot."

Curt fiddled with his hat. "His cooking, too."

Evangeline opened the oven door and peeked at the rolls. "He seems to be doing well at his store." The sweet scent wafted through the warm kitchen.

Sara turned toward the squeaking front door. "Here comes Elijah."

"Just in time. I think the rolls are about done," Evangeline said, reaching for a pot holder.

Elijah smiled as he entered the kitchen and shook hands with his guests. "Good to see you again, Tex. And this must be your son?"

"Yes, this here is Curt."

"Are you settled in at your new headquarters?"

"Almost. We got most of the buildings up before the bad weather hit. The grass was good, and the cattle got fat," Tex answered.

Evangeline dumped the hot rolls out of the pan. She waited a few minutes for them to cool before handing them to Sara to serve. "We were just talking about Tater and how well he's doing with the store."

Elijah savored the first bite of baked perfection before he spoke. "We do enjoy his company."

Evangeline poured more coffee and scooted her chair next to Elijah. "It will be wonderful to have mail service at our front door. We won't be so isolated anymore."

"Your mission's growing into a community," Tex commented. "Any chance the railroad could come this way?"

"We're hopeful."

"It sure will change the country for the best," Tex said, licking the caramel from his fingers.

Evangeline made no response. She wasn't so sure she wanted to see many more changes. For some reason, change had a way of raising havoc in her life.

As soon as Sara finished eating, she asked to be excused. Curt's gaze followed her as she left the kitchen with a covered plate in her hand.

Evangeline explained her quick departure. "Sara's delivering a roll to Doc. She might accompany him on his rounds this Saturday. She knows most everyone in the area."

Tex squinted, looking puzzled. "Wasn't she studying to be a teacher?"

"Yes, she did. Now she also finds medicine interesting." *Or was it Doc?* she suddenly wondered.

"She's a delightful girl. Very pretty, too," Tex said.

"Thank you. I'm certain she would appreciate the compliment. She's very precious to us," Evangeline said with her gaze on Curt. "By the way, you haven't said anything about Netty. It seems so long since I met her on the stage."

"Netty's doing just fine. She's anxious for me to come home for a visit. I'm thinking about going back for Christmas."

Elijah reached for another roll. "What have you heard about the Indian leases?"

"Been talking to Ed at the Bar Double B. We might combine forces, so to speak. Anyway, we're going to talk to the stockholders about it. Competition is mighty fierce." After a few seconds' lull, the silence was broken by the screech of the elder Texan's chair. "Well, I suppose we better get going and look in on Tater. Thanks for the delicious breakfast. We'll see y'all around," he said as he and Curt left the table.

Elijah pushed back his chair and stood to shake their hands. "If we don't see you before you leave, good luck. Stop in again."

After they left, Evangeline gathered the plates and cups, placing them in the dishpan. "I think Curt has taken a liking to Sara. He couldn't keep his eyes off her."

Elijah bristled. "Our Sara? She's too young for...for romance."

"I agree. She needs to grow up a little more. At least a couple of years."

"Maybe more," Elijah said, frowning.

"Say son, I saw you lookin' at Sara. Pretty girl, ain't she?" Tex commented as father and son walked over to Tater's store.

"Yeah, I think so. Educated, too."

"Hmmm...You know, if a white man marries an Indian woman, he has a right as husband to the Indian leases?"

"What you getting at?"

"Every Indian is entitled to land. I don't know if Sara's enrolled in the tribe, but if so, she's got land. Not only that, but you could lease her neighbors' land."

"Are you telling me to get married?"

"If you like her, what's the harm?"

"Well, for starters, Sara isn't interested in me. You heard Evangeline. She likes medicine, and she's probably fond of that Doc, too. Where does that put me?" Curt frowned, his voice becoming louder. "And she's educated. She's a teacher. She's not going to leave the mission to live on a ranch."

Tex laughed. "You just have to use your magic on her. If you can get a woman to fall head over heels, you can talk her into most anything. Now don't get me wrong, I loved your mama, but I got her to leave the East to live in Texas with me. Now that's true love, ain't it?"

"I can't believe what you're saying. I went along with your first caper, but quite frankly, I'm gettin' tired of your schemes. I don't think that's a good enough reason to get married."

Tex rubbed his whiskers, not rattled at the tone his son used on him. "Yeah, suppose I'm joshing."

Curt stopped and turned to his father, looking him in the face. "I'm worried about you. You're obsessed with grazing land. You need something else to occupy your mind. Why not get married yourself?"

"Me? I got no time for that." Tex stroked his chin again. "Although...you might have a point. I have been thinkin' a little about settling down. Good grub's awful hard to come by now that Tater ain't with us."

"That's your only reason for getting married again?"

"Your momma's been dead for quite a spell. Once you and Netty leave me, I'll be all alone. Got anyone in mind?"

"I'm no matchmaker. You're on your own for that one. But I hear tell they have dances on the reservation. Lots of pretty girls come to have a good time."

"I don't think a girl would be proper. I need an unattached woman. She's got to be pretty, and she's got to be a good cook."

"What about land?"

"That would be a plus."

"Now you're talkin'."

Tex heaved a sigh. "Where'd you pick up that conscience of yours, son?" He winked at Curt. "I could give the right someone a good life."

Curt smiled. "Maybe Tater would know. Bet some nice ones come into his store."

"Tater's done helping us. He really does like being a storekeeper. Can't figure out why, but he sure does. We'll ask him if he knows of anyone."

———

Tater's store was neat, just like the kitchen he used to keep when he cooked for Curt, Tex, and their ranch hands in the Black Hills. No odors of spoiled food emanated from the shelves or from the barrels. Only a whiff of sweeping compound and onion was discernible when they first entered. Tater had his back to them and was polishing a saddle when Curt and Tex walked in. He turned for a brief glance.

"What do you guys want?" he grumbled.

"Just stopped in to say hello," Tex said, breathing in the smell of new leather, which took him back instantly to his early days as a ranch hand. He had worked doggedly for many days in a saddle—such as the one Tater was stroking—to make enough money to buy a small spread of his own. He had raised a family and buried a wife there. His search for land had been insatiable since then. He suddenly reflected upon the conversation with is son and was startled at the lengths he would go to satisfy this compulsion. The thought dawned on him that he might be sick, but that just made him feel weary. A wife to take care of him would be nice.

"Usually you two are up to something." Tater kept on working.

"This time you don't have to do a thing."

"Oh yeah?"

"Well, I was just wondering if you knew some nice, unattached women."

"What for?"

"Oh, I was thinking of courtin' again," Tex said.

Tater turned and stared at him. "Oh, is that all?"

"Tater you sure have gotten bitter toward us lately."

"Don't like the way you acquire land. And I don't like being accused of doing no good."

"I paid your fine."

"Yeah, thanks a lot. Now, leave me alone."

"All I'm asking is if you know any eligible women!"

"If I did, I wouldn't tell you."

"Don't you think I'm good enough for a lady?"

"I just don't feel like thinkin."

Tex threw up his hands. "Alright then, what about some dances? Where can I meet someone in these parts?"

Tater grimaced. "Well, I suppose you'll find out anyway. They hold an annual Christmas dance not far from here. Lots of ranch hands attend. And they tell me there's lots of pretty gals there."

"Thanks, Tater. I knew you would come through." Tex pulled a list out of his pocket and handed it to Tater. "Fill this order for us. We'll be back to pick it up."

Tater took the order and glanced over it. "Found a new cook, yet?"

Curt shook his head. "No, not yet. Why do you ask?"

"You don't have near enough flour, coffee, or beans to last the winter."

"Well, put in what you think we need, then. Pa and me do our best, but it never comes close to your cooking."

"I believe that."

"We'll be back." Tex waved at Tater and left the store.

"Do you think it was a good idea to tell Tater what you're up to?" Curt asked outside.

"He's harmless. He's loyal, even though he doesn't always like what I do."

"So you're really courtin' again?"

"Sure. We'll go to the Christmas dance. Maybe you could ask Sara to go with you. Forget about marriage and the lease thing. I don't know what I was thinking."

"I doubt Sara will go with me, but I can ask."

"If she don't, we'll go by ourselves. I just bet we could join up with some ranch hands from the Bar Double B.

Curt slapped his father on the shoulder. "I'm glad you're coming to your senses. I was beginning to worry about you."

———

One late afternoon the week before Christmas, Tex and Curt peeled off their grimy clothes, filled two tin tubs with water in Ed's washhouse and settled in for a much-needed bath. They hurriedly scrubbed themselves clean in a flurry of sudsy, tepid water. A line of cowboys waited impatiently for their turn, shouting out their impatience. "Hurry up!

And don't use all the water!"

Once back inside Ed's ranch house, Tex and Curt donned their best apparel. "I feel like a boy on the prowl again," Tex told his son as he splashed on a spicy fragrance.

"Hey go easy on that stuff. You'll chase them away with that for sure."

"Too much?"

Curt tossed him a wet cloth. Tex rubbed off the excess and ran his hand across his newly shaven face. "Not bad for an old man," he said, looking in the tiny mirror.

"Settle down. It's not like you're getting married tonight."

"Yeah, I guess you're right. It's just that I haven't played this game since your mama died. I wasn't interested in anyone then. Ambition took her place."

"Misdirected ambition," Curt muttered under his breath.

Tex adjusted his tie and beat his Sunday hat on his knee for a dusting. "So you're going solo tonight, Curt?"

"Just like I told you, Sara's not interested in me."

"Sorry son. You'll find someone else."

"We'd better join Ed's hired hands. They're not about to wait for us. We're competition."

Ed came into the ranch house just as the father and son were leaving. "Sure you don't want to come with us?" Tex asked.

"No. I'm not interested. A quiet evening at home, that's my plan."

"Okay then. Thanks for letting us bunk with you for a few days."

"You're most welcome. You fellows behave yourselves. I expect not to see you till tomorrow morning."

Tex and Curt saddled their horses and joined about five ranch hands for a ride to the dance hall. The breath of horses and men hung heavy in the cold, biting air. It didn't affect the merriment that passed among them. The men laughed and rehearsed the night ahead of them, twirling and kissing their imaginary girls as they rode across the prairie. The thought of it all warmed their chilled bones. The stars overhead twinkled merrily, reaffirming the invitation for an evening of jollity.

The ranch hands razzed each other about the prettiest girl, deciding they all looked equally beautiful in the starlight. A few of the men shouted warnings to the newcomers. "Now, don't you move in on my gal!"

"Nor mine," another added.

"How do you know if they're attached?" Tex asked with a laugh. "Do you think they'd wait for the likes of you?"

"Well, just in case they're not married," the man said. "I just want the first chance."

"For marryin'?" Tex shouted back.

"No. No. Just a dance, a little squeezin' and maybe a little kissin."

A twinkle of light in the distance guided them over the crunchy snow. Soon the bass chords drummed in the chests of the approaching men. Tex swallowed the doubt in his throat. Usually, he had no reservations about anything, but now he was questioning everything. He shook the chills off his body.

The men dismounted and led their horses into a makeshift shelter containing hay. After they settled their horses and adjusted their kerchiefs, they stomped the snow from their boots and entered the lantern-lit hall. The building was already nearly filled with stylish ladies and bashful cowboys. A long table to one side held a feast of cakes, pies, meats, and bread. Several older women were assisting the guests with food.

Tex shuffled his feet as his eyes searched for a place to settle. Curt accidently bumped into him. "Go ahead, son. Mingle with the others. I might just...ah, visit the refreshment table for starters."

"You're not fooling me," Curt grinned. "You feel like a

fish out of water, just like I do."

"Maybe so, but you got the looks and youth on your side. Me? I got nothing. Now, get goin." Curt slapped his father on the back and disappeared into the crowd. Tex stood on his left foot and then shifted to his right foot, searching for someone to visit with. He wondered where all the people came from. They were complete strangers to him. He watched in admiration how quickly the ranch hands found fair maidens to swing around the dance floor. "What a silly idea for me to come with these young lads," he muttered, approaching a bench near the food table. He didn't think it was right for him to sample the home-baked goodies so early in the evening, but he felt he had to do something to keep from looking stupid.

"Good evening," a soft voice called. "Could I get you something?"

Tex lifted his eyes from the pies he was perusing and met the gaze of a middle-aged woman. Her black hair was swept back into a bun, and she had a flawless, bronzed face. He had caught only a glimpse of her dark eyes before she looked away.

"We have a good assortment. Anything you particularly like?" she asked.

"I...like most anything. Ah, maybe spice cake?"

"You're in luck. There's a spice cake right here." She picked up the pan and passed it in front of his face. The aroma of cinnamon and cloves appealed to him. "Want me to dish you up a piece?"

Tex nodded, suddenly speechless.

With a smile, she handed him a slice of cake on a plate and quickly poured coffee from a granite coffeepot. The liquid seethed and steamed as it threatened to slip over the brim of the cup. "You from around here?"

"Oh, about an hour's ride from the Bar Double B ranch." He fumbled with the plate and cup she handed him. "Actu-

ally, I live an hour even farther than that from the ranch."
He slurped from the cup a little too loudly and shrugged in
embarrassment.

"Sorry, I filled it a little too full." She stifled a giggle. "Are
you a cattleman?"

"Yup, Tex is my name. Tex McMurray. I'm here with my
son. His name is Curt." He precariously balanced the plate
and coffee in his hands.

"Pull up a chair and sit down at the table," she suggested, while pushing some of the baked goods to the side. "I'm
Louisa. I rarely attend dances, but my friends talked me into
coming tonight."

"Sounds like me. I've been widowed ten years. Don't go
out much, except for business."

"My husband's been dead five years now. Gored by a
bull," she said impassively.

Tex grimaced. "Sorry about that. You live on a ranch,
then?" His face brightened.

She nodded. "With my two sons. They're here tonight."
She pointed out two slim fellows on the edge of the crowd.
Tex guessed they were in their twenties.

Tex was about to ask her more questions when Louisa
left his side to wait on a young couple. He devoured the
spice cake on his plate and gulped down the last of his coffee. Before he was aware of her return, she snatched his cup
and refilled it. He wasn't used to a woman attending to him,
but he had to admit he liked it.

He drank his second cup of coffee more slowly this time.
He asked himself what he was going to do after he finished
with the refreshment table. He didn't want to sit there all
night. After several rounds of dancing, the guests began to
crowd around the table. Louisa hardly had any more time
to visit. He fidgeted; he was about out of coffee. Berating
himself on his lack of courage, he urged himself to leave and
roam the perimeter of the dance hall. Suddenly, he realized

why he hadn't attempted to court in all those years. Not used to feeling so alone and friendless, he happened to run into Curt. "Any luck, son?"

"I've danced with a few, but the cowboys continually cut in claiming I'm dancing with their girls. I'm not interested in anyone enough to cause a ruckus. What about you?"

"I visited with a lady at the refreshment table. But she got busy."

"Ask her to dance when she's not so busy."

"I think I forgot how."

"Practice on some of these other ladies, then."

Tex scanned the ladies visiting along the sides of the dance hall. "But which one? She might be married, and I don't want to be turned down or have an angry husband after me."

"Come along with me, and I'll introduce you to someone." Curt led his father to another area of the dance hall and introduced Tex to a pale, thin woman. "Cora Mae, I'd like you to meet my father, Tex."

Tex gently shook her hand and invited her to dance before he could change his mind. Surprised that she accepted his invitation, he escorted her to the dance floor. He breathed a sigh of relief when the band played a slow waltz, and he awkwardly took her in his arms. It had been years since he had held a woman so close. And she was a blushing stranger! Beads of cold sweat formed on his forehead.

He struck up a conversation to hide his embarrassment. Luckily, she was skilled at small talk and put him at ease. It took an entire dance to find his feet, so he asked for another round. The waltzes kept flowing, and Tex and Cora Mae kept dancing. They were even laughing at the conclusion of the fourth dance. Tex happened to glance at the refreshment table to find Louisa's eyes fixed on him. Enough dancing with this gal, he calculated. He escorted Cora Mae to her acquaintances and walked toward Louisa. Luckily, she wasn't

busy when he caught her eye. "Would you like to dance?"
She dropped her gaze. "I probably should stay here."
"They can get by without you for one dance." His courage mounted as he poured on his charm.
She smiled. "Well, if you say so." Tex extended his hand and thrilled when she placed her warm hand in his. "I'll have to warn you. I haven't danced in ages."
"That makes two of us."
"You looked like you were having no trouble on the dance floor a minute ago."
He blushed. "It comes back to you after a few turns to the music." His arms felt comfortable around her, but he was careful not to hold her too tightly. A floral fragrance and her warm, strong body encapsulated him for more than one dance until she begged to return to her duties. He let go of her reluctantly.
"We'll have to do this another time," he said like a young schoolboy.
"You dance well," she said. "I look forward to seeing you again."
After escorting her to the refreshment table, he melted into the crowd. When it was time to return to the ranch, he knew his life would never be the same.

CHAPTER 22

Maud and Frederick surprised Evangeline by announcing they were traveling to the mission for Christmas. Evangeline read Maud's letter twice to make sure she understood it correctly. *"I can't bear celebrating Christmas without Willow,"* Evangeline read aloud to Sara when she got home from school.

"Maud is coming here in the dead of winter?" Sara asked. "I can't believe she'd venture out this time of year." Sara poured herself a glass of water and fetched a cookie from the cookie jar. "She's really changed, hasn't she?"

"It must have something to do with Willow. But I wonder who will take care of Gertrude."

"Oh, Gertrude. I forgot about her," Sara said, catching crumbs in her hand as she sat at the table. "Willow's napping?"

"Cassandra took her for the afternoon. I'm sure they have thought of someone to watch Gertrude."

"Didn't you say she couldn't remember anything?"

"I did. She's been seeing a doctor, but I don't think he's made a breakthrough yet."

"Strange case. I know it's none of my business, but I'm curious about something."

"Don't be afraid to ask. We're family, remember?"

"Did Gertrude remind you of her son, James?"

"I felt drawn to her the first time I met her. I didn't know why at the time, of course, but I know now. I never would have guessed she was his mother."

"Could Maud and Frederick bring her here for Christmas?"

Evangeline shook her head. "I don't think it would be wise to disrupt her routine again. It was hard for her to get used to living with my parents. We're really going to make the holiday special."

"How do you mean?"

"Oh, we'll do the usual I suppose—the decorations, the food, the gifts, the music. I remember my first year at the mission. We made each other gifts, and we sewed up two quilts—one for Elijah and a lap quilt for Jeremiah."

"Let's make a Christmas quilt to hang in the dining area, Sara said. "Won't it look pretty as a backdrop for a large Christmas tree?"

"You may have something there. We have to get cracking, or we'll never get it done."

"When are Maud and Frederick coming?"

"Within the week. I suppose Mama could babysit Willow while we sew." Evangeline glanced at the clock and shrieked. "Oh, my! It's that late already. Sara, could you rush over to Cassandra and bring Willow home? I should put something on for supper. Elijah will be home soon." Sara left, and Evangeline peeled potatoes. She put them on to boil and placed venison in the skillet to fry. *We'll have a lot to talk about at the supper table,* she mused. Anxious for Sara to return with Willow, Evangeline paced back and forth from the stove to the kitchen window. She smiled when she saw Elijah with Sara and Willow.

Evangeline scooped Willow from Sara's arms and kissed the child before she plunked her in the high chair. "Supper's about ready," she called over her shoulder. Evangeline mashed the potatoes and cooled a plateful for Willow while Sara set the table. Elijah said grace, and the small family began to eat. Evangeline spooned mashed potatoes into Willow's open mouth.

"Mama sent a letter. She and Father will be here for Christmas."

"I don't believe it," Elijah said.

"It's hard to believe, but she misses Willow that much. I just hope they don't end up being snowbound somewhere. Mama would surely have a fit."

"When will they be here?"

"Shortly before Christmas. I want to make it special."

"You always make Christmas special."

Evangeline smiled appreciatively. "Thank you. But I mean extra special. Sara suggested we make a Christmas quilt."

"Do you have time to make a quilt?"

"We're going to do our best. Aren't we, Sara?" Evangeline noticed a melancholy expression on Sara's face and sighed. "We've talked about everything these last few weeks...everything but teaching. We really haven't taken the time to talk much about it," Evangeline said to Sara. "Has teaching been everything you imagined?"

"It's okay, I guess. Willow reminds me of a baby bird—the way she opens her mouth."

"She loves to eat, doesn't she?" Evangeline grinned at her daughter.

Elijah frowned. "Sara, I was expecting a more enthusiastic answer."

"I'm sorry." Sara lowered her head. "I didn't mean it the

way it sounded."

Evangeline flashed a warning glance at Elijah. "Don't be sorry. We always want you to be honest with us. We've been too busy to notice if you have been dissatisfied. Besides, I should have been here for you when you began. The first month or so can be disappointing."

"Oh, I'm not dissatisfied."

Willow gurgled with pleasure when Evangeline began spoon-feeding her applesauce. "Is something bothering you, Sara?"

"No, it's just...it's just that I have so enjoyed my time with Doc. I never considered studying medicine. I always thought I wanted to be a teacher just like you."

"You're having second thoughts?" Evangeline asked.

"I'm just wondering what it would be like to study medicine. I know it's not practical for me to even think about it."

Evangeline looked to Elijah for an answer, but he only shrugged. "We're surprised, of course," she began. "But you certainly are capable of whatever your heart desires. Both of us have great faith in you. Convincing the world might be another matter."

Elijah nodded.

"I know. That's why I've never said anything before."

Evangeline finished wiping Willow's gooey face. "I simply won't take that as a final answer. If medicine is what you desire to do, I'll do my best to make it happen." She lifted Willow from the high chair and handed the chubby, blonde child to Sara.

"It takes money to study medicine," Sara commented as she juggled Willow from one arm to the other.

"I can take care of that. I know that Mama and Father would look after you, of course." Evangeline's mind raced with ideas. "The best schools are in the East. You could begin your studies soon. In fact, I think you should go with them when they leave. That way you will be escorted on your journey—"

"But Evangeline, leaving now would put a burden on the mission."

"Don't worry about that. I'll go back to work; there are enough women around here to help with Willow."

Elijah had been listening thoughtfully. "Perhaps you shouldn't become too hopeful until Evangeline looks further into this idea."

"Elijah," Evangeline gently scolded. "Where's your optimism?"

"I just don't want her hopes be dashed to pieces."

"Don't worry about me. I've faced disappointment before," Sara told them.

"Too much, I'm afraid," Evangeline pointed out.

Sara kissed Willow and handed her back to Evangeline. "I promised to help Cassandra with a sewing project. I have to go now. We'll talk later?"

"That we will."

After Sara left, Elijah cleared the dishes from the table.

"Elijah, do you think Sara spends too much time with Doc?"

"I haven't given that much thought. Although, now that you mention it, she does seem to be with him very often—whether in his office or on his rounds."

"She teaches all day and then helps Doc on evenings and weekends. You don't think she has a romantic interest in him, do you?"

"I haven't observed that he's taken an interest in her. However, I have noticed that Curt seems smitten with her. She ignores him."

"I've noticed that, too. She's just too young to become involved. She probably *is* interested in medicine."

"Evangeline, do you feel up to all this?"

She nodded. "I do miss teaching."

"I know you mean well, but even if you get her into a

school, she's going to have a tough time. Have you thought of how others will treat her?"

"You mean prejudice?"

"Yes, we can't ignore that possibility," Elijah said. "I hope you weren't thinking of Carlisle. She could study nursing there, but I wouldn't recommend it."

Evangeline moved to the rocking chair with Willow. She kissed her forehead and began to rock. "I don't want Sara to be afraid to face the world. She has to understand she's an equal, even if others think she's not. It'll break my heart if someone hurts her, but I believe we have to take that chance."

"What you say is true. I want to protect her, too. It's like when we were married. The newspapers wrote terrible things about us, but I put them immediately out of my mind."

"You knew! I had no idea you were aware of what the papers wrote. I'm distressed you found out and never told me!" She glared at him.

"I wanted to protect you. When Maud was here, she asked me how you took the news. Of course, someone else showed me a newspaper before, but I don't pay a lot of attention to what the newspapers write. You have to realize they're out to sell newspapers. Printing the truth isn't always their intent."

"Well, I wanted to protect you, too." She smiled at him sympathetically.

"So how do we protect Sara without confining her here with us?"

"It's easy to remain here. It's safe and secure," Evangeline said. "I admit I've been guilty of taking advantage of that myself."

"I've been just as guilty as you," Elijah admitted.

"How do you mean?"

"I've been hiding from how I really feel. You probably noticed I couldn't commit?" he laughed.

Her eyes met his. "I guess I have."

"My mother and I had a good talk the night you arrived from Boston the second time. I should have received you with open arms. Instead, I practically ignored you." He hung his head. "She accused me of hiding behind my work and said I was afraid to take risks."

"That's kind of harsh," she protested.

He put up his hands. "No, it's the truth. I think back to when you were quite young. You left Boston to come all the way out here to the mission. That took courage—courage I didn't have." His dark eyes met hers. "You have found that courage again."

"I did, didn't I?"

Elijah smiled. "It's going to take that same daring to let Sara go. We know it won't be easy for her, but it's something she's willing to try. We have to support her."

"Sara does have courage. I'm so proud of her."

"She sure does," Elijah agreed.

Evangeline carried the sleeping Willow to her bed and then threw her arms around him. "Tomorrow, I'll begin writing letters to some schools I know of."

Elijah's eyes sparkled. "Something special is waiting for Sara. I just know it."

"And whatever it is, we'll all discover it together."

CHAPTER 23

Kat pulled the curtains aside to find that the boiling meat on the stove had caused moisture to accumulate on the glass window. She rubbed away the condensation and peered out at yet another storm. She had hoped for a calm day so she could get out of the tiny house for a walk. Jet had gone to the mission for supplies.

Her mind had been in turmoil lately. She agonized over her business, which teetered on the edge of success or failure. The last letter she received from her sister was far from reassuring. Her most trusted employees, Jake and Clem, had left for other jobs. Annabelle had explained that Clem and Jake were not cut out for restaurant work. The women were left to manage the restaurant.

The notice Kat had them run in the paper brought out a few undesirables, but no cooks. Kat realized she would have to hire Aggie. She shivered at the thought of that night when Aggie's sons had attempted to kill Jet, but she reminded herself that Aggie had sworn against having anything to do with their actions.

She sat at the table and began a letter to Annabelle. She was careful not to reveal her frustration. She suggested that Annabelle hire Aggie in hopes that it might save her business. Aggie was a good cook who would not let anyone push her around. Deadwood restaurants could bring in tough crowds, even without serving alcohol. Aggie could handle anyone out of line. However, Kat clearly stated she didn't want that cigar in Aggie's mouth while cooking. She hoped Annabelle could enforce that stipulation. She let the pencil drop from her fingers, distressed that some of her old friends would not be there when she returned in the spring. Clem and Jake had always been there for her.

Kat jumped up from her chair when she heard the sound of the team and sleigh. She was excited about the supplies Jet brought, but so much more enthused by the postal prospects. Maybe Annabelle had sent another letter. Perhaps Minnie had sent fabric or a new pattern. She tested the meat on the stove. Jet would surely be hungry unless he had stopped at the mission's kitchen to eat. But that was unlikely. It would have been safer to get home before another storm struck. Kat pressed her nose to the window until Jet drove up to the door. She then opened it and smiled at her husband.

"Miss me?" He grinned through the muffler wrapped around his neck.

"Of course." She laughed, rushing into the house with a bundle of supplies.

"Ah, you're more interested in what I brought."

"Well, that too."

He grunted as he manhandled the large sacks and barrels. "This should keep us fit for a while. Minnie sent this with me. I'll take care of the sleigh and the horses and then I'll be in. Oh, and here's the mail."

Kat's heart leaped with excitement. She thought it was

funny how little it took to excite her anymore. "Have you eaten lately?" She called.

"No. Couldn't wait to get home to you."

She laughed. "Good! I have boiled meat on the stove." She slammed the door shut to keep out the cold while she sorted through the bundle of mail for something from Annabelle. She frowned. There wasn't anything, so she opened the box from Minnie and found her scrawled note on top. She quickly read that the women at the mission were making a Christmas quilt to hang in the dining room.

"Make whatever pattern you want using the red, green, and white material I bought at Tater's store. All blocks should be twelve inches. Maybe one of these days, the storms will let up so we can get together and sew the blocks into a sampler quilt."

Kat quickly thumbed through the fabric, expressing delight at the assortment Minnie had sent. *Something to look forward to,* she thought. The cluttered boxes and barrels around the table required her attention. She placed the box of material on her sewing machine and put away the supplies. With the cornmeal Jet had delivered, she quickly mixed up a pan of cornbread and popped it into the oven.

Jet stomped his boots outside the door before he entered. "Sure smells good in here. Nice and warm, too. It's going to be a cold one tonight."

"Wash up, and supper will be ready."

While Jet removed his snow-encrusted coat and washed, Kat regaled him with questions concerning the mission. "Everyone seems snug as a bug there," he reported. "I guess they've had some colds. Doc's been busy with a few older people with the flu. Otherwise, I think everything's going fine. Minnie sent you some quilting stuff?"

"She sure did. We're going to make a Christmas quilt to hang in the dining room. I do hope we can spend Christmas at the mission."

"I do, too. A change of scenery would be nice."

"You mean you're tired of looking at me?" Kat retorted.

"No, that's not what I mean." He ruffled her red hair.

"Yeah, I know." She tore his hands away. "I'd like to see other people, too."

"I'll help you with the dishes tonight," Jet offered. "I have a feeling you want to begin your sewing project."

———

A week before Christmas, Kat and Jet woke to a clear blue sky. The sun was shining brightly for the first time in weeks. "How about a trip to the mission?" Jet suggested, hoisting himself out of bed and pulling on his clothes.

"Do you think it's safe to leave for the day?" Kat asked, throwing back the bed covers.

"It's the best day we've seen lately. Besides, don't you have some sewing to do with the ladies?"

Kat began hastily making the bed. "I suppose they're waiting for my Christmas blocks to finish the quilt. Let's get an early start. I think there are leftover biscuits from last night. That way I won't have to make breakfast or stoke the fire."

"What about coffee?"

"Can't you skip it this once?"

He grimaced. "I suppose. You get ready, and I'll hitch up the team. Rub some cold charcoal around your eyes and cheeks. The snow's liable to cause snow blindness. And take along a wide-brimmed hat," he hollered on his way out.

Kat dressed in her warmest wool skirt and a matching cardigan sweater. She placed the biscuits in a bag and dipped her finger in the ash bucket, searching for a piece of charcoal. She fished out a piece, looked at it with a scowl, and then smeared the lump of charcoal around her eyes and cheeks. The leftover piece she wrapped in a cloth for Jet. She plunked the wide-brimmed hat on her head, tied it down with a wool scarf, grabbed her box of quilt blocks, and left the house without looking in the mirror. When Jet first saw her with her smudged face, he pointed at her and laughed gleefully.

"Now, stop that," Kat demanded. "Are you playing a joke on me? If this is, you're going to be sorry."

"Honest, it works." He helped her into the sleigh and rimmed his own cheeks and eyes with the charcoal. "See? I did it, too. I hope this does the trick, or we'll be suffering for days."

"So you haven't tried it?"

"Oh, sure, a few times."

Kat shot him a burning glance. "I also brought along handkerchiefs to cover our eyes. I see you have fly masks on the horses."

"Hope it keeps down the glare. Got your quilt squares?"

"I do."

"Good. Then we're off."

The brisk air exhilarated Kat's spirits. She hadn't been anywhere for quite some time. She initially enjoyed the sparkling snow that graced the prairies, but the pure white landscape soon became monotonous—not to mention painful to the eyes.

Before they reached the mission, Kat and Jet resorted to draping a handkerchief over their eyes. The sun's glare off the endless sheet of snow threatened to burn them. "I see smoke from the chimneys," Jet muttered.

"Wonderful. The snow may be beautiful, but it sure is hurtful today."

Jet reached under his seat, producing a fistful of sleigh bells. He began to ring them merrily. The ringing sound drew a few inquisitive people from the comfort of their dwellings, Minnie among them.

"I declare! I didn't think I'd ever see you two again," Minnie said exuberantly. "Get on down, and we'll get you something to eat."

"Any coffee let in the pot?" Jet asked.

"He's been whining all morning about leaving without his coffee," Kat added while hastily wiping the smudged charcoal from her face.

"I have not." Jet protested.

Minnie just laughed. "Plenty of coffee and victuals for you, Jet. And don't worry about your faces. Just come on in. Everybody's waiting."

A young boy took care of the horses and sleigh while Kat scurried to find a mirror in spite of what Minnie had said. Jet entered the mission's dining room. Jet was soon served his coffee, and the cook's helper, a young boarding school student, placed platters of warmed food on the table.

"Where do we start? It's been ages since we last talked," Minnie said. "Are you staying the night?"

Jet nodded, and swallowed his coffee in several big gulps. "I think we'll chance it. My bones are saying we have two good days before another snow."

"Great," Minnie confirmed. "Kat, did you bring any completed blocks?"

"I sure did," she said, sitting down next to Jet. "They're in the box."

"After you eat your fill, we'll begin to put the quilt together." Minnie asked another student to fetch Evangeline and Sara. "Then tell Cassandra we're coming over to put the quilt together," she added.

As soon as they finished their repast, Jet excused himself to search out the fellows. Minnie left the dishes for Bea and the students to wash and walked Kat over to the sewing room. Kat opened the box she had brought along and showed the ladies her completed squares. Then they arranged all the completed red, green, and white blocks on a large table.

"Won't this be pretty!" Kat commented, gleefully perusing the squares.

"Yes, I think it shall," Minnie added, examining the blocks. "You have become quite the seamstress."

"We made several quilts at the Birdcage. I found out I truly enjoy quilting."

"I'm ready to sew when you have them arranged how you like. We've already cut strips for the border," Cassandra said.

Kat leaned back, soaking in the warmth of the room and the company of the enterprising women. She certainly loved her husband, but it was so comforting to listen to the prattle of women. She decided she had been isolated too long. She reasoned that Annabelle must have received the letter advising her to hire Aggie as a cook, and she hoped all was going well at the Birdcage.

CHAPTER 24

Aggie scurried around the kitchen at the Birdcage, battling the chaos. Leona wasn't the best at keeping anything neat. Pots and pans sat in a jumbled mess. Aggie could only guess where their matching lids were. She thought Annabelle, who was supposed to manage the business, seemed scatterbrained most of the time. Miranda had been assigned to help with dishes, but Aggie kept finding dirty dishes tucked away in the cupboard.

Aggie still couldn't believe Annabelle had hired her to cook. She knew Kat did not trust her, even though she had done her best to convince Kat that she had nothing to do with her sons' decision to attack Jet. In some way, Aggie saw this job as a chance to make it up to Kat. She was determined to do her part to make the restaurant a success.

According to Annabelle, business had declined lately in part because alcohol was no longer served at the Birdcage. Aggie didn't care either way. She had been around alcohol and ornery men all her life; she was confident she could have

269

handled both.

Leona stuck her head in the kitchen. "What are you cooking today?"

"I don't rightly know," Aggie said. "What have you been cooking?"

"Mostly taters and meat."

"I should try something different. Put a sign outside telling the customers what we have to offer."

Leona shrugged. "I suppose it wouldn't hurt none."

"You working today?"

"Annabelle said I'm supposed to help you out."

"Before you make the sign, get in here, wash your hands, and see if you can find a clean apron." Aggie scowled. "This kitchen is a mess. I'm trying to straighten it up a bit."

"Yeah, well, I'd rather be sewing."

"Maybe so, but first we've got to make us some money. We ain't going to make it if we don't get any business."

"So what's for dinner?"

"How about some fresh buns, fried chicken, gravy, and potatoes?"

"I don't think we got any chicken."

"Then run down to the butcher and get about four."

"Don't think our credit's good there anymore."

Aggie heaved a sigh. "Good grief. What did I get myself into? Go find Annabelle. I need to talk to her." As soon as Leona left, Aggie stirred up a batch of dough for buns. At least there was plenty of flour. Since working at the Miner's Restaurant, she had memorized every recipe she had ever cooked. The only drawback about working at the Miner's was that she didn't get to cook very often. Someone else still had the head cook job.

"You want me?" Annabelle rubbed her eyes.

Aggie figured she had just left her bed. "I want to fry chicken for lunch, but Leona says we have bad credit with the butcher."

"We do?" Annabelle frowned.

Leona nodded.

"I was wondering if you had some cash around here to go buy some chicken," Aggie said. "I guarantee that when the citizens of Deadwood smell my chicken cooking, they'll come in droves."

Annabelle blinked. "Okay, then I'll find some money."

Leona followed Annabelle, leaving Aggie rummaging around to see what she had to cook with. She wondered if anyone had made a pie lately. She opened the cupboard doors and found a few cans of cherries. She decided this would make for a perfect dessert.

By the time Leona returned with the chickens, Aggie had mixed up the pie crusts.

"What shall I do?" Leona asked flatly.

"Roll out the crusts, thicken the cherries, and we'll bake us some pies. Have you made any lately?"

Leona rolled her eyes. "No, I don't make pies. Neither does Annabelle."

"No wonder you don't have any business," Aggie said under her breath. After Leona had completed Aggie's instructions, Aggie sent her outside to write their menu on a board.

"I don't know how to spell very good," Leona confessed.

"Try." Aggie had more than she bargained for with frying four chickens, but somehow she managed with just two skillets. Within an hour, just as she had predicted, the restaurant filled up with hungry customers.

"Wow," Annabelle admitted. "This is the most money we've taken in since we quit selling alcohol. I can't wait to tell Kat!"

———

It took hours to clean the kitchen and, by the end of the day, the women were exhausted.

"Do we have to go through this every day?" Leona wailed, slumping in a chair.

"If we're going to have this job much longer, we'll have to. Otherwise, this place is going to fold."

"So we'll never get to open a shop and sew like we talked about?"

"Not now, but we'll keep dreaming. Someday it will happen."

"I doubt it. We don't seem to have any good luck."

"Christmas is only one week away. Do you celebrate Christmas, Leona?"

"Not too much. Never had any means to celebrate or anyone to celebrate with."

"I'll ask Annabelle about cooking up a Christmas meal here at the Birdcage. Wonder if she's thought about a Christmas tree? Surely she'll have one for Miranda."

"Can't remember last time I had a Christmas tree. My folks were poor and overworked."

"Would sewing perk up your spirits?"

"It might. What do you got in mind?"

"Sew us a Christmas quilt for our table."

"In a week? I don't think so."

"A partial quilt, then. Just a strip to go down the center of the table. It'd make it Christmas-like and all in here."

"Got no material."

"There must be some material around here with all the quilts that group made. Kat probably wouldn't mind if you snooped around for some."

Leona nodded. "If you say so. I'll have a look around."

"While you're doing that, I'll make a list of what we need. Hope Annabelle's got enough money to set us up in supplies." Aggie picked up a pad and pencil from the cabinet and went out back. She settled herself on a packing crate, groped for the cigar in her pocket, popped it in her mouth, and lit it before she began her list.

Luck? Aggie thought back to what Leona had said. In Aggie's opinion, luck had nothing to do with their success. Hard work would do it. Having a decent job was the best chance they had. She wasn't going to let that opportunity slip through her hands. She was going to dream up the best Christmas dinner Deadwood had ever seen.

———

Aggie arrived early at the Birdcage on Christmas day. Jenny had made a sign to advertise the special dinner and propped it against the building a week in advance. The staff became more eager as they noticed more and more people ogling the sign.

A light snow had covered everything during the night. Aggie trudged through the soft fluff to brush off the sign, secretly smiling in remembrance of her early years. A sense of peace overwhelmed her as she hummed a Christmas carol. She couldn't remember the words, but she recalled the melody from her childhood. Carolers around her town would stop by her home and sing to her family. No tree or presents adorned that old house, but she vividly remembered walking about town to look at Christmas trees in shop windows. And the snow—how she had loved the snow as a child!

She didn't know why she was in such good spirits this Christmas. She had no one to share gifts with this season except Leona, but they had agreed to save their money instead. She had a job, lived in a little house, and wasn't on the run. Her life could have been better, but she could have more easily faired much worse.

She hadn't heard a word from her boys. Rio and Jed wouldn't be celebrating Christmas besides downing a few bottles of whiskey. She had to admit their behavior was her fault. She hadn't taught them the right way to live. Her husband ruled the house, and she hadn't tried to go against him.

She pushed those dark thoughts out of her mind. *What's done is done,* she thought. All that was left was for her to improve her own future.

Aggie had decided to begin cooking early to ensure the geese she had purchased at the butcher the day before would have enough time to fully roast. She was so overtaken with holiday spirit that she had used some of her own money to buy everything on her list. Leona had scolded her that evening. "Remember, we decided to save money toward our own little shop."

Aggie had replied, "If we do well today, I'll take the money I spent out of the earnings. Call it an investment." Yet if she were wrong, they would be short on rent.

The goose had been roasting for about two hours before Jenny, Annabelle, and Miranda arrived to help with the potatoes, gravy, and dressing. The aroma of the cooking Christmas dinner dispersed into every nook and cranny of the Birdcage. Aggie couldn't remember the last time she had cooked a real Christmas dinner, and she guessed Leona couldn't either.

Leona came in shortly after Annabelle. "I just got this finished," she told everyone as she cleared the center of the table and spread out the colorful table runner.

Aggie wiped her hands on her soiled apron and came into the dining area. "It's great, Leona. Just how I had imagined." Aggie caressed the pinwheel pattern of red, green, and white. "We'll put the pies we baked yesterday on the table. When our customers finish their main meal, Jenny can dish up the pie from the table."

"Aren't you getting a little too fancy?" Leona asked. "Where did you learn all this?"

Aggie truly couldn't name the cause of her appreciation for homespun beauty. She never grew up with it. She certainly never had the opportunity to enjoy it while on the run. She could only shrug and say, "It just came to me, I guess."

The restaurant smelled of roasting goose and spice-scented pies when the first customers entered. Aggie had prepared for a big crowd. It was a gamble. From time to time, she peered around the kitchen door to see that the customers seemed to be enjoying themselves. To her, the happy and satisfied looks on their faces seemed to say it all.

After the meal, Aggie and the rest of the staff collapsed into the nearest chairs when the last of the diners left the Birdcage. "Whew, what a day," Aggie muttered. "Annabelle, add up the receipts and see if we came out ahead. I'm dying to know."

"I'll help," Jennie offered.

While they counted up the money, Leona sat down beside Aggie. "I've got to hand it to you. You outdid yourself today. What a meal that was! Hiring you as head cook was a smart move."

"Why, thanks, Leona. I didn't really mean to push you aside with the cooking."

"I don't mind. Like I said, I'd rather sew."

Annabelle shouted across the room. "We did it! There's several hundred dollars here. Won't Kat be surprised!"

"I guess we make a good team. We just have to entice them in here every day," Aggie said.

Leona massaged her sore knee. "Yeah, I guess."

CHAPTER 25

Evangeline couldn't wait for Christmas at the mission, especially now that her parents were here. Most of the decorating had been completed at the dormitory for the few students who remained at the mission for the holiday. However, there was no sign of a tree. This made her nervous because it was Christmas Eve, the day of the Christmas party. She thought back to her first year at the mission when she and Elijah had gone to the river breaks, chopped down a fragrant cedar tree, and hauled it back in a sleigh. The memory of that special day gave her an idea. Evangeline searched out Elijah and sprung her idea on him. "Remember when you and I went to the river breaks and cut a cedar tree the first year I was at the mission?"

Startled at her sudden question, Elijah lifted his brows and turned to look at her. "Yes."

"How about we volunteer this year to get the tree? I hope they still have the same sleigh."

"Any reason in particular?"

She slapped him in the shoulder, frowning. "I see you haven't changed."

"What? What did I do?"

"It was a special day for me, but not for you?"

He threw up his hands in frustration. "I don't...know. How do you want me to answer?"

What was she expecting him to recall? Evangeline had liked Elijah then, but he didn't seem to be infatuated with her at that time, which disturbed her immensely. "Oh, never mind. I just thought it would be fun."

"If you wish, we can go."

"Thanks. I'll tell the ladies."

Within a few hours, Elijah and Evangeline prepared for a trip to the river breaks. Elijah hitched up the sleigh—the very same sleigh Evangeline had remembered. It was first a gift to Jeremiah, which he then donated to the mission. Evangeline couldn't find the sleigh bells for it, so she instead sang Christmas carols and invited Elijah to join in. It took them several hours of tromping through the knee-deep snow to find the perfect tree.

"Do you suppose Cassandra will have hot cocoa waiting for us when we get back, just like last time?" Evangeline laughed at the memory.

"If I remember right, you weren't too fond of my mother back then," Elijah reminded her.

"Nor she of me." The husband and wife chuckled as they thoroughly enjoyed their outing together.

Once back at the mission, Elijah recruited a few students to help set the tree in its stand. Minnie brought out the handmade paper ornaments crafted by the students earlier in the month. "I guess we put this off a little too long," Minnie conceded. "We have been so busy putting the Christmas quilt together that everything else has gone unnoticed. At least we'll have something to eat. Bea has been busy baking all day. I think Maud is helping her out. Thanks for getting the tree." Minnie shook her head. "I was afraid Jeremiah was going to take care of it alone."

"Our pleasure. What else needs to be done?"

"Whatever finishing touches you desire. I must get back to that quilt." Minnie rushed out the door in the direction of the sewing room.

Evangeline thought the tree and the quilt would be plenty to make the room festive. Luckily, she had done some shopping before she had left Boston. Nothing was homemade, but she simply couldn't concentrate on making Christmas gifts this year. She had purchased a jacket for Elijah and assorted toys for Willow. She chose embroidered handkerchiefs for the ladies and colorful mufflers for the men. After all, it wasn't the gifts, but the fact they could all be together that would give the season its significance. Now, all she had to do was wrap them and place them under the tree.

Inside the warmth of her own home, she piled the wrapped packages on the kitchen table after she had finished them. It didn't take her long to change into a red and white dress Maud had insisted upon for Christmas. She searched anxiously through the window for Sara to help her carry over the presents, but she had a feeling Sara was with Doc, probably attending to another medical matter. She gave up hope of finding someone to assist her, so she grabbed a couple of shopping bags and stuffed the gifts into them. Darkness had already encroached upon the prairie by the time she left the house. Twinkling candles in the dormitory windows guided her to the Christmas gathering. She opened the door to a magical wonderland.

While Cassandra was showing off Willow in the ruffled Christmas dress she had sewn for her, Evangeline stopped at the refreshment table to pour herself a cup of hot cider. As she stood sipping the mellow mixture, she surveyed the room. The tree twinkled with glitter; the ornamental candles shimmered; and the finished Christmas quilt adorned the wall nearest the table. The room was saturated with the fragrance of cedar and fast filling up with family and friends. Evangeline reached for a piece of Christmas candy and popped it into her mouth. Bea and Minnie had worked for days to create such a sumptuous smorgasbord. *If I could only keep one moment forever,* she mused, *it would be this one—this state of happiness.*

The merry conversations were music to her ears. How grateful she was for these special people! Elijah circulated among the growing crowd, spreading his message of cheer and goodwill. Her eyes roved around the room, stopping on each little group until she spotted Sara with Doc. *I thought so.* They had been visiting privately ever since she arrived. *Medical talk? Or was it more personal?* Sara would be leaving for Boston soon. She knew that life without Sara would bring many changes. Sara was grown up. She had to live her own life now.

Kat and Jet circled the table and extended a friendly hello. *Kat looks stunning,* Evangeline thought. Her red hair, piled in curls, set off her silver gown. Evangeline wondered how Kat was adjusting to ranch life. *I hope she will remain strong for Jet's sake. He seems genuinely smitten with her.*

Tater and Curt came through the door with a commotion. They stomped off the snow that had accumulated on their boots. The crowd greeted them enthusiastically. Tater had become a beloved member of the mission community. His store and post office fulfilled a dire need for a break from their prolonged isolation from the world. His association as a land agent didn't last long. Evangeline and Elijah always suspected Tex had something to do with it.

Tex had returned to Texas to be with Netty. Curt, meanwhile, seemed to be at loose ends. Evangeline watched as he glanced in Sara's direction, also noticing his frown when he saw her with Doc. It reminded her of the tension between James and Elijah all those years ago.

"What you smiling at?" Elijah asked as he approached her. His eyes warmed in her presence.

"Just taking time to admire my friends and family. I don't see your father. Did you remind him to come?"

"I did. He left for the Cheyenne Agency this afternoon."

"I'm sorry. I thought he was becoming more comfortable with us."

"I don't think that's going to happen, no matter how much we want it to," Elijah said.

"We can't control our loved ones. I hope he will be happy and know how much we care."

Elijah's dark eyes saddened. "We have his murals in the dining room to remind us of him."

———

Christmas day had passed in a flurry of merriment, but now it was time for Maud, Frederick, and Sara to leave for Boston. Evangeline didn't want to say good-bye. She fed Willow her breakfast and put her down on a blanket. She pulled out a plate of cold roast from the icebox and sliced it for sandwiches so they could eat them along the way. She fought the panic rising in her throat, knowing that they would be leaving within the hour. She didn't know when she'd see them again.

"Good morning, daughter," Maud greeted, suppressing a wide yawn.

Evangeline turned when she heard her voice. "Didn't you sleep well?"

"No, not really. I guess it's because we'll be traveling for days. Who knows what problems we'll encounter along the way. Frontier travel is so abominable." Maud reached down and tickled Willow under her chin.

Evangeline laughed. "Now I know where my fear of travel comes from—you!"

"It's about time you got something from me," Maud said with a stern countenance. "It certainly wasn't my good looks." They both grinned.

"Thank you for coming for Christmas. I know it took great effort."

"You'll have to visit us in Boston, or I'll never see Willow as often as I like." Maud lifted the cup of coffee that Evangeline had poured for her and sipped with anticipation of its rejuvenating powers. "I don't believe I'll make this trip again. It's just too difficult."

"I promise I'll come for a visit, especially since Sara will be attending school nearby. Thank you for watching after her."

Maud stifled another yawn. "She's a good girl. We'll do what we can for her." Maud drank the last of her coffee and pushed back her chair. "I'll get my things and say good-bye to Minnie and Cassandra."

Evangeline turned to finish the sandwiches and wrap them in brown paper.

Maud practically bumped into Sara at the door. "Have you said your good-byes?"

"I have."

"It's my turn, then," Maud said. She left, and Sara picked up Willow. "You know, I think Cassandra is really going to miss me. I might have seen a tear forming in the corner of her eye. She turned away from me, so I can't be sure."

"I've never seen her cry before, but she really does love you. She liked to sew with you. Sewing is something she loves, and she could share that joy."

"I do like to sew. Does Maud have a treadle machine?"

"She does. The dressmaker uses it. Of course, Mama doesn't sew."

Sara snuggled Willow, kissing the top of her soft, downy head. "Willow will be grown by the time I see her again."

"Be careful Sara—she'll spit up all over you and ruin

your dress. She's been doing that lately."

"Oh, I'm not worried. She's such a sweet child, and I'll miss her." Sara heaved a deep sigh. "I don't know, Evangeline. Maybe I should wait and finish out my teaching term."

"You'll have babies of your own to snuggle someday. This is your time now. You have to take opportunities when they come along. If you don't, they may never come again." The glum expression remained on Sara's face in spite of Evangeline's encouragement. "If you back out now, you may never again muster the courage to go. I just about did the same thing once. When I was boarding the train to come west the first time, my response was to turn back and run home as fast as I could. But Father took my elbow and helped me forward, onto the train, and into a life of my own. Actually, I never realized the significance of that moment until now."

"I suppose you're right," she replied, unenthused.

"Once you begin to study medicine, you'll forget us."

"I will never forget," Sara said adamantly while looking out the window. "Oh, Elijah's coming for my trunk." She rose from her chair and handed Willow to Evangeline, planting one last kiss on the baby's cheek. Evangeline and Willow hugged Sara tightly. The two women linked arms and walked out the door to join Maud and Frederick.

Evangeline fought the pain welling up in her throat. She resolved not to cry. She could not make it more difficult for Sara to leave. Although she loved Sara like her own daughter, she refused to hinder the young woman from achieving such a goal.

Maud embraced Evangeline and kissed Willow as Elijah and Frederick hoisted her trunk into the wagon. "You will come and visit us?" she asked once again.

"I'll try my best," Evangeline said, forcing the words from an aching throat. "Though perhaps not until I must settle business affairs," she said as she kissed her father good-bye.

"We'll miss you." He winked at Evangeline, kissed Willow, and then shook Elijah's hand.

Evangeline encouraged Willow to wave to her grand-parents and Sara. "Oh, look, Elijah! Willow's waving!" She smiled through the falling tears. "But she may not remember who they are the next time she sees them."

"Not to worry, Evangeline. They'll just have to get to know each other all over again. Love transcends separation."

Evangeline nodded and leaned into Elijah's arms. Elijah enclosed wife and daughter in a loving embrace. Together they watched Frederick, Maud, and Sara as the wagon rumbled across the rough trail.

Times are changing once again, Evangeline avowed.